A FICTION

ATLANTIC
MONTHLY
PRESS

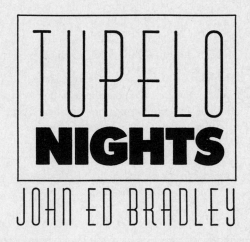

TUPELO
NIGHTS

JOHN ED BRADLEY

THE ATLANTIC MONTHLY PRESS
NEW YORK

Published simultaneously in Canada
Printed in the United States of America
FIRST EDITION

Library of Congress Cataloging-in-Publication Data

Bradley, John Ed.
Tupelo nights.

(Atlantic Monthly Press fiction series)
I. Title.
PS3552.R2275T8 1987 813'.54 87-22958
ISBN 0-87113-175-7

DESIGN BY LAURA HOUGH

The Atlantic Monthly Press
19 Union Square West
New York, NY 10003

First printing

FOR PIP

few months before he died, my father's father asked me to forgive him for not being able to climb the ramps at Tiger Stadium and watch me play football for Louisiana State University.

"The arthritis is bad," he said on the telephone. "But my heart, the lousy sonofabitch, is worse."

Because he was confined to his bed and rarely left the apartment over his clothing store on Union Street, he listened to all the games on KLLO, our hometown station. Hearing my name mentioned, he said, put something like a fat fist in his throat. And once, after learning I'd been named to an all-America team, he'd cried so hard he thought his lungs would burst. He had cried through the first five minutes of our Tulane game and beat his terrible, gnarled hands together and chanted "Girlie, Girlie, Girlie." When I asked him if carrying on that way meant he was proud of me, he started laughing and told me to go to hell. Then he hung up. I figured he was on the bottle again, and hitting it hard. When I called back, he answered the phone during the first ring and said, "Didn't I say it loud enough for you, John? Didn't you hear me? Go to hell."

Again he hung up before I had a chance to talk.

I once told a girl I knew that my grandfather and I had never spoken to each other after that, and she reminded me I hadn't really talked to him during that last call; he was the only one who had said anything. She laughed and tried to make me laugh, but I was hurt and embarrassed. Then she tried to hold and kiss me and love my anger away. "Here, John," she said. "Come here." She whispered a clever, dirty promise in my ear and reached to unfasten my belt buckle. When I pushed her hand away and said what I needed most was to go out into the day and clear my head, she hit me with a large leather-bound textbook on modern dance and said, "Go, and see if I care." Then she shouted, "Go, Johnny. See if I care!"

Her name was Sarah Sanford, but she liked to be called Sissy. I was less than a hundred yards down the street, headed for town, when I heard her calling behind me, "Didn't I say it loud enough for you, Johnny! Didn't you hear me! Go to hell, John Girlie! Go to hell!"

As it happened, I had no real place to go. So I walked. I walked through one of those days when the air, heavy and foul with the odor of river sludge and exhaust, felt as if it might explode into a gleaming white blossom of fire right in front of my face. A million other wild voices joined the girl's and screamed through the haze, and for all I knew nothing would ever feel or look or sound or smell right again. I walked aimlessly through downtown Baton Rouge for an hour or more—down Nicholson for about a mile and along the tracks to where they docked the steamboat *Bienville* that made weekend party runs to New Orleans, and then along the levee until I came to the old Southern Pacific warehouse standing hard by the back street. The warehouse was empty except for some torn-open sacks of beans and insulation and what looked like a mound of wet lime. In one dark corner, near a stack of wooden pallets, I saw a man sleeping on a sheet of corrugated tin, his hands shoved into his dirty trousers, clutching at himself. For some reason I thought I recognized this poor fellow, and I nudged him with my foot to wake him up. "Let me look at you," I said. "Look here, friend. Let me look at you."

His face was red and swollen. "Let me look at you," he said drunkenly. "Look here."

"Who do you think you are," I said.

"Who . . . Who do you think you are."

I was headed back to my apartment near campus when I saw a burgundy Olds 98 parked at the Pastime Lounge under the I-10 overpass. This was the same model Jason Girlie used to drive, and it was dressed as his had always been. Standing in the shade of the corner building, the car had tinted windows, spoked hubcaps, thin gold stripes down the sides and political stickers on the back bumper and, it appeared, a new coat of wax. I walked up to the car and rapped on the windshield. "You want to talk to me, Grandfather? What is it you want to tell me?"

There was no one in the car. And I knew there was no one in the car. Still, it wasn't all that difficult, especially with my eyes closed, to picture the old man sitting behind the wheel in one of his seersucker suits and bow ties, heating up the cigarette lighter for the unchewed end of his Macanudo cigar. "Talk to me," I said. "Tell me something." But before he could respond, or the picture I held of him could, I climbed onto the hood and slammed my right forearm into the glass. The pain that ran through my arm and shoulder was not good, but not entirely unpleasant either. The windshield didn't break or shatter as I'd hoped, so I put my best left into it and heard a sound like a pigeon flying blind into a patio door.

I looked through the glass and saw that the only thing behind the wheel was a stack of papers stuffed into manila folders. "You go to hell," I said and forearmed the windshield. Laughing, I said, "I'm not going to hell, old man, you go to hell. You go to hell." I hit the windshield again and again and finally bore a hole through the cracked pane. Blood wet my shirt-sleeves and moved down my arms. I scratched my face and blood streaked it. I slid down from the hood and drove my foot into the door on the driver's side. Unlike the windshield, the door would not give. I dented it with each kick but could not drive my foot through its metal wall and reach the picture of the old man sitting on the other side. "You go to hell!" I shouted. "You go to hell! You go to hell!"

I kicked away at the door until a terrible, hot pain shot up my legs and into my groin. The pain made it hard for me to stand, and I thought I might vomit. I went back to forearming the glass, and by the time the police arrived, their lights flickering a dizzy blue flame over everything, I had punched out all the side windows. I was crying, sitting on the curb with my legs pulled in tight against me, and there was blood everywhere. There was also one very distressed black man in a three-piece suit saying, "My car, what have you done to my car! What have you done to my car!"

One of the patrolmen said, "Hey, Bill, it's Johnny Girlie." And his partner said, "Well, I'll be damned. Johnny Girlie. It is him."

I felt sorry for the old man in the suit, the one who owned the car. When he learned who I was, he said, "Johnny Girlie. Johnny Girlie did this? Why me, John? Why do this to me?"

In those days, when I was just out of the game and it was still good to be bad in Baton Rouge, I was the friend of anyone who knew my name, and a lot of people who knew the game of football knew my name. There was nothing about me and the Olds in the papers the next day. The two policemen let me off after I agreed to pay the man in the three-piece for what damage I had done—about a thousand dollars worth—and after driving me in their screaming cruiser to the emergency room of Our Lady of the Lake Hospital. I needed thirteen or fourteen stitches on the back of my right hand, eight to mend the meaty forearm gash and a shot of Novocain to numb the awful throbbing pain in my feet.

Two or three weeks later, I graduated with a degree in general studies and moved back home to Old Field. I moved back believing I could start all over again now that football and school were out and Jason Girlie was dead and gone and my father was somewhere with him. I went back believing everything would be made right and simple and that I would be the reason for it being made right and simple.

"You always have a place here," my mother said the first night I was home. "I hope Sam always feels the same way, too."

She and the maid, Sylvie Banks, had prepared an enormous meal to celebrate my homecoming. At the center of the red oak table was a huge arrangement of silk and dried flowers surrounded by a dozen burning candles in tall brass holders. "When Sam gets out of college and comes back home to live," my mother said, "he'll get the same royal treatment. He'll get all his favorite food. We'll kill the fatted calf, won't we, Sam?"

Sam, then a graduating high school senior, sat gazing at a bowl of cucumber soup. If he'd heard her, he made no sign of it.

"Sam got drunk last night with his little friends," my mother said. "Tell Johnny you got drunk, Sam."

"I got drunk," Sam said.

"Tell Johnny what else."

"I threw up," he said, still staring at the soup.

"Your grandfather was the last person to throw up in the kitchen sink," my mother said. "That is, until Sam did it last night. Tell Johnny that's right, Sam. Tell him that's right."

"That's right," Sam said.

"And tell him what else."

"I slept on the floor."

"He slept on the kitchen floor, John. I found him at six this morning curled up by the trash can."

"Please pass the sweet potatoes," I said.

It is true that in his last years my grandfather drank too much and often let the bottle fool him into believing he was young and strong and could kick a little ass if asked to. Always when drunk the only ass he kicked was his own, and he kicked it pretty hard. He also let the bottle fool him into believing he was not a bad catch for some of the easy, less discriminating women of Old Field, even some of the young ones. I suppose those football Saturday nights in his apartment over the store, listening in bed to my games on the radio, were not all spent alone, for there were some who still recognized him as Senator Girlie from de Laussat Parish and who were foolish enough to think he had great sums of money safely deposited in the First City Bank of Old Field. Fool women knew that before divorcing my grandmother, Jason Girlie had owned a slaughter house and meat distributing plant, two liquor stores, stock in both the Oldsmobile and Pontiac car dealerships and a small sweet potato farm. Smiling and with one clenched fist raised to the camera, he had managed to appear in the Old Field *Times* about once a week, usually on the front page—at the ribbon-cutting ceremony for a new feed store or attending to the governor on his campaign run through town or looking over flood damage to the bean farms west of Bigger's Swamp.

What fool women did not know was that the parish courts had long ago split up his and my grandmother's estate, and that after serving only one term in the state senate, he lost in a landslide to an attorney thirty years his junior and retired in disgrace from what he liked to call public life. Another thing they didn't know was that Jason Girlie had squandered most of his money trying to make it rich in the oil fields off the Louisiana Gulf Coast. Gone for good was the more than two hundred thousand dollars he had dumped into a project headed by Ben Mawry, his legal counsel at the statehouse. He and Mr. Mawry had hired a petroleum engineer to devise a contraption to filter and cleanse dirty oil on the boats that serviced the offshore rigs, but the engineer turned up missing one day and so did my grandfather's money. His dream of making a quick fortune as an oilman died then, I suppose, and the rest of his savings went into an abandoned building in the middle of Old Field's run-down business district. He became the only man in town who sold Florsheim shoes and Sansabelt slacks. "This is pennies," he used to say. "This ain't money."

He called the place Girlie's Men's-and-Boy's.

When I was still in high school, my mother often took me and Sam shopping for clothes at the store, or we'd stop by just to say hello, but my grandfather was rarely there. I knew he spent much of his time drinking at Trudy's Yam Bar near the fairgrounds because sometimes, when we drove through that part of town, we'd see his Olds parked under the Yam's lighted sign that said RELAX, MAN, RELAX. Sometime after I had moved to Baton Rouge and made it through my first semester, he was thrown out of Trudy's Yam Bar for not paying his tab and stopped going to bars altogether. Sam still shopped with my mother at the store, and he told me they once heard somebody walking up above, on the top floor, and they knew it was him. Sam dialed his phone number and heard it ringing from where he stood at the checkout counter; then he heard it stop. When he put his ear to the receiver, Sam said, he could hear somebody breathing; he knew it was Jason. "This is Sam, Grandfather," he had said. And the old man had hung up. When Sam tried calling again, no one answered.

After that, my mother and my brother decided to let him be. They said he would get in touch if and when he wanted to, and they gave his periods of self-incarceration a name. A few times when I called home from school and asked if they'd seen him, my brother said, "No, the Senator's on another one of his sabbaticals." Other times my mother said, "He called just yesterday. Apparently his sabbatical is over."

The last ten years, arthritis had so twisted and disfigured his back and shoulders that kids in Old Field had taken to calling him the Old Hunchback and not Mr. Jason or Senator Girlie as he often insisted we refer to him. They created wildly imaginative stories about his origins, where he slept at night and why he chose to make periodic visits to our house on Ducharme Road. When the pain was so intense that he could no longer drive, he would call my mother and ask her to send me or my brother over. When he had to go to afternoon mass or to the K. C. Hall or to Bean's grocery, Sam usually took him, but only after a protest.

"Do it for me," my mother would say, "just this once. Do it for your mother."

And Sam would say, "But I did it for you last time, Ma."

"The keys are in the car," she'd say as he headed for the door. "I love you, Sam. I love you for this."

Once Sam had left, she would turn to me and say, "You really ought to be ashamed of yourself, Johnny. Your own grandfather."

A few days after they buried him, a writer with the Old Field paper called to say he was doing a report on Jason Girlie. He asked if I would meet him for breakfast and consent to an interview. I lied and said I knew next to nothing about my grandfather but would be willing to help all I could. We met at Bubba Toussaint's Grill off Beverly Boulevard and sat at the counter. The man put his tape recorder on top of the napkin holder and asked me how I remembered my grandfather, and I said the picture was always the same. I said it was of him and me alone in that fancy Olds he used to drive, and we were making our way through a field of sweet potatoes, out on the eighty acres he owned off the Sunset Highway. In the picture, I said, there were several head of cattle huddled under a run of pecan trees, most of them looking to eat the new green leaves off the lowest branches. We crossed a gully that ran clear to Bayou Claire, fifteen miles away, then up a short climb to the spot where a Houston wildcatter had contracted to set streamers of pipe deep into the belly of the earth. My picture of the old man also had a sound, I said, and it was the sound of a time that was gone and would never come again.

I said if I listened closely enough, I could still hear that seventy-year-old cripple clearing the silt from his pipes and spitting a big gob of phlegm and blood at me for saying, "There ain't a drop of oil in this place, Grandfather. And you know it."

The story ran on the front page of the Sunday paper, and it began with his life as a boy in Thomasburg, led up to what the reporter called "his middle-aged stumbling and bumbling around in the public arena" and ended with his final days of failure, the five years he spent in the apartment over the clothing store that went bankrupt three weeks before he put the busy end of a .16-gauge automatic shotgun into his mouth and pulled the trigger.

"Did he really spit on you," my mother asked the morning the story appeared. By the way her lower lip trembled, I could tell she was about to cry.

"Maybe he didn't mean to," I said.

"You should have told the newspaperman that," she said.

"Maybe. But then maybe I should've told him about the other things me and Jason talked about—like Jason saying he was proud of how he'd been all these years to Sam and me, and Jason saying he was a far better father to us than he'd ever been to your husband."

"Don't call him my husband," she said and pointed at me. "He was your father, too. Why can't you call him your father?"

"The real reason he spit on me was because I said your husband was a coward and an asshole and no different from him."

"Instead of calling him my husband or your father," she said, crying now, "you might consider calling him Jason's son. He was that, too, you know?"

"Husband, father, son," I said. "What's the difference? You married a coward who was also an asshole."

Jason Girlie's suicide came as a surpise to everyone who knew him, including his family, and we buried him in the yard behind Our Lady Queen of Heaven Catholic Church. It was the winter of my senior year in college, raining and cold, sometime in February. At his wake, the funeral director told my mother it was the largest crowd he had ever handled. This made my mother proud. There was a flower arrangement from the governor and one from U.S. Senator Russell Long, Huey's son. And these were the two she asked people to smell when they approached the open casket.

I told her those flowers were no better than and smelled no different from the ones Old Lady Hazzard and Jippie Babineaux and Joseph Maugham sent, but she pretended not to hear. I told her she was acting as if it was her father who had died, not the father of the man who had left her and me and Sam years ago, and she said, "You're out of order, John. You're way out of order."

When my friend Charley Paul Harwood arrived at the funeral parlor carrying a spray of wild flowers he had picked on his father's soybean farm and arranged in a rusty tin pail full of pond water, she said, "It was a very nice thought. Thank you," and turned away and pressed her nose against one of the blossoms on the governor's fan. She was, I suspected, trying to make me feel guilty for not carrying on as if his death were the absolute worst thing that had ever happened to me. She asked me if I'd heard what Father Ross was telling everybody. "Do you know he prayed for you?" she said.

"Father Ross gets paid to pray for people," I said.

"Not him," she said. "Your grandfather. Jason Girlie prayed for you."

Then she said, "Father Ross was telling Harold LaFleur and Mr. Strother and a few others—they were men who campaigned for him in the old days—he was talking about the time your grandfather sent you a telegram before the Alabama game in Birmingham. I think it was Alabama. The telegram said he was praying that you'd win and make the spread. And you called him from the locker room at halftime—from Legion Field, Father said—and told him not to do that anymore. He asked why not, and you said the players on the other team had grandfathers, too, and they were probably praying just as hard."

My grandparents were divorced when I was still in grade school, but no one mourned the old man's passing more than my grandmother. In the weeks after the funeral, Marie Girlie left her bedroom only to go to the bathroom or to get something to eat. My mother went to see her every afternoon after work, and they huddled together on top of the bedcovers and fingered the beads of their rosaries. There were two full-sized, four-poster beds in the master bedroom. Some nights, after cleaning Marie's kitchen and watching the ten o'clock news, my mother called to report she was staying over and sleeping in the guest bed. She was playing the role of friendly, understanding nurse and having the best time of it.

Once when she came home in the morning, she fixed a pot of coffee and brought it out to me in what we called the outdoor kitchen, though it was really just a large storage room set off from the main house and crowded with broken electrical appliances, sepia-toned photographs in cheap plastic frames, a chewed-up throw rug and a single bed without a headboard. I could see her wet lips. She wore makeup and smelled of baby powder and something else, something like calamine lotion. Her hair was wet and combed straight back from the forehead. You could see the clean lines the comb had made and the hard angles in her face, the way her cheeks seemed to hold the light. You could see the dull heaviness of her body, her wide hips and the way her soft cotton housedress made her breasts look as if they hung down to her waist. "What did you do last night," she asked, putting the pot on the front burner of the stove. "You see Charley?"

"We played some pool at Black Fred's," I said. "I got home after you'd already gone. How's Marie?"

"Marie's fine. She wants to know why you don't come see her."

I didn't say anything because I didn't know what to say. I

pointed in the direction of the stove and she understood. She fixed me a cup of coffee and came over and sat on the edge of the bed. "Every time I try to talk about him," I said, "you end up crying."

"Every time you try to talk about him, you make me cry."

"You cry because I bring up someone's name you can't talk about."

"Because you bring up your father's name," she said.

"That's right," I said. "I bring up my father's name."

When just out of high school, only seventeen, my mother had entered the Miss Lake Pontchartrain beauty contest in New Orleans and won. I was always much impressed by this and regarded it more highly than I did her brief but prosperous career as a fashion model in Dallas and New York. In the bottom of her antique chifforobe at home, there was a rhinestone-studded crown wrapped in blue velvet and a white sash that said MISS L.P. The velvet and the sash smelled of moth balls. As a girl, my mother had been very thin and big-chested, and she had long brown hair she kept in pigtails. After Sam and I came along, she was always dieting but never very success-fully. She wore white nylon girdles and white nylon brassieres that left deep red pinch marks on her back and shoulders. On the phone with friends, she sometimes talked about her figure as if it were something she had misplaced and never recovered. "What happens to people?" she said. "Will you please tell me what happens to people?" At church, or at any closed-in place as quiet as a church, you could hear her thighs rubbing together when she walked. To my ears this was a sexual sound, eliciting thoughts of the bedroom, and when my middle body responded to my lewd thinking, I blushed with embarrassment and my ears burned. I was confused. I invented conversations between my mother and me. "If you're so hot," I imagined myself saying, "then how come your husband left?"

"Your father," I imagined her saying. "Call him your father."

"If you're so hot, then how come he ran off with another girl?"

"You don't think I'm pretty, John? You don't think your mother's pretty? What's wrong with me, John?"

As a boy, I decided they had named her Miss Lake Pontchar-train because of her father-in-law's money. When I confessed this to Marie, she said I was wrong and should apologize to my mother for thinking such a thing. She showed me a picture of my mother in her wedding gown and traced her figure with the tip of her finger. She said Jason Girlie had not begun to get rich selling cars and liquor until after my mother had married and given birth to me. And she reminded me that my mother had come from "a very fine but uncelebrated family," people who lived simply and "without an ounce of fancy to speak of."

"Besides," she said, "my son had good taste. He certainly wouldn't have married Janie Maines unless she was a pretty girl. And what a figure she had, John! It was like an hour glass. You could have turned her upside down and told time by that girl's body."

I could not tell Marie that the real reason I thought Jason had bribed the judges of the Miss Lake Pontchartrain pageant had nothing to do with how shapely my mother was or how she looked in a wedding gown, but why my father had left. The few times I had asked my grandmother about my father's disappearance, she said, "One day you'll understand, Johnny. Give it time. Be patient."

But this was how my grandmother answered all questions that were impossible or too difficult to answer. Why did Jason drink so much? Why did the tomatoes come out so mushy and dull this year? Why do girls have what they have between their legs and boys have what they have? Why, Marie?

"One day you'll understand, Johnny," she said. "Be patient. Give it time."

Now my mother was holding the coffee cup to my lips, letting me sip and inhale the muddy aroma. "You think Jay's no good because he didn't come to his own father's funeral," she said. "Perhaps he had every reason in the world not to come to his father's funeral."

"You'll start crying if I tell you why I think he's no good."

"Tell me anyway," she said. She leaned against me and put her head on my chest. She was still sitting down, holding the cup of coffee in her lap with both hands. She had put her head on me that way because she didn't want me to see her eyes.

"You think I'll ever see him again?" I said.

14

"I don't want to discuss it, John. Not tonight. Please, baby. The day has been so emotional already. I'm tired of feeling things."

"But, Ma," I said. "You have to tell me."

When she didn't say anything, I said it again. "Tell me now," I said. "Tell me what happened. Tell me why he left."

"You want me to cry," she asked, and started crying. "You want me to cry again?"

"No, I don't," I said. "I just want to know about him. I want to know how he could leave the way he did and still live with himself. What kind of man can walk away from his family and just never come back? His father's dead. Don't you think it's lousy that he wasn't around for the burial? I just don't see how he can stand his own skin."

When she said nothing, I knew better than to push it any further. My mother had a famous way of letting you know when a particular discussion had reached its end. She stood erect and corrected her clothing. She ran her index finger along the space between her neck and her collar or pulled on the bottom of her vest to make sure it covered her beltline or pinched the crease in her trousers. She must've been satisfied that all was well with her house-dress because she went about straightening the mess I'd made of the bedcovers. She reached under the top wool blanket and tugged at the sheets, then she worked the blanket until it was as straight as she could get it. She said, "This old musty Army issue thing," and ran her hand over the blanket and across my belly. There was more light in the room, and I could see dusty black smudges under her eyes where her mascara had run.

"That blanket," she said, standing up. "It was his, your father's. I don't know what it's doing here."

"It's only a blanket," I said.

"Yes. But it was your father's blanket."

"That tells me a lot. That really tells me a lot."

"It tells you something," she said.

I waited until we were at the kitchen table, having lunch about three hours later, to ask if my father was in the Army.

"I never said he was in the Army," she replied.

15

"If the blanket belonged to my father, why didn't you burn it with the rest of his things?"

"I guess I forgot about it," she said.

"Will you burn it now," I asked.

"I might. Or bury it." Then she said, "Oh, baby. You're talking with your mouth full again. Please stop."

2

When I was still a boy, I learned that some things are best left unremembered and decided that it was okay to let go or simply forget a particularly difficult time if I didn't like it or considered it of little use. My mother, having once taken a course in child psychology at Newcomb College in New Orleans, believed that my inclination to eradicate certain unkind moments would retard my emotional development and lead to a definite, irreversible flaw in my character. "You have to address every misery," she said. "And you have to do it the best way you know how. Sometimes the best way is not the easiest, but you have to do it anyway."

"*You* might have to," I said, "but I don't."

A person had to take the bad with the good, she said, and neither underestimate the good nor overestimate the bad. She might have said that the good and bad in a person's life generally came in equal measure, and both had to be dealt with, but she didn't. If she had, she might've been forced to wonder seriously at the deluge of misery that hit her at such an early age—she was only twenty-nine when my father left—and she might've decided that God, in all his heavenly boredom, had plucked her and her alone out of the crucible and was having a fine time playing mean tricks on her.

I once bashed the front end of her Pontiac sedan into the rear of a slow-moving mail truck and, wanting very badly for it not to have happened, tried to purge the incident from memory by the next morning.

"How fast were you going," she asked me over breakfast.

"When?" I said.

"When you ran into that poor man," she said.

"When I ran into what poor man?"

"Pick and choose," Sam liked to say. "Johnny Girlie picks what he wants to remember and chooses to throw out the rest."

Of course I wasn't for a second able to forget anything as serious as a car wreck. But I had liked to pretend that I was. The truth, being the truth, was less mysterious: I was inclined to want to forget, but unable, as hard as I tried, not to remember.

My memory of my father was one thing I never pretended to forget or wanted not to remember, for there simply wasn't enough of it, and what there was seemed unfinished. For Sam and me, the whole ordeal was a lot like going to a movie, watching a few of the early scenes and being sent home before learning what becomes of everyone. You never knew if the hero ended up happy or sad, or if he lived in sickness and died or in peace and prospered. Somebody once told me that his friends called him Beau when he was a boy, and I spent an incalculable amount of time trying to find out whether this was something I had known and put away, or whether it was something I never knew and should feel lucky to have discovered. I didn't ask anyone about it. I mostly spent long hours alone in my room, staring into the darkness and calling what I knew of him before me, or sleeping and building a dream that brought him back to me and the house on Ducharme Road.

Even the smallest, least significant things my father and I did together came to hold places of great importance in my mind. I saw him driving his pickup truck and heard the sound of it, the radio going, and it was a picture and a sound that could make me laugh or cry or both laugh and cry at once. I saw the way he turned the dial trying to find some talk show out of Shreveport, and I saw the green light of the dashboard on his face and how handsome he was in it. He was the most handsome man I ever knew. The knuckles on his hands were hard and knobby, swollen from his days as an amateur boxer, and this added to his beauty and allure. Because his face was unmarked, I decided he must have been a good fighter; I decided he was never hit, never suckered. I decided he never lost.

I remembered him shaving with a straight razor in the morning before work, the steam on the glass and the way the white soap melted and ran in streams into the dark hair of his chest. I saw how he slept on his back with his right arm over his eyes and his left hand on his belly, and how his belly, brown and taut and with a slinky furrow of hair, moved with his breathing. Sometimes I could hear his voice as if he were seated right beside me, but other times it seemed to come from far away. Sometimes it was a deep and hollow sound that reminded me of someone knocking on the door of an empty room and asking to be let in. Even harder than making out what he said was hearing others speak to him and putting together their conversations. I could not, for example, hear my mother telling him *Okay, you take Sylvie home tonight, I'll pick her up in the morning.* Or, *Will you turn out the lights, will you please come to bed now.*

What time did was make it seem as if he'd always lived apart from the rest of us, even when he lived with us.

He disappeared when I was nine; in September, I think, or early October. I remember coming home from school and seeing both the family car and his truck gone. The garage door was wide open, as was the screen door to the kitchen, pushed all the way back on its hinges and kept from swinging shut by a ceramic Siamese cat. I walked through the house, turning on lights in every room and shouting, "Mom, you home? Dad?" But no one answered. When I reached their room, I saw her lying in bed with covers up to her neck. She was looking in the opposite direction of the door. She seemed to be looking at a picture on the wall or at the chifforobe. "Why are you in bed?" I said. "It's daytime. It's not even night."

"Let your mother rest," she said.

"Where's Daddy?" I said. "Where is he? What's wrong?" When she didn't say anything, I said, "Who took the car?"

"It's in the shop."

"What about the truck? Who took the truck?"

She pulled the covers even higher, then turned and faced me. It was dark in the room. I couldn't make out her face. "Are you sad?"

I said. I walked to the bed but she turned away. "Ma, are you sad?" I said again. "Why are you sad?"

"Go away," she said. "Leave me alone."

They found his truck a few days later in Holly Beach, a small hunting village in the southwestern heel of the state, about forty miles from the Texas border. It was an old unknown place that hardly figured in the flat brown vastness of the marsh country, but it was an old unknown place that had helped make my father a rich man. His Old Field law firm, J. Beauregard Girlie and Associates, had specialized in workmen's compensation and personal injury cases, many of which arose from accidents and disputes on the rigs off the Gulf Coast. His clients, for the most part, were uneducated men who lost hands and feet and arms and legs to the violent machinery of oil exploration and who later collected millions of dollars in consideration of their missing body parts and pain and suffering. My father spent some of his happiest days hunting for ducks and geese on his lease in the marsh west of Holly Beach, and it was while sporting by the sea that he met and recruited some of his best clients. After his disappearance, a search of the reed blind on the property turned up only a couple of unopened cans of Vienna sausage and a dozen or so empty shotgun shells. His truck was parked under a shanty set on creosote pilings, the same rental unit he used whenever he went to the beach during hunting season. They found his wallet and a bowie knife in the glove compartment, but the place itself appeared to be untouched. The beds were made, the dishes cleaned, the bathtub unsoiled. There was nothing to eat in the kitchen cupboard. The hot-water heater had not been turned on.

Without newspaper reports I would've known very little about his disappearance and the search to find him, because my mother refused to talk about it to me or anyone else. When the paper and its screaming headlines came every morning, I picked it off the front porch and hurried to the bathroom and locked the door. Stepping over the edge of the tub, I sat on its dry bottom and read the story over and over again. In one early article, the District Attorney said agents with the Federal Bureau of Investigation were working around the clock on my father's case, and the story included a quote from Jason saying he had not yet been contacted by anyone about ransom money.

In a story published ten or twelve days into the search, Jason said he would not give up hope that his son was still alive, and I took this to mean something that had never really occurred to me, that he might be dead. Other sources quoted in the story said there was no evidence of foul play and no leads to indicate that my father had been abducted. When I asked my mother if kidnappers had taken and killed Daddy, she said, "No, baby, no," and started to cry. "If ever you hear that," she stammered, "it's not true. Your father is not dead. He's not. He's not dead."

A few times when I was in the bathroom studying the morning paper, Sam knocked on the door, begged me to let him in and threatened to tell on me if I didn't. The first time I let him in, he said, "Read to me." I started to read that day's item about our father but he said, "No. Something else." So I turned to the comics and read as he pointed out the funny characters in each block of the strips. When I was done, I turned to the front page and he put his hands over his ears while I read aloud. "I said don't," he said, but I did anyway. I don't know why. I was four years older and thought I could do whatever I wanted.

When I showed him the pictures accompanying the story, he seemed uninterested. There was one depicting my father and grandfather embracing on the courthouse steps; the caption began with BETTER DAYS, then described my grandfather's victory four years earlier over incumbent Boyd Jones in one of the closest races in local election history. Both my father and grandfather wore seersucker suits and striped bow ties and dark wing-tip shoes. This was the only picture Sam liked, because both men were smiling. He asked me to read the caption again and again until he had memorized the words and could pretend to be reading along with me.

"You don't even know what it means," I said.

"I do, too," he said.

"Then tell me what it means," I said.

"I don't have to if I don't want to," he said.

"See," I said. "You don't either know what it means."

The newspaper coverage seemed to go on forever, but I doubt that it lasted more than a few weeks, or until the DA's office and the FBI decided that Jay Girlie had not been abducted by hoodlums and held for ransom but had, in all likelihood, grown tired of his life as a responsible husband and father and skipped town to begin again. They probably learned of a love affair with another woman—someone who worked in his office, who waited on him at lunch, who was a fan of his work in the courtroom. Even after the publicity surrounding the search had begun to die down, my mother refused to allow reporters in the house, and Sylvie always answered the phone. "Mr. Girlie's wife is not in right now," was her standard reply, including those times my mother sat in the darkened living room not twenty feet away.

The few times my mother met at home with sheriff's deputies and other law enforcement people, Sylvie drove Sam and me to the Girlie place in the country and let us hunt for lizards and water moccasins along the back bayou until she figured it was okay to take us back to town. One time, nearing our house on Ducharme Road, she saw strange cars parked on the front drive, braked quickly and reversed at high speed to the corner. Then she turned around and drove off in a hurry to South City Park, where Sam and I played on the swings and monkey bars and counted the leaves on the floor of the dry municipal pool.

"I want to go home now," Sam said. "Sylvie, please. It's time to go home." He started walking toward the car.

"Your mama said not when she's busy with those people," she called after him. "Sam! We have to wait. She said to wait."

Sam sat for about two hours on the backseat of the car, with the doors locked, before letting Sylvie and me in. His arms were crossed and his chin sat heavily on his chest. He looked like a little brooding monk. "I ought to get a switch," Sylvie said. "I ought to switch you good, boy."

"Switch me," he said. "It won't hurt."

I said, "If *I* switched you, it would hurt. Sylvie, can I switch him? He thinks he's so tough. You aren't so tough, Sam."

We were almost home when Sylvie pulled off on the shoulder

of Blue Hill Road and stopped the car. She reached over the vinyl seat and touched Sam on the side of his face, then she wet the tips of her fingers with her tongue and tried to straighten his mussed-up hair. Her eyes were wide and dark and sad. Her lips quivered and tears cut her dusty cheeks. "It's just that Sam don't like being famous people," she said, turning back onto the road. "Famous people got too many worries, too many bills to pay, too many dreams to keep. Am I right, Sam? Or am I wrong?"

"Right," he whispered after a moment.

"You can apologize now," she said. "You can tell us you're sorry for what you done and it's all forgotten."

"Sorry," he said.

"Well, sure you are," she said. "I never knew nobody so sorry as Sammy Dan. Poor Sammy Dan. Sorry, sorry boy."

It was Jason, more than anyone else, who was responsible for keeping the local news coverage alive and promoting the possibility that his son had been kidnapped. Having almost completed his first term in the state senate, Jason was back out on the campaign trail and trying to drum up votes for reelection. He didn't much mind having his name and picture in the paper, even under such dire circumstances, since early polls showed that he lagged far behind his opponent and would most likely lose. He needed this publicity.

When a New Orleans television station included him on a list of Louisiana's least effective leaders, he hollered, "Just spell the goddamned name right, boys. Just spell it right." And he spelled the name, "G-i-r-l-i-e." He was standing in the living room of his own house, and since Sam and I were the only boys around, we spelled the name—that is, I spelled the name, and Sam, still struggling to learn the alphabet, said whatever I said. Jason turned off the television and walked unsteadily to his favorite chair in the corner. He started to untie and take off his shoes, but after thinking about it for a second, he left them on, returned to the warm TV and put his foot in the screen. The set exploded like a cherry bomb. It fizzed and spit even after he'd pulled the plug from the wall socket. "That'll teach you," he said.

Sam ran into the kitchen, where Marie was writing letters at the table, and said, "Grandfather ruined the television. He kicked it with his foot. Come see. Hurry. Come see."

Jason, a few steps behind Sam, walked to the sink as casually as he would have if going for a glass of tap water. When Sam said, "Grandfather kicked it, he kicked it," Jason wheeled around and announced, "From here on out, son, it's Senator when you're talking to or about me. Do you hear what I'm saying? This Grandfather business has got to stop. That goes for you, too, John."

My grandmother, who had covered her ears with her hands upon hearing the television explode, objected with a squeal and mighty rustle of papers, but Jason cut her off. "And you—you don't call me anything, woman," he said. "Don't talk to me and don't give me a single damned minute of hung lip about it."

I would later learn that it was Jason, not my mother, who first contacted local police and reported my father missing and demanded a full-scale investigation into what he called "this act of barbarism, of human piracy, of theft of life." He was wild and unforgettable, shouting on a radio news program, "Find him, find him, find him!"

One night, a Baton Rouge TV station showed him trying to organize a modern-day posse to track down the kidnappers and free his son. How could he, the freshman senator and elected representative of the people, admit that his own offspring, his only child, had simply up and left his beautiful wife and children, abandoning them to get along in the world alone?

"If the body of law that governs this great land of ours fails to find my boy and bring him home to the people he loves and who love him," he said, "then this portly and smelly old body of mine won't."

By Jason's reasoning, admitting that his son had skipped town might lead voters to believe that this shameful behavior had everything to do with genetic makeup and could be traced back to the previous generation, and specifically to the Senator himself. Years later, when I was in high school, Marie told me that Jason had torn up the notepad of a reporter who made the mistake of asking if he'd ever wondered if Jay Girlie had just run off.

For almost three months after my father disappeared, my mother's daily routine included eighteen uninterrupted hours of sleep and six more in a catatonic state not unlike that of some dark creature in a monster movie; it was as if she decided to wake every afternoon only for the chance to fall asleep again. When finally she got out of bed one morning and declared herself "armed and ready to get on with this life," she began making even her most important decisions with little if any thought. Perhaps while asleep, she had talked herself into believing that making her choices swiftly would somehow set things on their proper course and give them less chance of failing.

"Don't think so blessed much," I heard her say once. "Just do."

To spare me the agony of having to answer questions at the public school a short two blocks away, she decided to send me to an all-boys Catholic school in the city of Lafayette, which was about forty miles from Old Field on the interstate. Every morning at six o'clock, she woke me by crawling into my bed and singing one of the songs she knew from church. If it wasn't the one I liked best, I said, "I want angels," and she immediately gave me angels, or at least the song about Saint Michael the Archangel. She fed me a breakfast of toast, scrambled eggs and hot chocolate, dressed me in a pair of khaki pants and a white button-down shirt and walked with me to the bus stop on the corner of Dunbar and Eleanor, where a plain yellow van would arrive with THE ACADEMY OF THE IMMACU-LATE CONCEPTION painted across its sides. This continued from late September until the end of the school year in May. Every morning, as the driver and his five little passengers watched, she wet the tips of her fingers and tried to straighten the cowlick in my hair.

Every morning she said, "Next year we'll be back at Park Place, back with your friends. I promise."

When I asked her if it was a real promise or just a pretend promise, she said it was a real promise, there was no such thing as a pretend promise. Then she said, "I promise it's a real promise, but you have to promise you'll always be my John Girlie, you'll always love me."

"I'll always love you," I said.

"And will you always come home," she asked.

"I'll always come home," I answered, knowing exactly what she wanted to hear and that saying it would give her peace and spare me further embarrassment. "I promise I'll always come home but only if you promise to be here when the bus comes back."

There were other parents who walked their children to the corner of Dunbar and Eleanor, but my mother was the only one who cried seeing the bus off. The other kids knew better than to ask why my mother carried on so. Even then I was known as an athlete and a fighter, with big hard hands and a mean knuckler, which was a famous way of extending the middle joint of the middle finger from the fist and throwing it into the other fellow's rib cage.

"See you later," I shouted through the open window of the bus, pulling away. "Everything'll be okay now, Ma."

"You'll be home when?" was often the last thing I heard.

I was not yet ten years old but already I felt responsible for her. She said, "You're the man, you're the boss around here now, John," and I accepted that as truth. When at night we read Hardy Boys and Happy Hollisters books, I would stop in the middle of a sentence and ask her something about herself, less out of curiosity than from a feeling of obligation. I knew that doing so made her happy. Pointing at the spot, I would ask, "What does it feel like having hair down there?" and she would answer, "Well, young man, it's like being special. Like being a lady." I knew a little about pubic hair, but I also knew that asking about such things inspired her to refer to me as young man and not as her son or baby or boy. So when I wanted to feel little and not so grownup, I'd ask about the past. "Did you really have a horse named Horse?" I would say and, hearing her say yes, would want to know how it felt to kiss Buddy Holly on the lips on the beach at Lake Pontchartrain.

I had a list of questions, and she said she had all the answers.

Our agreement, the only one we ever shook on, was that I told her everything and she told me almost everything. Her favorite thing to talk about—to me at least—was the period of nine months she carried me in her womb. Several times she had me place my hand on her stomach, close my eyes and imagine a tiny foot kicking my palm. She told me she used to sing to me in the bathtub at night, when she was well into the pregnancy, and I would play the drums with my feet on the wall of her belly. When I asked how a baby came to live in there, she almost always said, "God in heaven put him there."

The time I told her that my friends at school said a man put his thing into the place where there was hair and that got the baby going, she said, "God in heaven put him there, Johnny," and slammed her hand down on the dinner table.

She had all the answers as long as the questions did not focus exclusively on my father or suggest that his existence had anything to do with us. "Buddy LeRoid at school said your daddy puts his thing where there's hair down there and then the baby gets started," I said.

"Are you telling me the man who was your father is God in heaven?"

"No, ma'am."

"Only Jesus makes babies," she said. "Buddy LeRoid's a fool."

I always suspected her loneliness, her need to be touched and stroked and slept with. She often came into our bedroom and nestled close to Sam and me while we slept. Her presence was never unwelcome, though sometimes she insisted on waking us up. "Come on, baby," she said. "Talk to me. Tell Mommy something." She invited us to join her in her bed anytime we had bad dreams or simply wanted someone to hug. Sam never accepted her offer; he said her bed was too soft and hurt his back, though I knew there was more to it than that. He once told me that sleeping in her bed, in the place that had once been Daddy's, made him mad enough to want to hit somebody. It made him sweat, he said, and his stomach ached. Late at night in our own bedroom, when he sucked his thumb and hid under covers, I said only babies sucked their thumbs and hid under covers. "Okay then," he said, "I'm a baby."

If I kept picking on him, he would build a tent in the corner of the room by placing blankets and sheets over chairs and lamps. Then he would pretend to lock the door to the tent and swallow the key. When I said, "You're really not locked in there, I can break right through those walls," he said nothing. And even when I said, "I know you can hear me, Sam. I'm not stupid, I can even see you through the cracks," he still said nothing.

After a while I came to believe that the tent really was locked and soundproof and that nothing could hurt him as long as he stayed inside. On the inside, he could even talk about our father. "Daddy left us," he once said. "He took off forever and ever and ever."

"Not forever he didn't," I said, though I knew in my heart that what my brother was saying was true.

"Yes, he did," Sam said. "He left. He's gone. And he ain't coming back." Then he said, "Daddy's dead."

"If they kidnapped him it was for money," I argued. "Nobody called about money. We still have all our money."

He was lying on his back, staring at the ceiling of sheets. "He's dead," he said. "To me he's dead. I know he's dead."

One day after my mother scolded me for asking a question about my father—it was a silly question, I remember; I wanted to know if he had a battleship tattoo on his chest—I built a tent of my own, one nearly twice as large as Sam's, and refused to come out for more than twelve hours. My mother placed a jar of M&Ms near the entrance of my tent hoping to lure me out. "John," she said, "your mother's going to call the police if you don't come out this very second. Do you want me to call the police?"

Sam, whose shadow I could see on the ceiling of my tent, said, "No one can talk to you when you're inside, Mom. Johnny can't hear you."

"Come out, Johnny. I'll tear your tent down if you don't come out. I'm going to count to ten. One . . ."

"You're deaf in there," Sam said. "Johnny's deaf in there."

I was deaf until she placed a plate of hot turkey and sweet potatoes next to the M & M's. My favorite meal was hot turkey and sweet potatoes and M & M's. Sam said, "You don't hear food talking, you smell it. It wasn't your ears that ruined it. It was your nose."

"It was ruined before it even started," I said.

"Your tent wasn't real," he said. "Mine was a house."

3

When I was in college, Charley Paul Harwood and I often hunted the marsh at Holly Beach and stayed in the little Hotel Cameron just across the sand road from the house where they found my father's truck. It was a good place to go after the fall semester and football season because it gave me a chance to hide and sleep and catch up on what I'd missed during five solid months of football. Sometimes we took girls along and rented two rooms. If they came along prepared to rough it, the girls liked the morning quiet with the windows open to the smell of the dirty sea and the wind blowing back the white cotton drapes. You could walk on the short balcony and look out past the road and the run of shanties at the drilling and production oil rigs way off on the horizon and at the long brown beach littered with beer cans and bottles and grass sacks that held the discarded heads of boiled crawfish and shrimp.

When the smell was bad, as it often was, closed doors and windows could not keep it out of your room, and the girls who were not prepared to rough it complained of nausea and asked to go home. Either that or they wanted to travel the road north to Lake Charles and the Holiday Inn, where there was room service until three in the morning and a wet bar by the swimming pool. At the Hotel Cameron, there was no room service and no wet bar. You brought your own bottle or bought one at the tackle shop. For food, there was the Café Noir off the two-lane strip coming into town, and it served Cajun and Creole cooking that most girls objected to: rabbits in a mushroom gravy seasoned heavily with cayenne pepper and spring

29

onion tops, and baked duck with cornbread dressing made from the
ground hearts and livers and gizzards of the birds, and on Sundays
there was always barbecued garfish and a bloody pork sausage or
boudin. The girls either said they didn't care for the wild flavor of
the game, or they asked permission to be excused and sat in high
chairs at the bar or out on the pine deck that faced the water. This
complaining was why Charley and I usually made the trip alone and
took only one room. We liked the strong, high taste of the food and
the fecund odor of the marsh, and it was better to hunt with the
intention of getting a few shots in than to hunt wondering about the
girls we'd left sulking back at the hotel.

When we were alone and the hunting was good, I rarely
thought about my father. We left the Hotel Cameron hours before
daybreak and ate honey buns and strips of salted beef on the ride
to the lease. Charley's father leased the property from a man named
Fontenot who ran a couple of shrimp and oyster boats. Fontenot
hated the hunt season and had little to say to hunters except when
they were late paying for the right to use his land. After killing our
limit, Charley and I sometimes stayed in the reed blind and watched
the birds move and feed in the rice fields on the distant edge of the
marsh. When he was drinking, Charley liked to call them in and wait
until they had set on the muddy pond before firing a blind overhead
shot and scaring them off in a panic. Ducks blessed with any memory
never returned, and those with no memory at all came back a few
hours later only to be scared away again. Several times we had stayed
until sundown and drank from bottles of cheap whiskey and talked
as loudly as we could, keeping everything but the moronic poule
d'eau out of our shooting range. If my mother's Pontiac remained
parked on Fontenot's pebble drive after dark, the old man would
paddle his pirogue out to our blind through the wooden decoys we'd
set afloat, and tell us it was no good hunting at night; it was illegal.
He was French and spoke with an accent that made him difficult
to understand.

One thing I did understand was the way he said, "Out, out!
You people, out!" Another was the resolute manner in which he

raised what looked like a machete from under his seat and waved it over his head.

At the Café Noir later in the evening, we turned over our kill to the cook, and he, in turn, had the waitress seat us at a table looking out on the Gulf and give us a bottle of homemade fruit wine that tasted good and sweet and gave you a numbing buzz after only a few swallows. We laughed telling the story of Fontenot to the rough-necks and tool pushers at the bar and stayed until the cook left the kitchen, walked across the sprawl of small oak tables and white wicker chairs and pulled the plug on the Pabst Blue Ribbon neon in the front window.

"See you tomorrow," he'd say as we headed for the door. "And bring what you shoot."

When the hunting was lousy, as it always was when there were girls along, I could think of nothing else but my father. I could think of nothing else because I spent most of the time walking the beach or the little sand roads and talking about what I knew of the place. And practically all I knew of the place had been related to me by my father when I was just a boy.

In relating what he'd told me, I was placing myself in his shoes and adopting the roles he had played, which invariably had left me feeling sad and upset. I missed him.

I told them how I had once watched a boy put the barrel of a Remington 12-gauge automatic shotgun into the mouth of a dead hammerhead shark that had washed ashore and pull the trigger. I described how the blast had exploded the head of the shark and let loose several dozen crabs that had been feeding on its insides, and how I'd managed to run down seven or eight of them and steamed them with a couple of ears of corn over a hot bed of charcoal.

Charley liked this story because it gave him the chance to take on my original role. "Well, Dad," he'd say, "were they good?" And I'd say, "Hell, yes, they were good. Steamed corn is always good," just as my father had said so many years before.

Later on, after night had fallen and the rigs lighted up like small white fires on the far water, and the girls were beautiful in the way they always were when away from home and in a place they had never been before, I would stand in front of the old, wind-scoured house on the beach road and tell the story of my father's disappearance and give Charley a chance to say, "You never saw him again?" And for me to say, "No. I never saw him again."

Charley especially liked this story because it sometimes worked so well that he got the chance to share a bed with a pretty girl and hear wild waters roll in his sleep. This was back when he was still considering a life as a priest in the Catholic Church, and through the thin layers of sheet rock and insulation that formed the wall between his room and mine, I could hear him say, "No, Julie, no. When I say, 'Go in peace to love and serve the Lord,' you say, 'Thanks be to God,' not 'Yes, I hear the angels sing.' Come on, please pay attention."

Once I heard a girl say, "Oh, Charley Paul, shut up and kiss me."

The girls liked the story about my father's disappearance because it showed that their taste in men was not so bad and that putting up with the stench of the marsh had its rewards. "You're both so sweet," a girl once announced as she threw her arms around me.

Charley said, "We've been called a lot of things but never sweet. Ain't that right, Van Gogh?" And he clutched his crotch.

Van Gogh was the name Charley had given to his penis.

My father's stories were not so good for everyone. The others laughed or felt their hearts pound, but the talk always left me feeling like a fraud. I had used these stories to get close to a girl, to convince her that I was not so wild a bastard for a bastard who was wild and that I was worth trusting. My behavior on those hunts when women came along nearly always left me embarrassed and full of regret. Some nights, after hearing myself try to impress my friends with sad, funny tales about the memory of my father and his times at Holly Beach, and after realizing I was a fraud who deserved the worst kind of death, I went and sat alone on the balcony at the Hotel Cameron and refused to let anyone near me. I thought drinking tumblers of rum and Coke and watching the little house across the road would work to get the picture of my father out of my head. But I was wrong. The trick—the only one I could ever count on—was to take off my clothes and get in bed with someone who could help me forget where it was I had come from and how it had all worked out. The trick after that was to close my eyes and sleep and wake in the morning and leave without stopping for the roast venison at the Café Noir and without once looking in the rearview mirror.

One night the sadness would not go away, so I sat on the balcony wearing nothing but a pair of camouflage pants and felt the damp breeze send a rush of goose bumps across my bare chest and back and arms. I heard the girl in the room ask me to please come to bed, it was late, and a voice that was mine say, "I'm coming, just wait, it won't be long now." Then from across the sand road I heard another voice. There was the blue light of a lantern in the window of the house, and behind it a voice I seemed to recognize. "You come here thinking you'll find me but you won't. You won't find me," I thought I heard the voice say. Then, "You'll never find me."

I was certain that it was my voice saying, "If I wanted to, I could find you," because the girl said, "Who are you talking to, Johnny, is somebody there?" There was a bottle at my feet, and I took a swallow from it. Then I took another and watched the blue light in the window of the little house go out and everything turn dark. "If I wanted to," I said and stopped. But I guess I decided I wanted to say something else. "I never wanted to find you, old man. Maybe you thought I wanted to find you, but I never did."

Then I heard the door to the balcony open and turned and saw the girl standing in the frail light of the moon. She was holding a sheet to her breast, letting it flow and cover the rest of her body, and the sheet looked wet and pink in the light. Her hair fell down to her shoulders and looked wet and pink on the side nearest me and flat and dark on the other side. She stood without moving, looking beyond me at the house across the road. "There was a light in the window," I said.

"You thought it was your father," she asked.

"I don't know who it was," I replied.

After she had gone back into the room and dressed and come

out onto the balcony again, she said, "Let's go see him. I would very much like to meet your father."

She held my hand. We walked down the stairs and through the lobby of the hotel, past the old lady working at her ledger behind the great mahogany desk and past the men in quilted overalls and fur-lined hats playing dominoes on the bare wooden floor. We walked through the swinging glass door and stood in our bare feet in the middle of the sand road. There was no traffic on the road. There was the air and its foul smell, and the moon, and the green and blue and white lights in the windows of the cabins and trailers set high above the road on pilings and girders of steel; and way off I heard the flat, metallic hum of the oil rigs.

"You said you didn't care if you never saw him again."

"I said I never wanted to find him." I replied. "There's a difference."

She was quiet for a moment, then said, "It wasn't him you were talking to. He's not here, Johnny."

"I know he's not here."

The house was dark. She held me by the arm and led me up the stairs. She knocked on the door. She knocked twice with the flat of her hand, then four times with her clenched right fist. I looked across the road at the Hotel Cameron and our room and the bottle on the floor of the balcony. There was the sound of the bolt lock being disengaged, and of a chain being drawn. A voice said, "Is there something you want?" and she said, "We were wondering if a Mr. Girlie was here." The voice said, "You want Mr. Girlie," and she said, "We were wondering if he was here. Is he in the house with you?"

The voice said, "There's no one I know of by that name, Miss. Not here anyway." And she said, "Thank you. Thank you very much. I hope we didn't wake you."

The next morning she woke me before dawn and told me it was time to go. She kissed my lips and my chest and told me it was time to go. Then she went down my belly and kissed me where I wanted to be kissed, and she said, "Let's go, Johnny. It's time to go. Please let's go."

After leaving Holly Beach, driving my mother's Pontiac down the road that cut the marsh in one lonesome ribbon, I felt better and was able to laugh. Climbing the highway, there were no gas stations for what seemed like a hundred miles, and no restroom facilities for the girls who sat under blankets on the back seat, drinking beer and playing cards. Almost every time the girls threatened to relieve their bladders on my mother's seat if I didn't pull over, I stopped the car in the middle of the road. If you could see forever down the monotonous blacktop strip and spot nothing but the tiny white forms of egrets feeding on bugs along the center line, you knew that parking in the middle of the road was not imperiling the lives of the women squatting in the space between the open front and back doors. But if there were shining white beads of light standing in the place where the egrets should have been, and you knew these shining white beads to be the lights of an automobile, it was a better idea to pull off the highway and find an abandoned dirt or board road leading to the spot where a derrick had once stood. After finishing their business, the girls piled back into the car and returned to their game of cards and bottles of beer.

More than once I had driven less than five miles back down the road to Old Field when I felt someone's tight little fist banging on my headrest and heard one of the familiar pained voices demand that I pull over this very minute.

"I like watching a girl squat and pee," Charley once said after we'd dropped off our dates. When I said nothing, he said, "It's the only real difference between them and us, if you think about it. They can't stand up and do it like we can."

I thought about it. "I can think of some other differences, Charley. That's not the only one."

He saw that I was serious. And because he wasn't drinking, I knew that he was serious, too. "You think they're better than us?" he said. "Women, I mean. Sometimes I think they're better than us, John."

"They're different, that's for sure."

"Don't laugh," he said. "But I used to squat to pee. I'd sit on the toilet like a girl instead of standing over it like I was born to.

Until kindergarten it's all I knew how to do, and I blame my old man for it. Malcolm was too religious and ashamed to show himself in front of me, so my mother, who was a little more liberal, would take me with her to the bathroom. We went to a shopping mall or something, and there I was with my mother in the bathroom. Everybody was squatting in those stalls, so I was squatting, too."

I was quiet. I knew he was waiting for me to say something that would hurt and humiliate him. But I didn't. And after a few minutes he said, "I'm glad you didn't laugh, John. Thanks. Thanks a lot."

"You're welcome," I said.

Because she didn't trust Charley driving the Jeep, my mother had insisted we take her car. But she neither liked nor approved of our trips to the marsh. Long before, she had sworn never to visit Holly Beach or eat wild game again, particularly duck, even at a restaurant. Charley and I gutted our kill and arranged the birds in uniform rows along the bottom of a ten-gallon cooler, then covered them with chipped ice. My mother refused to look when I opened the plastic lid and asked her to come and see what we'd done. "You won't believe how beautiful they are," I said, but she shook her head and turned her back to me.

"I'm not interested in what you found in that place," she said. "If it came from Holly Beach, I don't want it in my house. Do you hear me, John?"

By depriving herself of these small pleasures—of sharing in her son's success with a shotgun and eating what he killed—she was punishing her husband, and it did not matter that her husband, wherever he was, had no idea that he was being punished. All that mattered was that she and I both knew it.

"Did you take girls this time," she would ask when I got home.

If I said yes, she said, "Did they have their own room, or did they stay one with you and one with Charley? If one stayed with you, aren't you feeling terrible about yourself right about now, John Girlie? Aren't you feeling just a little guilty?"

She called me John Girlie when she was mad at me and simply John or Johnny when she wasn't. Whenever she was asking about one of my nights out with a girl, I could count on being called John Girlie.

"Or did all four of you sleep in the same bed?" she said. "Come on. Talk to me. Tell me something."

I always told her that Charley and I shared one room and the girls shared another, but I was never sure that she believed me. She had me strip off my soiled and bloody hunting clothes and deposit them in the laundry bin. One day I caught her checking the front pouch of my underwear. "What are you doing, Ma?" I said. "What are you looking for?"

"Girls today," she said and dropped the shorts into the washer, "are so very evil, John. They're so evil. And don't tell me they're not. Girls today give of themselves indiscriminately. And I don't mean just petting of the breasts. Girls today allow anything imaginable and they don't stop and think of the consequences."

"Not the girls I know," I said.

"You're so stupid," she said. "You're so blind."

There was no arguing with my mother over girls today. It was much too late to come to their defense, and her son of all people— her son who was stupid and blind—did not qualify to speak on their behalf. "I hate it when you talk that way," I said.

"Because it's true, you hate it."

"It's not true," I said. "It's a lie and it's degrading. I hate it because I'm good, Ma. I'm a good person. I don't do what you think when I'm with girls. I know how you raised me."

She always brightened up when I mentioned this. "It wasn't easy," she said. "But I did it, didn't I? I did pretty good raising you and your brother, didn't I?"

"You did great," I said. "And that's why you should trust me."

"Oh, baby, I do," she said. "I do. I really do." Then she put her face against mine, with her warm cheek flush against mine, and she kissed the air in front of my ear.

should not let on that I was ever obsessed with my father's disappearance and the search to find him. A few months after he left, I quit hoping someone would discover the reasons why he decided to leave us and never come back or send word of where he had run off to. In this world it is possible to leave at any moment and never return, to go away and begin again, and dying is not the only way. This is what my father taught me. In time, I stopped coming home from school half-expecting to discover his truck parked in the garage and Jay Beauregard Girlie himself sitting in his favorite chair in the living room, waiting for me to walk through the door and give him a hug. I no longer came home and checked the mail, hoping to find a postcard from some exotic, faraway place and his manic chicken scrawl saying all was well, the beaches were white and pure as confectioner's sugar, the sun high and good, no need to worry, love to all, Your Father.

Later, in high school, when I visited the bars on the weekends and ran the streets looking for girls, I sometimes saw him through the huge picture windows of the cafés in town, standing some distance from the maître d' and the waiters in their black formal dress and the people laughing over dinner. I saw him as I knew him when he still lived at home, not as he would have looked with almost ten years on him. Whenever I saw him so clearly that I wanted to stop, Charley needed only to remind me that it was whiskey talking, and I'd feel better.

Those times that I demanded we stop anyway, I stepped out of the car and headed across the thoroughfare, not even looking for traffic. When at last I reached the door and entered the building and saw that the man who was my father was just a man who vaguely resembled him, I felt much better though slightly exhausted from the heavy, unexcellent pounding of my heart.

"He isn't worth it," Charley said. "He quit on you, he quit on your mother, he quit on Sammy. The man's a fucking quitter, John."

"Fucking quitter," I said. "Fucking coward. Bum."

"Probably left for a piece of ass—some young tight quick piece of ass. Probably out there somewhere making money, making babies, pretending he's someone else. Probably thinks he's a free bird."

"I hate him," I said. "I hate him."

"Damn right you hate him," Charley said.

Exactly three months and a day after my father left, my mother decided it was time to clear the smell of her husband from her bedroom. She poured his cologne down the toilet and flushed it again and again until the handle stuck and Mr. Happy Leoswane, the plumber, was called on to fix it. She and Sylvie stored some of my father's clothes in two oversized cedar chests in the outdoor kitchen, then after a few days a pickup truck arrived, and two silent young men loaded the chests onto the bed of the truck, secured them with long pieces of hay-baling twine and drove off as my mother and my brother and me watched from the living room window. A few days later, my mother and Sylvie sent every article of bed linen to the cleaners to be laundered, along with the rest of the clothes he had kept hanging in his dressing closet, including his best suits and hats and the fine Oxford dress shirts with his initials, JBG, sewn on the cuffs.

When the laundry came back in white cardboard boxes and clear plastic wrappers, my mother had Sam and me add it to the top of a great pile of his private things she had made on the back lawn. If we spent too much time looking over the heap of my father's private letters and papers and favorite books, photographs and record albums, she made a terrific fuss and threatened to punish us both. When we asked her what she was doing—why the pile—she said she was doing what she must and told us to please try to understand. "It may seem like a silly grown-up thing to you now, but one day it won't," she said. "One day it will seem very simple and the right thing to do."

Then she said, "You'll forget it ever happened."

"No, I won't," Sam said. "I'll never forget."

"You'll forget," she said.

"Not me," Sam insisted. "I'll never forget."

"Oh, Sam," she said. "Apologize to your brother and me. Tell us you're sorry for being such a meanie."

"I won't," he said. "Because I'm not. I'm not sorry and I'm not a meanie. And I'm not going to apologize."

"You're a baby," I said.

"If you won't apologize," she said and slapped his legs with the flat of her hand, "I'll have to spank you with a belt. Johnny, run and get your mother a belt."

"Spank me then," he said and took off running down the hall to the bedroom and his blanket tent. I could hear him shouting at the top of his lungs, "I won't forget, I won't forget, I won't forget!"

When his shouting stopped, my mother turned to me. "He'll forget."

"I'll make him," I said, making a fist.

"He'll forget," she said again.

I suppose I knew then without any doubt that my father was never coming home again—not any time soon at least—and I suppose I also knew that she knew why he had left and perhaps where he had run off to. I might have given her a tougher time about her silence and the building of the great pile had I not feared that upsetting her would give her good cause to run off, too.

One night, after my mother went to visit Marie in the country without telling me beforehand that she was going out, I went to her antique chifforobe and was surprised to find that she had not emptied it of all her clothes, jewelry and prizes for winning the Miss Lake Pontchartrain beauty contest. If my father, who loved me, could leave without a word, so could my mother. On bad days, when I was feeling depressed, I almost expected her to go and wished that it would happen; if she planned to leave, I wanted her to do it right away so that I might be left alone to start over and get on with my life. If I was to be rid of my father, and also of my mother, I wanted it to happen quickly. And I seemed to think that the pain would be less severe if it were sooner than later.

On a night when the house was quiet and I figured everyone was asleep, I went outside with a flashlight and looked for things in the great pile that were most special to me and worth keeping. I pulled out one of my father's monogrammed dress shirts and put it on over my clothes. The tail of the shirt reached down past my knees, and the sleeves were almost double the length of my arms. I pulled out a small prayer book with a red silk cover and gold-trimmed pages that felt as light and dusty as the wings of a moth. My father had turned away from the Catholic Church years before marrying my mother, but he kept the book because there were pictures he liked of angels and songs he'd known as a boy. The angels were not cherubic but tall and majestic, with wings of gossamer and strong, handsome faces. Most of the songs began with "Sweet Jesus" and ended with "Save me, Lord." Out there by the great pile, I sat on the cold ground and read by the flashlight and heard my father's voice. He was singing, and you could feel how hard he strained to reach the high parts. It was the way he had sounded on that one Christmas Eve night when he went to Queen of Heaven and sat between Sam and me and sang so everyone could hear him. He sang because my mother had told us singing was like praying twice unto the Lord, and she had said his attendance at midnight mass was the only Christmas gift she truly wanted.

I sat on the lawn hearing his big voice again and imagining a pride of angels descending onto the lawn. I imagined them coming through a bright break in the sky and trailing a flood of light. A hard shudder ran through my body, then I felt the kind of warmth I would later learn also comes after too much drink. My body went limp. The ground was no longer cold, and the white beam of the flashlight was lost in the tremendous rush of light. Above my father's voice, I thought I heard the innocuous chatter of the angels, as pure as the wind in the trees. I heard the limbs of the trees creaking against the bright storm, the small branches rubbing together and whispering like insects. I thought I also knew the smell of the angels' wings, the scent of the divine essence, sweeter than sweet roses. When I looked into the gray of their eyes, as I was certain I had, I saw images of eternity—a bruised cloud, a rolling river. I saw time move and dance as it does when you want it to hold still and not spin out like some great road before you. I leaned back and rested my head on the bed of grass, blinded by all I wanted to see and saw and would never see again. After a while my father's singing became no louder than the voices of the angels, and the wind died, and the hole in the sky sucked back the light until it was dark and night again.

The next morning I woke in my bed to the sound of sirens and slammed car doors and Senator Jason Girlie saying my mother's name over and over again. He said it without anger or a mean spirit but with the most impossible sadness, as if he were looking upon the death of someone he knew and could find no words to make sense of it. I looked out my bedroom window and saw the flames taking the pile and how the ashes and violent sparks rose through the bare branches of the trees. It was a fire twice as tall as the heap of everything she had been able to find of my father's, and when I pressed my nose against the glass, I could feel the heat. My mother was wearing a housedress and work gloves and was raking things half-burned into the flames. My grandfather and several firemen in yellow slicker suits stood behind her, pointing at the sky and plotting some strategy to keep the fire from moving across the lawn to the house. "I knew she was going to burn it," Sam said behind me.

When I didn't turn to face him, he said, "I know a lot of things you don't know, Johnny."

"You didn't know," I said. "Nobody knew."

There was the odor of burned plastic, heavy now, moving like a cloud through the window and into the room, a terrible smell. There was no smoke in the house, only the odor, and it made me cough. "You don't know anything I don't know, Sam. I'm older than you are."

"I knew last night when you went outside," he said. "You thought she was sleeping but she wasn't sleeping. She was sitting in the living room in the dark. You thought I was sleeping, too. But I wasn't. I saw her when I followed you."

I turned and saw how very proud he was and knew he was telling the truth. "I bet you woke her up," I said. "You're looking for an excuse for following me and waking her up."

"You fell asleep on the ground," he said. "She told me to hold the door open and she went outside and she picked you up. She took off Daddy's shirt you were wearing. I held the door open, and she carried you in and put you to bed. You don't even remember anything."

"Where's the book?" I said. "Did I have the book?"

Sam walked to the window and stepped up on a wooden foot stool to see outside. "What book?" he said.

"The prayer book," I said. "You know the prayer book."

He pointed at the fire, pressing the tip of his finger against the glass. "It was Daddy's," he said. "It wasn't yours."

A few days later, my mother's parents drove the three hours west from New Orleans to Old Field and rented a room at Tap's Motel. Marie said they were welcome to stay at the Girlie place in the country, but Grandfather Maines said they didn't want to get in anybody's way and would treat the trip like a vacation. The real reason they decided to take a room, everyone knew, was because Grandfather Maines was a rare Louisiana Republican who, at any moment day or night, was wont to ridicule and challenge Jason Girlie's liberal politics. At one memorable Sunday dinner, he had taken a manly bite from a turkey leg and, with his mouth full, threatened to beat the living shit out of Jason for supporting the desegregation of public schools and then run down the hall to the bathroom and thrown up before reaching the toilet. Grandfather Maines's weak heart often gave him numb shoulders and a tingling sensation in his arms, and around Jason he often fell into fits of rage and trembling. "This is it, Mother," he would shout, "this is it," meaning he thought he was going to die.

Marie decided it would be good for everyone if Sam and I stayed with Grandmother and Grandfather Maines at Tap's and left my mother alone to work out her anger at the house on Ducharme Road. One thing she wanted to avoid, I suppose, was putting the two old men under the same roof and hearing old man Maines accuse old man Girlie of producing a son who was not only a fool and a coward but a worthless bag of slime for having left his wife and children. Another thing she probably wanted to avoid was having old man Girlie ask old man Maines why he and his wife had taken more than three months to come and sit by their daughter's side.

Tap Billedeaux's motel and eatery was just across Landry Street from the Water Time Lounge, and at night you could watch the drunk, hooting couples sitting on the hoods of their big-wheeled trucks parked on the oyster-shell lot. The motel got busy at about two in the morning when the Water Time closed and these same couples moved into Tap's rooms and played loud, late-night televisions to drown out the noise of their sinful fucking. Our room had two double beds—one for Grandfather and Grandmother Maines, the other for Sam and me—but when the TVs and lustful shouting started we all huddled together in one bed and pulled the covers over our heads. The weird sounds that came through the walls made Sam cry and suck his thumb, and it set my grandparents off into discussions about people.

"People are so rude and inconsiderate," Grandmother Maines said.

"People just better learn when to sleep," Grandfather Maines said, more annoyed at being awakened than embarrassed over what was going on in the room next door. "I'm paying to sleep in this room and people better not forget it." Then he shouted into the blankets, "People better not forget it!"

"You know, boys, people weren't that way when I was growing up," Grandmother Maines said, putting her arms around me. "People had more self-respect."

"Don't believe it," Grandfather Maines said into the blankets. "People always been idiots about each other."

My mother visited us at Tap's each morning, and we had breakfast together at the pancake grill. We crowded into a booth, and my grandparents promoted conversations about what it was like when Janie, the youngest of their five children, was a little girl growing up on St. Charles Avenue in New Orleans's fashionable Garden District. They no doubt thought talking about a less difficult time might make their daughter feel better and get her mind off her husband's disappearance, but they failed to see how patronizing their efforts were.

· "Remember how you used to want to wear dungarees to church and your father insisted you wear that pink dress we bought on sale at Low's," Grandmother Maines said. And Grandfather Maines, always contrary, said, "Oh, Estelle. That's no story. Remember the time she won the perfect attendance certificate for the entire school year. Now that's a story. That's a triumph."

"I have a suggestion," my mother said. "Why don't we eat and not talk? I'm so tired of talking and being talked to. Let's just sit here and eat and pretend to be normal people. Okay? Let's act like normal people for a change."

"But even normal people need to talk," Grandmother Maines said. "It's part of life. It's part of being human."

"You're a smart one," Grandfather Maines said. "Ain't she a smart one, boys? What do you say, Sam? Your Grandma Maines's a smart one?"

Sam peeled away the crusty brown rim of a hotcake and pretended not to be listening, so Grandfather Maines answered for him. "We should all be so smart," he said.

They didn't stay long. I doubt that my mother discussed with them the subject of her missing husband, and I doubt that they had the courage to bring it up. It was as if they had heard about a death in the family, arrived months late for the funeral and, finding no body, decided there had been some mistake. If ever there was evidence of how little my mother and her parents knew and needed each other, it was this week-long visit. They left after my mother told them, with all the grace and conviction of someone who'd just graduated from charm school, that she loved them very much and appreciated their concern.

"That's what parents are for," Grandmother Maines said, and Grandfather Maines said, "If you can't be yourself with us, Janie, who can you be yourself with?"

Jason Girlie took care of the bill at Tap's, and in so doing infuriated Grandfather Maines, who rubbed his numb shoulders and stomped his feet and swore never to return to Old Field. Grandmother Maines reminded him that his little girl lived there, and he said, "Well, remind her where it is we live. Because this is it, Mother. This is it." And he tapped his chest at the place of his heart.

One night several weeks later, when I was sure that both Sam and my mother were asleep, I left our room and went outside and stood over the spot where the great pile of my father's belongings had been. Jason had sent a man over to clear the rubble and rake away the ashes, but there remained a scar on the ground. Against the beam of my flashlight, it was black and jagged and huge. I kicked at the center of it with my bare feet, and the cloud of dust that rose filled my lungs. I could taste the scorched earth and feel the heat of what was lost. The night threatened rain. Thunder clapped in the sky, and lightning made the clouds visible. There were no angels.

In the morning, my mother came to my bedside and said what she always said when she thought I was feeling depressed: "Are you the man in my life now, Johnny?"

I said I was, and kissed her good morning.

5

My friend Charley Harwood grew up telling people he wanted to be a Jesuit priest in the Catholic Church. From the time he was six or seven until a week or so before he turned twenty-one and went off to a seminary in Connecticut, Charley made the morning mass in a suit and tie and newly polished bluchers and received holy communion. Every Tuesday night, he and his father, a charismatic who could speak with the gift of tongues, attended a prayer meeting in the Queen of Heaven rectory and prayed for the salvation of what Mr. Malcolm called the dearly troubled world. Charley was serious and angry when he said the only thing that might keep him from becoming Pope was the matter of his heritage. He was not only an American, but an American who came from a small, hick town in Louisiana. As long as he lived, he said, he would never forgive his father for leaving Italy after the Second World War and settling down in Old Field.

When I reminded him that his father was born and raised in Old Field, and that the girl his father had loved and married was born and raised in Old Field, Charley said to hell with Old Field and to hell with Louisiana. And to hell with his parents.

I suppose what I liked most about Charley Paul Harwood was that he was the only person I ever knew who truly loved everybody and hated them at the same time.

We first met at the junior high school in town, on my first day of class. He was in the library showing a girl named Geri Sturgess the correct way to receive and swallow the holy Eucharist. Because Charley had eaten all of the pressed wafers of wheat he'd stolen from church, he was improvising with barbeque-flavor potato chips. For a chalice he used a Dixie cup with a pencil drawing of an ascending dove on it. He took one of the dusty red potato chips from the cup, held it with both hands over his head and said something in Latin. Then he said "Body of Christ" and delivered it to the girl's tongue, after which she said "Amen." He was very religious about all this, apparently intent on placing the chip squarely in his lovely parishioner's mouth without fumbling it. After a while Geri Sturgess took the communion without chewing and working her jaw muscles, and this seemed to please Charley immensely. When a crowd gathered—including Mrs. Handley Hayes, the librarian—he asked everyone to please get in line and say the Act of Contrition in silence before coming up for the blessed sacrament.

"And there will be no pushing and shoving," he said. "I don't give a shit how hungry you pigs are."

He had emptied out the first bag of chips and was just starting on a second when the principal stormed in and pulled him out of the library by the fleshy pink lobe of his right ear. Charley made the sign of the cross with his free left hand and told everybody to go in peace and love and serve the Lord. The principal had Charley's right hand pinned against his back, and every few steps he delivered a blow with his knee to Charley's hamstring. "Father forgive them," he said on his way out. "They know not what they do."

Far down the hall, I heard Charley shout something, but for the distance and echo I had a difficult time making it out. I thought he had said "Meteor, meteor, meteor," but someone who knew better later said he was saying "Confiteor, confiteor, confiteor."

When we were seniors in high school, Charley told me he no longer believed in God but would attend the seminary anyway after four years of theology at Tulane. He didn't want to disappoint his father, who had already begun enlisting sponsors to help with his son's priestly education. Charley was pitiful when he talked about all the years he would waste at Tulane and the seminary in Connecticut, and he cursed without ever really knowing what he said or how he sounded when he said it. Everything was goddamned this and goddamned that. Studying theology in New Orleans was, he said, "a big goddamned stupid sonofabitching waste of time." Then he said, "And John, you know how I hate to waste time."

He wanted me to say that I didn't believe in God either, and when I told him that I did, he started to cry and beat his fists against the edge of the old-time, claw-foot bathtub at his house. I was standing in the doorway, watching as he stuck his head under the faucet and turned up the spigot.

"You oughta not go," I said. "Not everybody can be a priest. Your father'll understand. He's nothing but a bean farmer, for crying out loud. He never even went to high school."

"Don't ever talk to me." He slammed his hands into the blue-tiled wall. "Just get out of here and don't ever talk to me, do you hear? Don't ever talk to me."

As a graduation gift, his parents bought him a Jeep CJ-7, a sturdy but impractical vehicle for what they called "the long trip north." Charley reminded them that New Orleans was only a few hours east and asked them not to forget his requisite four years of theology study at Tulane. But their excitement could not be restrained. "Think Connecticut," Malcolm said. "Think seminary. I do."

"What will we call you?" his mother said. "Won't it be something to hear your own father call you Father Harwood? And me, too, your mother who could not be more proud? Father Charles Paul Harwood, the son of farm people, baptizing children, hearing confessions, blessing the dead. Isn't that wonderful? Isn't that a wonderful idea?"

Almost every Saturday night in the spring of our senior year in high school, we used the Jeep to drive to Lafayette and a college bar called Mother's Mantle and another called the Keg. If we were able to convince the bouncer at the door that we were old enough to get in, then able to convince a couple of girls to drive with us to the Harwood's soybean farm near Grand Coteau, about fifteen miles away, it was a good night and Charley would be the first to go to confession before ten-thirty mass the next morning. He told me he confessed the mortal sin of fornication, and when I said this was one sin he hadn't committed, he told me he also confessed the mortal sin of not telling the truth. "At the end I always tell the priest that I'm sorry for all my sins, including those I do not remember. The I-do-not-remember part covers everything I choose to forget and will never tell anyone. You can lie to a priest if you tell him you're lying. That's about the only thing I like about being Catholic."

Charley got a degree from Tulane in art history, much to his parents' disappointment; his enrollment in the theology department lasted less than three months. One summer day after his freshman year, he knelt before Malcolm and his mother and swore to them and to God in heaven that the switch in curricula did not indicate an end to his dream of becoming a priest. His heart was a Catholic and a priestly one, he said, and he simply wanted to learn a few things about paint, paintings and painters before committing himself to the monastic life. "Besides," he said, "at one time my hero, Vincent van Gogh, wanted to be a priest."

Charley pronounced Van Gogh this way: Van Gock.

"I have never heard of this Van Cock," June Harwood said.

"He was a redheaded painter who cut off his ear and sent it to a prostitute," Charley explained. "He was what you call an Impressionist."

"My impression is that you are worshiping a false god in this Van Cock," Malcolm said. "What's happened to you, son?"

"Did he bleed to death when he cut off his ear," June asked.

"I don't know," Charley said. "I find out next semester."

After graduating from Tulane, Charley went to the seminary but quit attending class after a few weeks and stopped pretending he wanted to be a priest. He moved to Boston and found work waiting tables at a discotheque, where on busy nights he often cleared more than a hundred dollars in tips. He felt and behaved like a rich man. He bought a water bed and a set of fine china from a mail-order catalog, and he bought a videotape recorder and a couple dozen pornographic videotapes. He called Malcolm and said the priesthood was infested with homosexuals. Every night at the dormitory someone had stuffed pictures of all-male orgies under his door, and a young black seminarian had approached him in the Grotto to the Blessed Virgin Mary and exposed his erect penis. When his father began to cry on the phone, Charley said he told him, "Daddy, I swear I didn't touch that fellow. He was sick and ungodly. He wasn't what's good."

Charley moved back to Old Field in late November of that year and by Christmas was dredging graves in the cemetery at Queen of Heaven, working to pay back loans for his college education. One night he stopped maneuvering the incredible arm of his backhoe long enough to ask me how big a douche bag I thought he was. When I said pretty big, he said, "Not even pretty big. I'm a really big douche bag," and he said he'd lied to his father about the young seminarian at the grotto. "The only photographs of homosexual men I ever saw," he said, "were at a fuck shop in New Haven." He said he used to go there to pick up prostitutes and buy cocaine and to look for ways to hurt himself. He said the only person he ended up hurting was his poor father, who had lost his gift of tongues and quit attending the Tuesday night prayer meetings. The injury he had done to his father was the main thing that made him a really big douche bag, he said, rather than just a pretty big one. Lying to his old man that way was the worst thing he had ever done, and he would never in a million years get over it.

"You'll get over it," I said, hoping to cheer him up.

"Fuck you," he said.

"I'm trying to be nice."

"Then fuck me," he said.

I cannot say with any certainty why I was so attracted to Charley Harwood. I guess I liked him as much as I did because he loved to hunt and drink whiskey and tell stories that made no sense but made you laugh. He said things I would never say, and this to me was evidence of his superior courage. He had balls. He was like one of those ancient hearkening fools we used to run into at the annual Yam Festival—they had nothing but bullshit to sell but sold it so well you bought what was available and did not for a minute feel suckered or rotten about it.

"That Harwood boy," my grandmother said after first meeting Charley at a Christmas party, "what a tragic puppy. How is it you like him, Johnny? You two seem entirely different."

"You mean why," I said. "Why do I like him."

"No," she said. "*How* is what I mean. I don't know how it is somebody like you would want to spend time with somebody like him. He seems so wickedly incorrect about things."

After I graduated from LSU and moved back to Old Field, Charley often came by the house to try to make me feel better about having returned to a town I had sworn I would never come back to. When I spent too many hours alone in the outdoor kitchen, reading travel magazines and maps and trying to decide what I should do with myself, he came over with a string of bream and small-mouth bass he had caught at the farm pond and cleaned them in the double-basin sink, then fried them in a black cast-iron skillet and served them with hush puppies and cold tomato wedges. If I didn't answer his calls for a week or more, he wrote me long, detailed letters accounting for most everything he had made of the time, including his predawn ritual of sitting up in bed, lighting a stick of marijuana and masturbating while watching one of his pornographic video-tapes. In one of his letters, he told me how much he liked the blue images and the simplicity with which men and women were able to undo each other without the compromising struggles he knew of sweet talk and dinner and promises of love and one day marriage. These people were the way he would like to be, he said, bound to no one and without rules on how to get along.

Once he undressed in front of me and played with his penis until he was able to get an erection. "Well?" he said.

"Well what?" I said.

"Is Van Gogh a redhead or what?"

"I'd say he's a redhead," I said and watched him put his clothes back on. "In fact, I'd say he's almost a bluehead."

"I knew you'd say he was," he said. "Even I myself am impressed when Van Gogh gets that demented look in his eye."

He rarely asked me about football. And he was good about never reminding me that most people went to work when they got out of school. The only thing he ever reminded me of was our agreement to hunt the marsh at Holly Beach at least twice a month during the season, and to catfish at Bayou Maldone every other Sunday.

Once I asked him if he thought I should get a teaching job or look for something in sales at the newspaper, and he told me he thought both ideas were pretty bad. "You've got the rest of your life to hack out a living," was what he said. But it seemed that my only alternative to getting a teaching job or looking for something in sales at the newspaper was enrolling in a graduate program at another state university and putting off having to decide whether I should get a teaching job or look for something in sales at the newspaper.

My mother suggested I substitute teach at the high school a few times a week. The day I called the assistant superintendent of schools to ask about putting in an application, the man was in the mood to talk about football and the end of my career. He wanted to know why I had chosen to give up an opportunity to play as a professional, and I was not in the mood to tell him.

"You talk to Mr. Prentiss," my mother asked later that afternoon.

"Yeah," I said. "I talked to him."

"What did he say?"

"He said I threw away a chance of a lifetime."

"You mean football?"

"That's exactly what I mean," I said. "He said I let a lot of people down, including his son, my biggest fan. He said I wasn't very smart to give up the money and would be a bad role model for kids."

"That wasn't a very nice thing to say," she said.

"No, it wasn't. That's why I told him to go find a tall tree and a rope and hang himself."

"You never wanted to be a substitute anyway," she said.

A few weeks later I got a job as a roustabout at the Texas Eastern Pipeline Company on the edge of town, out near Prairie Ronde. I worked the graveyard shift, from eleven at night until eight in the morning, then drove back home to one of my mother's breakfasts of hot beignets powdered with sugar and café au lait in giant red-clay mugs. After a shave and shower, I would sleep until noon, then wake and eat again, then go back to the outdoor kitchen and sleep until Charley came by and said it was time to get up; the doves were moving out at the farm. He said the doves were moving because he knew it sometimes worked to get me up and out of Old Field—out to the land his father leased and farmed—and into something beautiful and good.

It really was something beautiful and good on those days when we drove in his Jeep along the dirt roads and through the wide open bean fields and argued about everything and nothing but got along just the same. His favorite way of driving the Jeep was to let the vehicle drive itself, and we never knew where the thing would go and when it would choose to stop. Sometimes when it went across a cattle guard and into the back hay pasture, bouncing along through the tall green grass and kicking up a storm of hoppers, it strained and coughed and seemed to be on the verge of death. "Calm yourself down," Charley said and rubbed his hand on the dashboard. Other times on the levee with the sleepy, slow Bayou Maldone on one side and the bright green and gold world on the other, it skipped and sang and carried on as if able to generate enough power to lift off and fly. "You got an attitude problem," Charley told the Jeep.

At the back of the farm, near a tumbledown feed shed surrounded by weeping and corkscrew willow trees, Charley often stopped the Jeep and hit a line or two of cocaine before starting down the dirt path that cut through walls of briars and brambles and ended at the Harwood family cemetery. Surrounded by a rusty iron fence, it was a little yard crowded with dead Harwoods dating back to the early 1700s. Hard weather had reduced some of the names incised on the stone tablets to gray, illegible lines, but Charley knew where every member of his people lay and when they had come to be buried. He also knew the spots reserved for his mother and father.

"June will be next to the old man," he said. "I only hope that dead those two will have more life in them than they do now."

One day, drunk on Thunderbird wine, he stretched out on a piece of ground near the corner of the yard, folded his hands and placed them on his chest. His face was white from having drunk so much, and his lips were chapped and blue. He needed not tell me that this was where he would be laid to rest, but he did anyway. "You got shade in the morning, sun in the afternoon," I said. "I like it here." He looked as dead as a living person could ever hope to look, and when he closed his eyes and held his breath for more than a minute, I found myself wondering if perhaps he really had died right in front of me. Then it began to rain, slowly at first, the drops falling like fat pebbles, but after a time in hard driving sheets. I ran for cover under the willows, but he stayed on the ground, playing dead, and he didn't flinch. I finally roused him by pouring wine on his face and pressing my foot on his crotch. "It was incredible," he said. "For as long as I could stand it, I was reaching out and touching the face of God. And he was reaching out and touching mine."

In town after a day at the farm, the Jeep always took us either to Bubba Toussaint's Grill or Black Fred's New Pool Hall, which was just up Union from the building that had once been my grandfather's clothing store and apartment. Sometime after Jason Girlie's death two years earlier, the property had been sold to a carpet and rug outfitter who turned the upstairs apartment into a meeting house for the local Alcoholics Anonymous. Almost any night of the week you could drive by there and see a huddle of long sad faces looking down on the traffic below but refusing to acknowledge you when you offered a friendly wave or pumped your horn. A town as small as Old Field, with maybe fifteen thousand living between the west loop of Lindy Road and where the gravel started on Thomasburg Road headed east, and you rarely saw a long sad face you recognized. Charley said it was weird, and I said it was worse than weird, it was horseshit.

"Who are these strangers?" he said.

"Lushes," I answered.

"Fucka buncha lushes," he said.

Since I hated driving by my grandfather's old place and Charley knew it, he let the Jeep take us to Black Fred's by way of Blues Alley that ran by the courthouse and parallel to Virgil Charles's high stone fence. Somehow the Jeep knew to park behind the pool hall or behind Maxwell's Newsstand and the guitar shop next door. "Stay here," Charley always told the Jeep before we went in. When we came back out he said, "Thanks for hanging around and keeping your goddamned mouth shut. I hate it when you don't keep your goddamned mouth shut."

I told him he treated that Jeep like a horse and would've tied it to a hitching post had there been one nearby, and he said, "You're too literal for a person with a college degree, John."

Black Fred's had two front show windows that let you look inside and see Booboo Raymond and his girl playing eight ball and Doc Verrazano taking his first Scotch after a day at Charity and somebody who just stepped off a Greyhound hunched over a bowl of chicken gumbo, looking up every now and then to see if the eight-eighteen to West Jacobs had arrived. The only thing fancy about the pool hall was the Wurlitzer jukebox that played the Neville Brothers and Chuck Berry and all the old Elvis Christmas songs. Only one of the tables was level, and all had initials and clumsy hearts carved into their legs. There was a long oak and brass bar that looked as if someone had beaten it with a logging chain, and in front of the wall mirror there was a run of liquor in smoky brown, red and green bottles.

In those days you could still buy one of the famous hamburgers made by Cheryl, the cook, and a side of fries for a dollar and a draft in a nice-sized go-cup for a quarter. There was only one bathroom, and although the lock on the door was broken, the toilet worked, as did the condom vending machine over the sink.

Black Fred, who was white, called most men "Gents," even those he'd known all his life. Every woman who ever walked through his great oak door was "Miss Ma'am." Charley Paul Harwood alone he referred to as "Young son."

I was "Mr. Beauregard Girlie's boy."

"There was some Miss Ma'am in here two, three hours ago looking for Mr. Beauregard Girlie's boy," Black Fred said one night when Charley and I sat down at the bar. "She wanted to know if we were friends, you and me."

I ordered a coffee and a slice of apple pie, and Charley ordered Beam Black Label on the rocks. "You told her you knew him?" Charley said.

"I told her I knowed him after she got Cheryl to make her a burger. I had to remind her this was a place of business and not no dance club."

"She had a body," Booboo Raymond said from over by the wall. He was putting some chalk on his stick, getting ready to break. "She had a pair meaner than Sandra here. She had on some perfume that made my nose burn."

"Tell him she was a colored girl," Sandra said.

"She weren't no colored," Black Fred said.

"She was about as colored as Sandra here," Booboo said as he broke. "I couldn't stop looking at that big mean pair she had."

"If she wasn't colored," Sandra said, "nobody is."

"This Miss Ma'am was beautiful," Black Fred said.

"She was a two-toned colored if she was one," Booboo said.

Black Fred said the girl ate one of Cheryl's famous burgers and drank a ginger ale and sat at the bar for about thirty minutes before going outside and flagging a cab. He said he knew for sure she was a white girl because Jake Comeaux was driving the cab that picked her up. Black Fred reminded me that Jake Comeaux hated the entire Negro race because his daughter had run off with a black man. Jake Comeaux, he said, would not let a black sit in his cab unless it was to drive him to his own lynching.

"I got a feeling she was one of them high yellows," Booboo said.

"She had one of them accents," Sandra added. "She thought because she'd been schooled she was better."

"She left a two-dollar tip," Black Fred said. "Generally you don't get that when they sit at the bar. They think if you got to walk is the only way you deserve to get a tip like that. Sometimes they leave you something if you talk and tell stories, but she didn't say a thing. She just wanted Mr. Beauregard Girlie's boy. She got dressed up for him. She put on smell-good for him."

Charley was laughing. He always laughed when Black Fred got to talking. "She put on some smell-good for him," Charley said. "She was beautiful. She wanted Mr. Beauregard Girlie's boy."

"I bet she did," I said. I was laughing, too.

"She was uppity," Sandra said. The way she looked at Booboo, with a pair of hard eyes and a cigarette hanging from the corner of her lips, you could tell she didn't think any of this was very funny. "That colored girl talked like she owned something."

"It was a pair she owned," Booboo said, bending over for a shot on the two ball. "It was a pair meaner than Sandra's here."

Sometimes the girl who had come by looking for me was not black. Sometimes she was Oriental or a German blond, and sometimes she limped or spoke seven different languages. She was always a girl with a better body and larger breasts than Sandra Boulier's. She always gave Black Fred a big tip, and she always smelled of expensive perfume, and she always left in Jake Comeaux's cab. The girl wasn't always even the same girl to all of my friends in the bar who saw her and created her again when Charley and I came in. One afternoon Sandra saw a black girl, Black Fred a girl with bright red hair and freckles, Doc Verrazano a girl he saved on the table at Charity and Booboo a girl with a gorgeous rear end shaped like a giant catawba leaf.

One thing they always agreed on was that she was looking for Johnny Girlie. Sometimes there was a dispute over whether she left a phone number and address on her business card. But on those rare occasions when everyone agreed that she had left a card, everyone said it was a shame the card had been lost. It was just too bad, Johnny. Everyone said I should hang around a few hours, eat something, shoot some pool. Maybe, if she was smart, she'd come back. At least it was something to hope for, they said.

"If she's lucky she'll come back," Black Fred said.

"They never come back," I said. "Why don't they ever come back?"

"Places to go," Charley said. "Things to do."

We never closed down Black Fred's. After playing some eight ball and running the table on Booboo, Charley liked to head out with a quart of beer and ride around town until he decided it was time to stop in at Mabel's rooming house on Cherry Street. Although I never once saw her, Charley knew a woman who rented one of Mabel's rooms, and he dropped in a few times a week for what he called a grudge tumble, meaning the sexual act was inspired less by love than something like hate and the need for two people to abuse each other. The woman, he said, was married to a tool pusher who worked the offshore rigs fourteen days at a stretch, came home for seven, then went back out for fourteen more. Charley stopped at Mabel's terrible old house only when drunk or stoned, and he never stayed more than half an hour. Most nights I waited in the Jeep until he was done with what he had to do. Other times I walked down the street and waited in the statue garden at Saint Jude or went down Beverly Boulevard to Bubba Toussaint's Grill for a coffee and cigarette at the counter.

One night when Charley appeared in the bolt of yellow light from Mabel's kitchen door, stumbling down the steps and across the lawn, laughing his wild laugh and tugging at his crotch, I figured that any second somebody would empty the chamber of a rifle into the back of his head and drop him in a quick, shadowy heap. I waited for the woman's tool-pusher husband to shout from the upstairs window, "That'll learn you," and the woman to scream against the approaching wail of sirens. I knew and waited for all these things, but it was like knowing and waiting for all the bad there could ever be and none of the good. Nothing ever happened to Charley. He did what he did with the woman and came down feeling like hell. He came down and told me to drive, to take him out to his father's farm, and we drove with the top of the Jeep pulled back and the warm air rushing all around us and neither one of us saying a word.

Somebody finally said something and it was Charley. "Why do I keep going back to it?"

"It must be good if you keep going back," I said.

"It's only good because it's wrong," he said. "If it was right and mine, I wouldn't want it. I'd get rid of it."

"One day her old man will find out and kill you."

"If that weren't the truth then it would be right. And if it were right it would not be any good."

"You don't make any sense, goddamnit, Charley."

At the farm pond he stepped out of the Jeep, took off his clothes and poured what was left of the beer down his lower belly and groin. He stood in the flood of headlights and washed himself, rubbing in the beer like soap. He hated her smell, he said. It stayed on him even after the beer bath and walking through a run of cedars and down to the pond and wading out until the water reached his chest. "I should remember to keep some Lava soap in the Jeep," he said. "I could scrub her off Van Gogh and make him feel like a redheaded rascal again."

When he was done in the pond he walked dripping wet to the bean field, lay his shirt and pants on the ground and dropped between the dirt rows. I joined him after a while and fell to my knees, then lay on my back and rested my head on the ground. He was wet and naked, and his breathing heavy now. His belly moved up and down, and you could smell the smell of sex commingled oddly with the smell of the beer and the pond water. I tried not to think about the weird odor, tried to smell what I was seeing—the night and the dimpled white of the moon and the shadows the water oaks and sweetgums cast over the soft dirt.

"If I died over fucking, it would be okay," he said.

"No it wouldn't," I said. "It wouldn't be okay for anybody."

"All I want is a good woman. I don't want her to smell."

"You don't know what you want," I said. "You don't know anything about it. You're dumb and you're stupid and sometimes I wonder why I run around with you."

After he caught his breath, he said, "You run around with me because we understand each other. And there's nobody else."

"That's true," I said. "It's only me and you."

He was laughing when he took off running as fast as he could across the wide, moonlit field, running over the bean rows and away from the Jeep parked at the edge of the pond. I watched how far he could go taking two and three bean rows at a time. He seemed to be headed out of what light there was and into the dark. Way off now, only a small dark thing moving across the rows and rows of beans and away from the light, I saw my friend Charley Harwood. And I heard what he was shouting.

"Confiteor, confiteor, confiteor."

few weeks after I became accustomed to working the graveyard shift at Texas Eastern, I began having trouble sleeping the nights on my days off. My mother said if I stayed awake all day and let my body run down, I'd have no trouble falling asleep at night. After turning out all the house lights but the one over the kitchen sink and the flood light on the back patio, she came to the outdoor kitchen with a pitcher of warm milk, steaming in the bright winter cold. I watched her through the window and saw the way she carried the tin pitcher with both hands and used her back and elbows to open and shut the screen door.

She poured two glasses and sat with me and gave me a pep talk about how important it was for a young man to get eight hours of rest each night. Sometimes she rubbed and kneaded my back and legs and said a prayer to the Virgin Mary, whom she often called on to provide minor miracles. "Blessed art thou amongst women," she prayed. "And blessed is the fruit of thy womb, Jesus."

When we finished drinking the milk and catching up on the news of the day, she sat in a chair in the dark and watched me undress.

Every time she watched me undress it was as if she were seeing me for the very first time. If she was feeling especially proud of herself, she said it frightened her to think that she had carried me for nine months. If she was feeling low or lonesome for something, she told baby stories and laughed at the memory of Sam and me as infants and sometimes she cried. After I stripped down to my boxer shorts and got under the blankets, she came over and sat on the edge

61

of the bed and told me it was okay if I wanted to come in and watch television if I had trouble sleeping. She said she would leave the back door unlocked just in case I couldn't fall asleep, but that it wasn't good to talk that way; it was negative and implied that I would have a difficult time getting my eight hours. I thanked her and kissed her good-night and watched her walk through the garage and across the patio with the empty pitcher. The cold turned her breath into clouds of vapor, and rising into the back floodlights it looked blue. I told myself it looked like the wings of a hundred cherubim, and sometimes that helped me sleep and dream of how it was playing football before a crowd on its feet and everybody screaming and what a hero I once had been.

Those nights I couldn't sleep, I dressed in a pair of sweats and jogging shoes and ran down Ducharme Road to Dunbar and up Dunbar to White Avenue, and under the long run of live oaks and mimosas on White to the Dupart Country Club. I ran raising my knees high, carrying an invisible football tight against my body, stiff-arming invisible opponents who stumbled and fell trying to defend against my many moves. I liked pretending that I had scored my glory as a running back and not as a linebacker, that I had eluded the tackles and not made them. I ran across the nine-hole course with its small lakes and sand traps and bridges designed to accommodate electric carts. The course made for good running because the ground was pretty in the night, rolling with a face of dew and everywhere a soft light from the street lamps standing on the periphery of the property.

Out of the club I turned back and ran up White and Dunbar again, along the quarter-mile row of uncut privet blocking the light of the moon and stars and making it hard to see anything at all. I ran, sprinting as hard as I could, with my lungs burning and my mouth like cotton and a tightness in my groin. I ran up to Ducharme and all the way down the winding road to the great, manicured lawn in front of the house. I ran around the side of the house, screaming obscenities to help suppress the pain in my lungs, and hurdled a redwood bench on the patio before finally bursting through the door of the outdoor kitchen. The hard, cold floor received me as one might expect a hard, cold floor to receive a man who weighed considerably more than two hundred pounds, and I grunted against it. After the pain in my lungs went away, I showered without turning on the bathroom lights, and the hot water felt like needles on my back. I toweled myself dry and went back to bed until the muscles in my legs quit throbbing and twitching and the bright lights in my head dimmed to darkness and I slept or failed to sleep.

Mostly I failed to sleep. I lay in the dark and thought about football and how I was going to miss it. I thought about the fall afternoons in Baton Rouge and the old savage feeling I used to get in my stomach before boarding the bus at the dormitory gates and heading out to the stadium with the blue turning lights of a trooper's car leading the way. I thought about the time Billy Streeter cried in the back of the bus and called the name Jesus over and over again, seeing the huge beast of a crowd part as we pulled up to the cobble-stone street outside the stadium. Streeter had cried because he was a freshman, only eighteen and playing in his first game. When they were freshmen and suiting up for the first time, they either cried or lost control of their bowels; having done the other myself, I preferred to see them cry. Reaching from the dressing room door to the door of the bus were two lines of state troopers and university policemen holding hands to keep the crowd back, and when we walked down the narrow path, young boys shouted our names and everybody reached out to touch us. I remembered a girl in a purple feathered hat, jeans and a sweater on which she had pinned small, black-and-white pictures of the LSU players. She had clipped the pictures out of the souvenir program, and each pin entered the left eye and exited the right. I remembered how she had said my name and pointed to a picture over her heart. "Ain't it you, Johnny?" she said. "Ain't it you?"

That was football as I remembered it on those nights when there was something in my mouth that made it impossible to swallow. It was also running wind sprints in the greasy half-dark of summer and pushing the eight-man sled with coaches McCombs, Wharton and Klandle barking like dogs and screaming for you to bark like one, too. It was not easy pushing the sled and trying to breathe and bark at the same time. None of it was easy and all of it was hard. I thought I was going to miss it, but how good it was to have done it. Not everyone had.

Other times I remembered the night after my last game. In the parking lot at Tiger Stadium, my mother and Sam had prepared a tailgate party. The trunk of the Pontiac was open to a spread of fried chicken, potato salad, carrot and celery sticks, crab and onion dip and sweet dough turnovers filled with candied yams and apples, but I was too tired to eat. My mother fixed me a mint julep and sat on a lawn chair and played with the corn-yellow chrysanthemum pinned to her lapel. Sam, who'd said little since meeting me at the players' gate, drank beer and walked from one poorly lighted end of the lot to the other, kicking debris and mumbling under his breath. When my mother began pulling the petals off the head of her corsage and saying "Loves me, loves me not," I said, "Are you and Sam acting strange tonight or am I just imagining things?"

She continued to pick apart the flower. "Loves me, loves me not."

"Who loves or does not love you, Ma?"

"My boys love me," she said, suddenly perky.

"Glad you got that out in the open. Of course we love you, so what? What's going on with you and Sam?"

"John," she said, looking away, "your brother and I decided something. Or maybe it was your mother deciding and Sam smart enough not to question her."

"Who wants to bet that what you've decided has something to do with me?"

"What we've decided is that you can't play games forever. It's time for you to come home."

"You want me to quit football."

"It's not quitting, baby. It's coming home. I need you there. In just a few months the house is empty and Sam gone to college. I just think it's time for you to be a man. And how can you suggest that coming home's quitting? Don't you think it's time to put away your childish things. Please, let's put them away."

"I could go pro, Ma. I know a lot of people who'll say it's quitting."

"A lot of people didn't bring you into this world."

"Well, at least two people did."

"And only one is left. And she wants you home."

Neither she nor I said anything more until Sam returned to the car, then we both spoke at the same moment. "Don't you think it's time for Johnny to put away childish things," she said just as I told him, "You know how high I could end up going in the draft, Sam?"

"You see," my mother snapped. "They call it the draft as if it were for military service. How juvenile can you get?"

Sam bit into a drumstick, then threw it among the trees at the edge of the lot. Then he opened another can of beer, took a swallow and threw it toward the trees. "I'm not saying it's your turn at home, John," he said, "but my time's up. Four more months and I'm out of there. I'm traveling."

"He talks like it's a prison sentence," my mother said. "When he was a boy, I had Sylvie wash his mouth out with soap whenever he misbehaved like this. I only wish she was here right now."

Sam bit into another piece of chicken and flung it to the trees. "The next thing she'll want to know," he said, "is if you have the courage to do right?" He washed down the chicken with a swallow from the julep pitcher. "You have the courage to do right? Do you love her or do you not? It's got to be one or the other."

"This is silly. Ma, do you know what it means to go pro? It's easy money, first thing, and I don't know what's so childish about that. A few years and I'm set for life."

She was still pulling the petals off the corsage and letting them drop to her feet. "The right thing is never easy," she said.

Sam broke into wild laughter. "The right thing is never easy," he said. "But the wrong thing, now that's easy. The wrong thing is always easy!"

"Your husband made a lot of money," I said. "It was easy."

"So easy and so much," Sam said, "she's still living off it."

"Easy?" she said. "I'll tell you what's easy. Prostitution is easy.

You just lie on your back, spread your legs and pretend to be enjoying yourself. But that doesn't make it right."

"Sometimes you forget I'm your son, Ma," I said, "the way you talk to me. You forget who you're talking to."

"Well," she said, "sometimes you make me feel as if you've forgotten who I am."

"For God's sake don't do that," Sam said, and reached for another piece of chicken. "She's the one who brought you into this world."

"I haven't forgotten," I said.

"She's the one taught you right from wrong," he said.

"Yes," I said. "She's the one."

"Then it's decided," she said, turning to watch Sam throw a chicken wing high into the night sky. "I'll make sure Sylvie cleans the cobwebs out of the outdoor kitchen. I'll have her scrub the tub and change the sheets. Everything as it should."

There was also Charley Paul Harwood to help me through those times when I couldn't sleep. Late at night, when he wasn't watching blue movies in the bedroom he occupied at his parents' house, I usually found him shooting pool or playing pinball at Black Fred's or at the Queen of Heaven or Saint Jude graveyard digging holes with his backhoe. In the beginning, Charley took the job to reimburse those members of the congregation who had contributed to his schooling. At eighty dollars a hole, he was able to pay off his considerable debt in little more than six months. But rather than give up his new occupation and work with his father at the farm, Charley stayed on at the church and picked up extra jobs in the yard at Saint Jude and at the new cemetery on the edge of town, Bellevue Memorial Park. He said he liked the work because the hours were flexible and among the dead he could feel something he believed to be God's presence. His favorite digging time in summer was after midnight, when it was cool and less humid and he knew his noisy operation wouldn't disturb the regular daily functions of the church. In winter the bitter cold of the yard gave the ground more snap, he said, and it took him half the time to go five feet down, four feet wide and nine feet long. He also credited the cold weather with helping to lighten the weight of the vaults he dropped in the holes.

"The frigid air gives everything a perfect fit," he said. "The vault fits the hole better, the coffin fits the vault better, the body fits the coffin better. It's like the life cycle, John, only it happens to be about death."

I always felt a little spooked visiting Charley at one of the graveyards. He talked about the ghosts he'd seen during the course of his evening digs and laughed describing their reports from the underground. Among those he claimed to have seen were the Eigersen twins running sprint relays on top of the plots occupied by the Sibille sisters, Jane and Laurie, who in 1962 had been killed in a traffic accident on their way to Mont Mars. Also at Bellevue, Charley saw Saul Dohman eating the young buds off the camellia bushes and Barney Fautier drinking from a mud puddle in the shell road winding through the yard. Both Saul and Barney, he said, were dressed in the three-piece polyester suits they were buried in.

"It was classic asshole attire," he said. "Even in death, they look like geeks."

Charley once made me stand in an open grave at Queen of Heaven to make sure he had reached the requisite five-foot mark. The floor of the earth was several inches above the top of my head, and I told him he'd gone way deep. He started the old John Deere tractor and maneuvered the scoop of the backhoe like a third arm, quickly filling the hole with another foot of soil and packing it with the flat of the blade. "One night this dead bitch, Mrs. Hamilton, she came up here and you could see the little brown hole in the side of her head where she shot herself," he said. "She had the gall to ask me what I was doing. When I didn't answer, she hopped down in the dig and started taking her clothes off. You could see these veins poking out all over her skin. I told her she smelled like earthworms and she just laughed. She had this look, I think she wanted to fuck me down there in the dirt. I told her I didn't fuck dead people, but she ignored me. When she asked me again what I was doing, what that thing was, I said it was the mechanical equivalent of my dick. You should have seen her haul ass out of that hole."

Some nights we'd sit on the ground with our feet dangling in the hole and smoke pot or share a bottle of whiskey. He said cocaine was a little better than marijuana and far better than whiskey because there was nothing like hitting a couple of lines while sitting on the floor of a grave and waiting to throw picks and shovels and clods of dirt at the restless dead who wandered over looking for a vacancy sign and a new place to sleep. Once, stoned at Bellevue, he ran around pulling up the plastic and real flowers in all the vases at the heads of the graves and tossed them down in the hole he was digging for Scooter Mason, one of our old friends from high school. Leukemia had killed Scooter after a long, unworthy battle, and Charley had been at his bedside when he died. According to Charley, Scooter's last words were "Dig her deep, friend." Because Scooter died without a family to make arrangements for the burial, Charley withdrew a large part of his savings and bought a nickel casket and a plot under a giant flowering dogwood. After digging down ten feet and filling the bottom of the grave with flowers, Charley added a thick layer of soil and Spanish moss for extra cushion.

"Scooter was a hardheaded sonofabitch," he said. "This'll keep him comfortable."

The oldest cemetery, Queen of Heaven, had statues and figures of everything from an alabaster lamb sleeping on its side in the section called Babyland to the marble Dalmatian standing watch over the crypt of some poor dead fireman. Some of the older dead had been buried above ground in tombs to protect them from high flood waters, but the newer dead rested in sealed concrete vaults buried under ground. There was a stone lion over my grandfather's grave in the east wing of the yard, and Charley said it scratched for fleas every Saturday night. On Monday mornings it growled because that was when the black men from the Sanborn Heights projects came by with their push mowers and cut the grass. "Jason Girlie was a racist and you know it," he said.

"I know he was a drunk," I said. "He liked his Scotch."

"That lion sure smells of it," he said.

Charley was not always so high-spirited while working, not always full of stories about his encounters with the dead. One cold winter night when I couldn't sleep, I found him kneeling in the statue garden at Saint Jude, at the foot of the angel Gabriel lording over the figures of deer, rabbits and chipmunks arranged in eternal postures of repose. I walked through the uniform rows of stone tablets, across the ivy circle at the center of the yard and past the great redwood cross and bone-white statue of Jesus and came to stand before my old sad friend in a pool of fractured red and green light streaming down from the stained glass windows of the church. It was not yet ten o'clock, and the mournful strains of a pipe organ moved in the cold air, accompanied by the proud singing of the parish church choir. It was lovely in the cold, and everything seemed clean and new from the dusting of snow earlier in the day. I smelled the wonderful aroma of burning pine mingled with that of fresh pastries from the bakery down the street.

Charley, still kneeling, made the sign of the cross. He made it as if he meant it and said, "You ever get to wondering what we're doing in this town, always hanging out? All we do is hang out."

"Sometimes you dig graves and sometimes I scrub floors," I said. "We work sometimes, and sometimes we sleep and eat and drink, and sometimes we just hang out. We don't always hang out."

"A while ago," he said, "I was thinking about how I just don't know anymore. I just don't know. Then I started thinking that I never really did know and never really cared if I knew or not."

"Know what?" I said.

"I don't know," he said. "I don't even fucking know what I don't know. That's how confused I am."

We both started laughing, but nothing seemed very funny.

"What else have you been thinking?" I said.

"I've been thinking about what would happen if all these poor fuckers really did come alive and told me what they were thinking."

"I don't think you have to worry about that."

"I think they'd tell me to leave Old Field," he said, "and go up to a city somewhere and try to be something that made more

69

sense than a gravedigger. Before this priest business, I thought about show business. It was one or the other. I could do blue movies and swing that thing. I got the body for it. I got Van Gogh, remember?"

"Yeah," I said. "I remember."

"I want to reach out and embrace the world and then gobble it."

After I thought about Charley Paul Harwood embracing the world, I said, "Charles Harwood's one ambitious boy."

"My ambition's between my legs," he said. "Good boys get good nooky. You know that."

"You can always leave."

"That's right. I can go."

"You can leave now or leave tomorrow. Go up Highway 2, go north. Nothing's permanent. You know nothing's permanent."

"Nothing's permanent, my ass," he said.

I looked at his dirty face and at his dirty hands resting like a pair of dirty birds in his lap. "I think you'd better—"

"I'm really not in the mood to care what you think," he said. "I don't need you of all people telling me what to think."

"Johnny Girlie's one sad sack of shit," I said, and then I said it again. "He's one miserable low-life sonofabitch."

He stood up and brushed the dirt off his jeans and, with the tail of his shirt, wiped the dirt off his face. He was suddenly sorry for treating me badly, and he wanted me to know it. When he put his dirty hands on my shoulders and squeezed me, I pushed them away and said, "One miserable low-life sonofabitch." He put his hands back on my shoulders and I pushed them away again. He was laughing now and so was I, and this time it all seemed pretty funny.

"Tell me I'm forgiven," he said.

"You're forgiven."

"Tell me I'm one sad sack of shit."

"You're one sad sack of shit," I said.

"That's right. I'm one sad sack of shit," he said. "All I do is bang that woman at Mabel's and dig graves and go back and bang that woman at Mabel's. This is my life."

"It's a terrible life."

"That I don't even know her name is really terrible," he said. "When I'm in there and we're finished, I look around the room for her name on letters, but there aren't any. I look in her shirts to see if maybe she put a name tag on the collar, but there are no name tags. She has some magazines but she buys them at the drug store. If she had the sense to subscribe there'd be the little white strip across the bottom with her name and address. But she doesn't. She reads the dumbest magazines, *Cosmo* and *New Woman*."

He had talked it out and was feeling better now, and he said he wanted to take a ride and go someplace but said he was in no mood for Black Fred's. He let the Jeep take us screaming down the gravel road near the Harwood farm in Grand Coteau, then south on Highway 2 past the stockyards and the ripe smell of manure and past the strip joints way off the road. After we crossed the Samms River, the Jeep made a quick U-turn and headed back in the direction of town. On the western edge of Old Field, the Jeep stopped off Lindy Road, and we sat up high in our seats to look over the fence of corrugated tin and see what was playing at the Yam Drive-In. I saw two women driving a little red sports car through the mountains of what was probably northern California. They were both blonds heading out on the road through the mountains. Then they were checking into a motel and putting a key into the doorknob of Room 101 and opening the door to discover a heart-shaped bed covered with long-stemmed red roses. Then they were reduced to two naked blonds kissing and undoing each other in Room 101 of a hotel in what was probably northern California.

"A couple of lesbos," Charley said.

"It makes me want to cry," I said.

"We don't stand a chance in the world," he said. "People come out here in the snow and park and freeze watching lesbos make out. Look at that shit. We don't stand a chance. I tell you, Johnny, not a chance."

"Not in this world. We weren't made for it."

"Get us out of here," he told the Jeep. "Just get us the hell out of here. Goddamnit to hell, get us out of here."

He dropped me off at the front of Saint Jude, and I started

across the cemetery to where I had parked on Beverly Boulevard. I no longer could hear the choir singing and the organ playing or smell the wonderful aroma of baked pastries and of firewood burning. It was cold and the snow started to fall through the wintry cathedral of black tupelo trees, swirling in spots like bubbles of carbonation in a soda pop bottle. It was beautiful. Everybody said it never snowed in Louisiana in January but it was snowing, all right, and it was beautiful. It was what my mother always called a picture, something meant to be kept forever, hanging on the bedroom wall, remembered.

I don't know what compelled me to stop in my tracks and turn my face to the sky, open my mouth to the snow and bite at it, but I stood there a long time eating the clean white flakes of snow, tasting nothing but coldness and thinking nothing had ever tasted better. My ears burned and my hands were numb and useless. All of a sudden I felt a weird and inexplicable need to skip and dance through the perfect lines of tombstones and around the crucified stone Jesus and back to the statue garden and the good angel Gabriel and embrace the dead who were, like me, living. I thought of the Eigersen twins and Jane and Laurie Sibille at Bellevue, and I thought of Scooter Mason on his soft pillow bed and of Mrs. Hamilton, hungry for love, and the small brown hole in her head. I thought of them dancing under the tupelo trees with me, dancing in the snow, and of my grandfather at Queen of Heaven and the stone lion scratching its fleas. I sat on the ground—the snow coming through the tangle of branches above—and I saw or thought I saw something moving toward me, moving across the graveyard.

It was Charley coming to scare me, I told myself, coming back to scare me and dig another hole. But no, it was not Charley. It was something dark in a cape or a long coat or blanket stopping at the foot of a grave and kneeling on one knee and bending, all the way over to rearrange the flowers in a glass jar leaning against a tablet made of red marble. As quietly as I could, hiding behind statues and tree trunks, I walked over to see who it was. And I saw that the dark figure was a woman who had removed the scarf from her face and pulled back the fur-lined hood of the cape. She was a woman standing in the snow, feeling the gnawing ache of the cold, mourning the dead who refused to die. Who was she mourning and how had he died? And how was I so certain it was a man she was mourning? Why did it matter?

She did not stay long, not that time she didn't, not the first time I saw her in the yard at Saint Jude. I watched from where I sat unmoving on the frozen ground and saw how hard she cried and could not stop crying. I saw the way her body heaved, and I heard the terrible, terrible sound she made. She was a woman, but I did not know how beautiful a woman or that I would come to love her and how my life would be forever changed because of that love. I did not know a thing about it. I watched her wrap the scarf around her face and pull the fur-lined hood of the cape back over her head and walk away from the place she had come to. She walked through the snow and the tupelo trees and disappeared in the dark of the boulevard.

I stood over the grave and ran my fingers over the red marble tablet. There was no date on the stone, and there was no name, either. The top of the stone was worn smooth and chalky, and lichen grew along its weathered face. The woman had come to cry at this grave, and then she had left. I had watched her go and then stood up again and opened my mouth to the snow that kept coming down. The tupelo trees creaked and groaned, and I thought I heard them, was certain I heard them, call my name.

7

On the night of his twenty-fourth birthday, Charley Harwood said it sometimes seemed to him that he was never twenty-three years old. Stoned and crazy after too much cocaine, he said he couldn't remember a minute of the day before the one he was then living, or the one before that. It was like a dream he'd had once but could not remember except for the feeling that something important had happened. He laughed and said it almost drove him crazy trying to find out what that important something was. I told him to think of that year as being like a dead person buried in one of the holes he dug.

"Asses to asses," I said. "Duss to duss."

There is little I do not remember about those days when I was living again in the town where I grew up. I remember, in the beginning, how it was late at night at Texas Eastern, with all nine compressors working to receive the great flow of natural gas into the station and push it out, and how at dawn the birds moved on the prairie and the sun was a violent orange blur melting down the fog and making the ground steam. Around seven-thirty, I'd walk up to the front gate and wait for the day crew to come up the drive, and by then, knowing it was time to leave the station, I no longer felt so tired and sleepy and lonely for company. I always drove home with the windows rolled down and the air drying the pockets of sweat on my shirt and pants, my scalp itching from the heat. I remember how much I hated the work but liked being away from people who wanted only to talk about football and remind me of myself.

In town, I liked to stop at the Phil-a-Sack for a honey bun and a pint of milk and to visit the pretty, young Vietnamese woman who worked the counter. She laughed the morning I told her my name was Girlie, and I left thinking about what it would be like with her parked somewhere on the edge of town and the sweet tightness and the sweet smell of it. I remember the way the hot bath in the little bathroom of the outdoor kitchen drew in my testicles and made me cough, and how the water burned my hands and feet and left them looking blue under the fluorescent lights over the sink. When I was bathing, Sylvie sometimes backed through the open door with a pitcher of cold milk and put it on the floor next to the tub without once looking at me lying there in the hot, steaming bath. When she left, I reached over and drank the milk with great thirst and let it spill down my chin and roll down my chest and belly and into the water. The milk was like spinning threads of silk in the water. More than once I thought about Sylvie as I had the pretty, young Vietnamese woman and felt the thought where I should not have felt it. "Go away," I told myself. "Make yourself go away."

When I could not talk it away, there was one other way I knew of to get rid of it.

From the very beginning to the very end of my time in Old Field, there is little I did not keep and store in my memory. I remember, for example, the sad animal look on Charley's face when we sat in the dark of his bedroom watching television, the picture of a man and a woman wrapped around each other like some strange, fleshy genus of human ivy. It was Charley who said, "Except for the life in this room, everybody in Old Field is dead." I remember asking what about his mother and father and my mother and grandmother, and Charley saying, "There is no life in this town but yours and mine, John, and sometimes Sammy Dan's when he comes home from school and gets away from all that silly fraternity boy bullshit."

"He's a Kappa Sig," I said.

"So?"

"I hear they're not as bad as some others."

"Yes they are," he said. "These Kappa Sigs are no different from your Kappa Jigs. I'd like to take one and cut off his head and then shit in his neck. It would be a good example. I hate those people."

"I'd like to see you try that on Sam."

"Boula, boula, boula," Charley said.

He knew it made me sore talking about Sam and his reluctance to come home to Old Field on weekends and holidays. Sam was a junior then, full of his own private vision of himself as a man, and he rarely called my mother. She called him every Sunday morning after mass and said, "Son, we never hear from you, why don't we ever hear from you?" I suppose he apologized then or explained that he was studying hard and late, because the next thing she said was, "Well, that's no excuse. I don't buy it." When I called, it always seemed as if we were separated by more than sixty miles of interstate; there was little to say and no proper way in which to say it. Once I asked him what he wanted to do when he got out of school, just trying to make conversation and show that I missed and cared about him and hoped that everything good went his way.

"All I know," he said, "is that I'm not going back to Old Field. And I'd appreciate it if you didn't push it, John."

"You don't have to come back to live," I said. "And I hope you don't think I was suggesting that. It would just be nice if you stopped in and visited once in a while. Me and Ma miss you."

"I'll never go back," he said in a near whisper.

"Not even to visit?" I said. "This is your home. Your mother lives here, Sam. I live here. How can you never come back?"

I was quiet and he was quiet. Then he said, "All I want is to be happy. Don't you want to see me happy?"

"Wouldn't that be something," I said. "Sam Girlie happy. Sam Girlie having the time of his life. What a weird, wonderful change that would be." I started to say something else, but he hung up.

Although it took nearly a month of that year for me to discover her name, I first saw Emma Groves when I was twenty-three. I saw her in the graveyard behind Saint Jude on the only night of the year it snowed, and I saw her again the next night and the night after that. I saw her every night for two weeks and at the same time, about forty-five minutes before my shift at Texas Eastern started. The first five or six times I saw her, I stood behind the trunk of a tupelo or hid in the shadows of the Newbring family tomb. The next week I played a game of situating myself as close as I could to the grave with the red marble stone. I sat on the ground with my knees pulled in tight against my chest and my arms wrapped around them and tried to talk myself into thinking and feeling like a gravestone.

"Stones don't move," I told myself. "Stones don't blink. They don't giggle. They don't belch. Stones don't even think."

One night she looked in my direction, and I shuddered and let out a mousy whimper that she apparently did not hear. Another night I had to relieve my bladder so badly I almost did so in my work khakis. To get around it, I thought about football and needing to piss during practice and telling McCombs about it and hearing him laugh that rotten laugh of his and say this was where my days as a boy ended and my days as a man began. "Hold it," McCombs had said. "Put it out of your mind and hold it." I managed to last until Emma left the yard, but then realized how ridiculous discipline was at a time like that and let everything go on the grave of Albert S. Young, loving husband and father who departed this life on January 21, 1942. The piss steamed and crackled when it hit the cold ground.

"Stones don't relieve themselves," I said aloud. "You're a pretty bad stone for a stone your size."

After a week, a warm front moved in off the Gulf and melted the snow and ice and left everything dead and brown again. She arrived wearing a dress and shawl or simply a pair of jeans and a pullover sweater. She walked along a worn dirt path through the graves, a path she probably had made herself, and kept her eyes on the ground, careful not to step over some poor soul imprisoned below. After making her visit, she unceremoniously turned around and headed back along the path to the boulevard and the place she had come from.

I once got close enough to smell the soft fragrance of her perfume, like the one clear dew drop you pull from a honeysuckle blossom, and see how perfect her face and hair and body were in what moonlight fell through the tupelo trees. Once she laughed and said something to the grave, and I thought it was a pretty voice and a pretty laugh, and that she was pretty for someone so sad.

I also thought that if given the chance I would make her love me. After the first week of hiding and watching, it was already true that I loved her, or loved what she was. She was a sad, dark specter in the night, a lost and broken angel, and she was mine. I wanted to take all that she was and carry it with me and belong to it, as it would belong to me. At night on the road to work, I rehearsed all that I would tell her once I found the courage to confront her from the shadows and speak my name. I would tell her how stupid I felt waiting some nights at Bubba Toussaint's Grill, sitting at the counter as if before a great altar and praying for the strength to approach her when the time came to take my place in the yard. I even rehearsed all that she would tell me once she heard my story. She would laugh hearing me tell how my chest boomed like thunder whenever I saw her walking under the lamps of the boulevard and making the iron gates of Saint Jude, and how once, seeing her move across the spread of stones, coming this way, I had taken off my belt and unbuttoned my pants and shorts and slowly, using both hands, unburdened the terrible swelling in my lap. I would tell her how it felt to spill myself on the ground, smelling the faint ammonia smell and fearing she might smell it too.

"You did that just watching me," she would ask.

"I did," I would say.

"Aren't you embarrassed," she would ask.

"Of course I'm embarrassed," I would say.

Whatever I told her, she would laugh and know only happiness. She would come to me and hold me. I would get the chance, I kept telling myself, to make her love me.

When I asked Charley if he'd ever seen a woman at the grave in Saint Jude marked with the red uncut stone, he said no, he hadn't but he had seen two red-faced little kids playing grab-ass under the cross of Jesus in the middle of the yard. Charley was working then at Bellevue, preparing holes for four young black men killed in a wreck on Highway 2. "I saw a real woman in the graveyard at Saint

Jude," I told him. "She was as real as you and me, and she was beautiful."

"Just another of the dead," he said.

"She was real," I said. "I'm sure of it. And she was beautiful."

"I've heard them cry. Nobody cries like the dead."

"I'm telling you she was real," I said. "And she was beautiful."

"It's been a long time since I saw a real woman. And I can't tell you how long it's been since I've seen a real woman who was also beautiful."

"Come on, Charley. You know the grave I'm talking about, the one with the red marble tablet and nothing on it?"

"I should know," Charley said. "I dug the sonofabitch—I dug it back when I first started. I wanted it in Babyland here at Bellevue. But you can't tell somebody where to bury their kid."

"It was a kid?"

He nodded and said, "I told the priest they were upsetting the order of the lives of all those who'd died before this little boy, and he told me to mind my own business. What I didn't tell him was that I'm a line artist and I've got symmetry to think of. You start digging holes four feet long in the place where you've got all these eight-footers and you got a bunch of shit."

"You're full of shit," I said.

"I'm an artiste." He'd been smoking grass; you could smell it in the air. He kept a bottle of Johnnie Walker under the tractor seat and had probably been hitting that, too. He was as drunk or stoned as a man can be.

"You sure it was a baby?" I said. "Positive?"

"It was a baby with a baby head and baby feet and legs and baby arms and a baby heart. It even had a baby pecker, if you can imagine that. It was a little tiny baby without a sin on his soul. Someone said crib death, but I heard from one of the priests that the mother dropped him taking him out of the tub. He was all slippery and she went to dry him off and dropped him. He popped his little watermelon on the side of the tub there. You know what that's like?"

"Don't tell me," I said.

"The kid's father was standing there, and he tried to stuff the brains back into the boy's head. This is what one of the priests told me. After that he went crazy and wound up in the nuthouse at Pineville. That's where the queers got to him."

"You can shut up now, Charley. I don't want to hear it."

"It was goddamn gruesome, and it was terrible. I don't joke about things like that dead baby, John. But these black fellows dead on Highway 2, I can understand somebody wanting to laugh about it. They were probably nice men. They were all drunk, heading for some juke joint out by Summer's Point, and ran into the concrete side of a bridge, doing a hundred. The engine of their little Plymouth Fury went through the floor board and the front seat and wound up in the trunk. Don't ask me how the brothers wound up."

The next day after work, I bought a toy dump truck at Tiny Meaux's Five-and-Dime and put it on the boy's grave, and when she found it she turned it over in her hands, studying it as if it were some weird rock that had fallen out of the sky. The day after I placed a little kid's rubber football against the stone, and she played catch with it walking home under the lights of the boulevard. The ball went up and came down, went up and came down, and not once did she miss or even bobble it. In all, I left a small play store on her son's grave—an elaborate box kite, two model airplanes and a tank I assembled myself, a chemistry kit in a fancy wooden box, five of my favorite Hardy Boys books, a kicking tee, a wind-up robot and a squirt gun. The most expensive thing I left was a tricycle; it cost forty dollars and had racing stripes along its sleek red body. She received each gift with great joy and said "Thank you" to the night before heading home. It wasn't until she was way down the boulevard that I felt safe enough to say "You're welcome."

One day the lady at Tiny Meaux's asked who the lucky boy was, and I told her it was a sick cousin up in West Jacobs. "You're Janie Girlie's son, aren't you?" the woman said.

"I could be," I said.

"What do you mean you could be?" she said. "Either you are or you aren't? You can't could be."

"I could be but I can't," I said and left the store.

After that, I decided to start shopping elsewhere and to buy gifts for the woman, who was living and could enjoy the presents, instead of for her son, who was dead and could not. Next time I bought six yellow roses and a large crystal vase at the Village Square, and picked out a greeting card with a plain blue border and no greeting. I wrote a short note and signed my name, then drove out to Saint Jude feeling something like a hive of bees swarming around where my heart should have been. I couldn't catch my breath and my legs ached and tingled like they do after a long run. It was a mild, green day and I was alive in it. I was alive in it as I had been in few others. I left the glass jar leaning against the stone and placed the roses in the new crystal vase next to it. I prayed that I would meet this woman and make her love me, and tried to picture the little boy in the grave, happy and pink and taking a bath, but I confused the image with that of the four black men whose bodies were wound into the engine of a midsize automobile. I felt my stomach turn over and knew I had no right standing there, praying for someone I never knew and hoping the prayer would make me worthy of meeting the dead kid's very much alive and beautiful mother.

It was about nine in the morning and there were people in the yard, walking down the drive on their way to Toussaint's Grill for the special breakfast plate and to the bank building and on up Memphis Street to J. W. Smith's, which was still advertising itself as the first air-conditioned laundromat in the state of Louisiana. I walked back to the boulevard and started the car and was letting it warm up when I decided that leaving the note might not have been so smart. I hurried back and stuffed the card in my shirt pocket, then drove back home for beignets and café au lait with my mother and a good hot bath.

When at last I turned in, I covered myself with a soft blue comforter of eiderdown and slept with the oscillating fan set on high cool. I thought even as I slept that night could not come quickly enough, that some men rise in darkness to face the day, and that I, of all people, was one of them. But when I woke, it was to sunlight and the hard, desperate sound of my mother's voice.

"What is this card?" she said from where she stood next to the bed. "Wake up, John Girlie, and tell me what this card is."

"What card?" I said.

"The card in your shirt pocket," she said. "I was checking the pockets of your clothes before putting them in the washer and I found this card. This isn't like you, baby. This just isn't like you."

"I haven't done anything," I said.

"You haven't done anything?"

"Okay," I said. "What have I done?"

She read from the card, her voice tight and angry. It was someone else's voice, I told myself; this voice does not belong to my mother. "All I know is that I cannot stand back and watch you this way any longer. I cannot do it because I feel stupid and criminal. It's not like I'm some freak watching you undress from outside your bedroom window. I saw you here one night, the night it snowed, and I have come back again and again just to be near you and see you and feel your sad sorrow. I wish you were never for a minute sad and see that you are not always. Please know that I think only good thoughts about you and who you might be and why you come every night to this place. These flowers are for you and the toys and things were for your boy who I never had the good fortune to meet. All this is hoping I might meet you and be your friend. Please don't think bad of me. Am I wrong in doing this? Is it bad? My name is Johnny Girlie. I grew up in this town of Old Field and I used to play football at LSU."

"That last part," I said. "I meant it to be funny."

"You sound like a fool. It isn't like you."

"I didn't mean it foolish. It just came out that way."

"Where have you seen this person?"

"At the graveyard. Saint Jude."

"And you want to meet her?"

"What's wrong with that?"

"What's wrong with it?" she said. "You want me to tell you what's wrong with it? Is that what you want?"

I nodded my head, but she wasn't looking at me. She was looking at the card. "What's wrong with it is that this person is just not for you," she said.

"What does that mean, she's just not for me?"

"You don't even know who she is," she said.

"I know enough. I know how good she looks. She goes to the same grave every night. She's got red hair, or it looks red from what I can see. She's a picture."

"Emma Groves is not a picture," my mother snapped in the voice I'd decided was not hers. "She's trash."

"What's that supposed to mean?"

She still did not look at me. "It means she's older and she's had more men than you could count. She's just not for you. She's the most horrible, promiscuous little piece of trash. She's a—"

"I just saw her, Ma. I wanted to meet her. I thought she was beautiful. I never cared about how fast she was or how old. I never thought about counting her men."

My mother tore up the note and threw the pieces on the bed. Then she headed for the door. "She's not for you, okay? Tell me okay, John Girlie? Say okay and it's final."

"Okay to what?"

"Okay she's not for you."

"I don't have to say okay to that," I said. "Why should I say okay to that? Of course she's not for me. I don't know who she's for."

She pointed at the torn-up card. "Tell me she's not for you. Tell me okay she's not for you."

"I didn't even know her name."

"It's Emma," she said. "Her name is Emma Groves." It was someone else's voice she was talking with. "Okay she's not for you. Okay she's not for you. Tell me okay she's not for you."

I pulled the blankets over my head. "Okay," I whispered, "she's not for you."

"Louder."

"Okay she's not for you."

She was shouting. "Again. Okay she's not for you. Again, John. Again! Tell me okay she's not for you!"

"Okay, she's not for you," I said. "Okay she's not for you."

I pulled off the down cover and saw her standing by the door, watching me watching her. She looked pale in the light of the room,

and heavy and wide, a stranger. If her voice had belonged to someone else, I thought, her body could too. This was not my mother.

"Okay she's not for you," I said. "Okay she's not for you. Okay
she's not for you."

Even her smile was strange. It crossed the bottom half of her
face like a long running sore; it was raw and ugly. "Get up and get
dressed," she said. "Lunch is almost ready."

I stayed in bed until Charley came by and stood over me and
asked what was wrong. I told him not a goddamned thing was wrong.
When he went to turn on the lamp on the bed stand, I said not to
goddamn touch it. He said okay, he goddamn wouldn't, and then
he left, slamming the door behind him. I sat up on my elbows and
saw him through the window, heading across the patio in a bloody
pair of camouflage hunting pants and a faded surf shirt. I hurried
outside after him, still naked, and called his name, but he never
turned back. After a minute his Jeep started and I heard him gun
the engine a few times before hitting Ducharme Road in a flood of
gravel.

"Come goddamn back here," I shouted, knowing he was gone.
"Come goddamn back and talk to me, Charley. Come goddamn talk
to me."

I stayed outside a long time, and moved out from the shadows
of the trees and over into the sun and let it warm me. I sat on top
of the patio table and leaned back and felt the white hot sting of
the nails in the redwood. "Johnny, you're crazy," I heard Sylvie say
through the kitchen window. "You're crazy, John."

The bright sun reflected against the bricks of the patio and
prevented me from seeing much of anything. I stared into the vast
white sky and the sun was huge and terrifying, and I shut my eyes
against it. Even with my eyes closed, I saw a plain of white spinning
light, and it flipped over in my mind and made me feel as if I was
falling. I held on to the sides of the table and tumbled through the
light, tumbled like something dry and brown caught on the wind,
and it was a good feeling. When I sat up again, I was drunk and tired
and could hardly open my eyes. The sun was all around me, pressing
against me, but it was still cool out, and a fine, salty Gulf breeze

blew. I felt a rush of goose bumps on my legs, and it moved up my chest and neck and arms and gave me a shudder. I was so relaxed, so loose limbed, that I felt giddy and started to laugh. It was just a little laugh, but I had no control of it. I felt myself getting hard, and I had no control of that either. I looked to see if anyone was at the window and, through the great wall of sun, saw the shadow of someone behind the kitchen screen. I was hard now, and I was laughing with no control. "What are you doing?" my mother said. "Johnny, what are you doing out there?"

"Nothing," I said.

"Johnny Girlie," she said. "Johnny. Johnny Girlie."

The white sun was on me. The white sun was everywhere. "I'm doing nothing," I said. "What did you think I was doing?"

From the counter at Bubba Toussaint's Grill, a person of average height could swivel on one of the high chairs and see past the register and the potato chip racks and the near-empty, five-gallon jar of dried Gulf shrimp, and glimpse the bowed white head of the stone Jesus in the yard at Saint Jude. It was a Jesus the lawn boys from Sanborn Heights never bothered to clean, even when they worked extra hard trimming the ligustrum hedges, polishing the brass nameplates on the front and back gates and sprinkling pesticide on the mounds of fire ants that sprouted along the great iron fence. Pigeons sat idly and shit on the head of the stone Jesus, leaving its face, neck and shoulders more green than white. Somebody wrote a letter of protest to the editor of the Old Field *Times*, creating quite a stir among readers but failing to draw any response from the clergy at Saint Jude. Twice a year the Jesus received a thorough whitewashing, and that was enough for the priests. Had a little pigeon shit ever hurt anybody anyway, Charley Harwood wondered as he read the item in the paper. After all, it was just a statue, and not the Good Lord Jesus himself.

"Where was it they strung up the real one, anyway?"

"You're the guy who wanted to be a priest," I told him. "You should know."

"You didn't answer my question."

"Calvary," I said.

"Oh, yeah," he said. "Calvary."

Because Bubba's food was rotten and worked over your system with all the punch and fury of a dirty prizefighter, and because I had long ago pledged allegiance to Cheryl's burgers at Black Fred's New Pool Hall, I rarely ordered anything more than a cup of coffee and a single twenty-five-cent cigarette from the pack Bubba kept open behind the counter. He called the cigarettes his public Picayunes and sold them at enormous profit, clearing about four dollars a pack. Bubba, who was black, ran an all-night place with lots of grease, smoke and bum chatter. Few whites or middle-class blacks frequented the grill, perhaps in fear of the outlaw biker gangs that occasionally stopped for take-out jars of smothered red beans and rice and go-cups of Ezra Brooks. The bikers, headed for the Gulf of Mexico, liked to eat in the parking lot and pick a fight by scraping a nickel across the door of somebody's new car. They also were known to threaten to rape and kill the wives of local police who showed up in a torrent of dust and tough language.

My grandfather, Bubba once told me, made both of his opening campaign speeches while standing on a stool at the counter. Later, Bubba said, when voting time came around, Jason Girlie returned with fire on his breath and five dollars for every hick, bumpkin, field hand and freak who promised to walk with him down to the nearest precinct and vote for "free school books, new roads and free anything else you fine, fine people of Old Field want."

The night I first met Emma Groves, I went to Bubba's and had a coffee at the counter and asked Bubba's son Terrence how business was going. Terrence, who looked unkindly on customers who took seats at his popular eight-stool counter without ordering something to eat, said business couldn't be better and asked if it was true that I had taken sick in the head and spent my nights hanging around graveyards. I assured him this was not true but explained that a man of religion could get in some good prayers at night among the dead. "Being religious yourself," I said, "you can forgive a man his need. You can forgive me, can't you, Terry?"

"No," he said, "I can't."

"Ah, come on, Terry. Why not?"

"Because," he said, "I heard about you and that spooky woman."

"What spooky woman?" I said.

87

"The one who keeps going in the yard, out with all those people already dead and buried in the ground. You better watch that shit, John. That spooky shit's trouble, man."

"No trouble, Terry," I said. "I sort of like it spooky."

Suddenly he was angry. "Don't call me Terry, John. It's Terrence."

I liked his old man's coffee and cigarettes, but the younger Toussaint and I never got along. I dropped a few quarters on the counter and said, "Nickel tip's for you, Terry."

I was walking toward the door when Terrence Toussaint announced, at the top of his lungs, that it was long past time my picture was removed from the wall. "Got to go," he said. "Got to come down. Can't have people living in the past no more, can we, John?" The photograph, hanging in framed deference over the grill among a renowned group Bubba called his Wall-of-Famers, showed me, in an LSU uniform, diving at the camera and one quick second away from achieving an amazing belly flop. My colleagues were a dozen or so local dignitaries: the deceased founder of the Yam Festival, a javelin thrower whose district record had long been eclipsed, Jason Girlie, a neighborhood handyman who ate breakfast every morning in the same corner booth, the mayor and his secretary, the five current members of the City Council and a lovely young girl whom Bubba often referred to as Little Miss Beautillion, the reigning queen of the debutante coming-out ball sponsored by local black churches.

"Go ahead and take it down," I said. "I don't care."

"You care," Terrence said.

"No I don't," I said. "I don't give a shit."

"Can't expect a person to be a hero all the time, can we, John?"

"No, Terry," I said, wanting more than anything to climb over the counter and tear his throat out. "I guess we can't."

The grease and smoke and suffocating bullshit at Bubba's had given me a headache. Out in the lot, the pink and green glass shades of the lamps hanging over the counter radiated a weird, frosty glow, and all but a few of the people sitting hunched over soup bowls and steaming cups of coffee were strangers. Their every gesture seemed staged and highly deliberate—from scratching their underarms to wiping their mouths with plain paper napkins—and they moved in agonizingly slow motion. From behind the wheel of my mother's car, I watched Terrence climb a stepladder to remove my picture from his father's collection. He held it out before him, waved it like a cheap door prize and said something to the people at the counter, probably asking if anyone wanted an old black-and-white photograph of a football player who no longer played football. Only one person moved, a rheumatic old man walking toward the bathroom door. Terrence said something else, and still no one moved. Then he looked through the window and waved at me, and I waved back. After he pulled the picture out of the frame, folded it in half, then quartered it and stuffed it in a bucket of scraps, I drove less than a hundred yards down the boulevard and parked near the back gate of the cemetery.

The fog was getting thicker by the minute, but now that Bubba's was behind me I liked the night. I liked it because somewhere beyond the cold, a woman named Emma Groves breathed and laughed and walked and talked and carried the weight of her beauty as only a woman named Emma Groves could. The night was all right because she lived in it.

She came, of course, though always there was the fear that tonight would be different, that something would keep her away. She came walking under the trees and through the graves as if pulled by a force greater than her own will—pulled by the grave with the red stone, or was it by my own power? For a moment I was certain I'd actually drawn her to this place, pulled her from her home at such an hour, made her larger than the night itself. She came as she always came, beautiful and terrific, and saw me there, standing at the head of the grave, mumbling to myself and afraid as I had never been before. I loved this woman. Already I loved her. She saw me and continued to move this way, never stopping or veering from the path she had always taken—through the Braden and Archer and Scott families, past the feet of Jodie Arceneaux and Louella Talbott and Dean St. Cyr and up the drive to the stone Jesus, then turning and walking by the dead Paul Theodore and the dead Susan Jane

Reardon and the dead Aubrey Beckett. She came and stopped at the foot of the grave, and I leaned over and ran my fingers over the cold smooth top of the stone.

"You're Johnny Girlie," she said and offered a hand to shake. It was a warm, thin hand that felt good in mine.

"My name's Emma Groves."

· I felt nervous and weird, taken aback that she knew my name and had spoken with such kindness, but managed to say, "I'm the one who left those toys and flowers." Then, "I wasn't sure what color roses to get."

"They were beautiful. Thank you."

For several seconds, the long beat of a heart, I looked at her standing a few feet away and saw precisely what I was getting into. Something told me that if I did not turn my back and walk away, I would never again be able to. This occurred to me with startling clarity, and I wasn't prepared for it. My tongue was thick and muddy as I struggled to make it work. God, how clumsy and wrong I must have seemed to her. But it was not only the person of Emma Groves I saw in that one clear moment among the graves at Saint Jude. I saw a picture of the future that was meant to be and would come and would surely find us different from who we were then. In that one piece of pure time, I saw beyond the dead and the tupelo trees, and beyond my fear, and I was in that other faraway place. And Emma was there too.

"I just wanted to meet you," I said.

"Well." She shrugged, as uncertain of what to say as I was. "I'm glad we met, John. Thank you for coming. It was nice of you to come."

"I wanted to meet you, Emma. And I wanted to ask you if you would go to dinner or some place with me."

"To dinner?" she said. "You want to go to dinner?"

"Oh, no. Not now. But sometime. We could go to a restaurant and maybe see a movie or drive to Summer's Point and have a beer. Really, we could do anything, go anyplace, whatever you want."

She was serious. Did she question my intent, the forthrightness with which I delivered my lines? Her hands were balled up and resting on her hips, and already I loved her. "Are you asking me for a date, John?" she said. "You come here, of all places, and you stand there. You wait for me, someone you've never met. And you ask me for a date?

"That's right," I said. "I'm asking you for a date."

"Well. Okay then. I'm glad." She let her teeth rest on her lower lip, and she moved from side to side. She bent over and removed a scrap of newspaper from the tall grass of the grave and, when she stood up again, she was smiling. "I was wondering when you were going to stop hiding," she said.

"What?"

"When you would stop hiding," she said, louder this time. "I was wondering when you'd stop."

"Hiding?"

She nodded and said, "Some nights you looked so funny all bunched up on the ground trying not to move. I thought about asking you what you were doing, but I didn't want to embarrass you. I thought it was cute. I wasn't scared."

"You should've said something."

"I didn't want to spoil your little game," she said.

"But I wish you'd said something."

"I thought it was fun. I promise I never was frightened. I knew who you were from the start."

"You did?" I said with a dry throat.

"I saw your picture once in the paper. I remember because I'd thought it was so strange, the way you were diving right out at the camera and making that mean old face. I'd never seen a picture like that before. Didn't it hurt when you hit the ground? What sort of pose was that, John?"

"I just wish you'd said something."

"I won't tell anybody."

"You won't tell Charley Paul Harwood?"

"Who's that?"

"Charley. He's my friend who digs the graves."

"I won't tell Charley. I promise."

"And my mother and anybody you might run into at the New

Pool Hall. I don't want them to know what a little silly ass I made of myself trying to meet you."

"I've never been to the New Pool Hall, and you weren't an ass. Not even a little silly one."

The cold wind blew and her long red hair moved behind her like a cloud, danced and shimmered in the lamplight, and she pushed away what strands fell across her face. She was looking at the ground at her feet—at the place of her son. "Let's talk some other time," I said, embarrassed. "I'm really sorry. I'll be going now."

"Oh, don't." She reached to stop me. "Don't go."

"I thought you'd want to be alone for a while."

"A minute's all," she said. "What's a minute?"

She put her hands together, forming a steeple, and she began to pray. I moved off in the shadows and sat at the foot of a tree. She spoke directly to the ground as if someone were stretched out on the grass listening to her every word. I wondered how it was that the living were able to speak so plainly to the dead. She told her son how her day was going—"I ran out of tokens for the washing machine and had to borrow some from that sweet little Jewish couple down the hall"—and never once did I suspect her of being insincere, of carrying on this soliloquy for my sake.

Had someone drifted through the cemetery and asked what this strange handsome woman was up to, I suppose I'd have explained that she had lost her son, but look, he was sleeping here, down in the ground below. "And sweet," she said, giggling. "I've met this new fellow, the nicest new fellow."

Having just met her, I already had given myself to her side. I believed in her sorrow. Who so loved another that she would continue to mourn him for months after he was gone? If what she was doing was way out of the ordinary—and it didn't matter to me if it was—I had neither the heart nor the desire to do anything about it. "His name is John Girlie," she said, and then turning to where I sat under the tupelo, asked, "John Girlie? Is there a middle name, or is John Girlie all there is?"

"It's John Jason Girlie," I said. "After my grandfather."

"I like it," she said back to the ground. "Don't you like it, sweet?"

She sat next to me in the car, with her hand on my knee. I could feel her warmth and happiness. Every mile or so, she erupted with a burst of bubbling laughter and stopped herself by pressing her hand to her mouth. "It's like I've always known you," she said. "Do you have this feeling that you've always known me?"

"I suppose," I said, honestly. But when she became sad, I said, "I mean, I do. Of course I do."

We drove down Memphis Street and turned on Union. In front of the place that had been my grandfather's store and last dwelling, I stopped and pumped the horn and saw the curtains quickly pulled back in the upstairs windows. There were several dark, unfamiliar faces pressed against the glass, looking down on the street. I lowered my window and said "Girlie, Girlie, Girlie," and we drove on, Emma's laughter and mine growing louder as we picked up speed.

All the stores and restaurants were closed, and the large, broken face of the First City Bank clock, the hands permanently frozen at 6:13, blinked in the darkness like a stroboscope. We passed Virgil Charles's place and Maxwell's Newsstand and the New Pool Hall, and when I started to say something, she shook her head no and said, "Hush, John. Hush." She had decided it was no longer necessary to maintain a conversation. All that was necessary were nods and shrugs and hand gestures and grunts, grunts coming when the fog sat especially thick on the road and made the driving difficult.

I knew the town. Blinded, I could drive it and overcome every hard curve and pothole. I knew that sometimes Mr. Haywood Sloane sat up nights in his living room reading books on the Civil War, and that from the road you could almost see the movement of his lips through his open picture window, and his arms flailing like those of a conductor before a symphony orchestra, and the gentle gray dance of his soft gray hair. I knew who slept and who watched television, and I knew a few who made love in the light of their rooms, though only a few. I knew the corner where Sally Cousins worked, Perot and Vine, and the number of the room at Tap's Motel where she made her sale. I knew where four old hands from the Bearings & Fittings plant met twice a week for high-stakes poker, and that on those evenings their wives went to the back lot at Howard Posner's furniture warehouse and sat for hours sharing smokes and cheap wine and swapping lies about the men they'd held. I knew every billboard along Highway 2, and I knew the dizzy red, white and blue of the barber pole at Garbo's that never stopping turning. I knew that on weekends Pepper Beaugh's janitorial crew cleaned the bank and the private school, and that sometimes, to save on the electric bill, they worked by the light of giant kerosene and colored-oil lanterns. The light of those lamps was brilliant and warm coming through the windows, pouring out like painted dust. And I knew, when I saw it, what a lucky boy I was to be awake and alive to see it. I knew everything about that town.

I knew the pretty and the ugly of it. I even knew where to go and park if you wanted to kiss a girl. But that was not where I went with Emma Groves—not right away it wasn't. We drove through Sanborn Heights and the rows and rows of old unpainted shanties, some of them yawning with their load of sleeping humanity, others sad, some burning yellow porch lights, others cracking and creaking when the wind blew. We drove down Maple until the asphalt turned to gravel and the gravel to dirt. The packed dirt road ran along the southeastern edge of Bigger's Swamp, and seeing that swamp with Emma Groves was like seeing it for the first time. It was dark and wet and seemed, like a great hungry animal, crouched and prepared to strike. And its prey was Emma Groves and me. We hit Highway 2 at the head of the swamp and drove west until we found the clearing and the new industrial park and the used car lots and then the train depot. From there we took Blue Hill Road and moved on to the stockyards, the odor heavy and sour now and the cattle, rubbing their bloated sides against red board fences, making a sound like children crying. We drove past the strip joints—the Home Turf, the Cajun Crane and the Gallopin' Jugs—and finally we reached the Samms River.

It was to the river we drove, and parked and talked until morning.

There was light on the water when she finally got out of the car. The cold fog was like spirit wings in flight, and it seemed to move around her and away. I asked her was she hungry, did she want breakfast. She said no, but would I come over here. She was standing by the water. I stood next to her and saw that she looked weary and her mouth was dry. Her lips were full and thick, and she wet them. She ran her fingers through her hair.

I said may I hold you. She said yes you may.

How was it, being twenty-three and full of luck, that I knew my life, or what on my terms amounted to a life, was over then—that nothing I ever did or touched or saw would equal what I did and touched and saw that first morning with Emma? Was it my life I lost then, or was it simply all the days I had lived before that one by the river? Everything about it was clumsy and wrong. I was clumsy and wrong. The way I fought through her clothes was wrong, the way I handled her flesh. My clumsy wooden hands held her as though she were a young bird struggling for life. "Soft," she said. "Softer." The way I made her lie on that hard cold bed of soil was wrong, the way I looked at her and talked to her and felt for her. The river moved, and the sound that came out of me was like something in a dream, lost and faraway. I left my shirt on, my socks. Had a baseball cap been handy, I might have worn it. "Gentle," she said. "Gentle now."

She laughed at me, and the river moved, and the morning fell upon us like a prayer.

At breakfast my mother said, "How was work?"

"Fine," I said.

"About our talk yesterday about that person," she said.

"What person?"

"That woman."

"You mean Emma Groves."

"You know who I mean."

"It's over, Ma. It's done."

"I want you to know something, baby. I want you to know how

I knew about it—I mean, how I knew it was Emma Groves you bought those flowers for. I'm sorry I hurt you. I didn't mean to hurt you."

"It's over and done with," I said again. "You don't have to tell me. You don't have to say a word about it."

"But I want to," she said. "You're learning what it means to be a Girlie, John. People at Tiny Meaux's were talking. Everybody knew where you were taking those toys. People were watching you from the parking lot at Bubba's—just like they've been watching that poor woman make that walk for a whole year now. I know it's pitiful, but it's how they entertain themselves. They feed on that woman's misery. They forgot why she goes to that yard. They forgot who's in it. And I don't know what can be done about it."

"I wish you'd stop talking," I said.

"They should do something about it, baby. It's terrible. The pastor at Saint Jude should lock the gates at night. That's what should be done about it."

"You shouldn't have called her names," I said. "You don't even know her, Ma. I remember how it was around here when Daddy left. People are not themselves sometimes."

She put her face in her hands.

I said, "It's over and done with, Ma. Let's let it go. Leave it alone."

"Oh, Johnny," she said and slammed the flat of her hand on the table. "When will you learn that it's never over and done with?"

9

When I was thirteen, my mother accepted an invitation from a man named Butch Perles to accompany him to the annual Crewe of Corinth Mardi Gras ball. My mother would not have considered accepting had Marie not insisted that Butch Perles, a lonely widower and her insurance man, and my mother, the sole guardian of two growing boys, seek each other out. Those were the days in late winter when Marie stopped by our house three and four times a week with boxes of French cream puffs and chocolate eclairs from Sanders' Bakery and ice-cold buttermilk in glass bottles. She usually arrived in high spirits, wearing either a mink stole or a great rabbit coat and a mortician's mask of makeup to hide her years. Convinced that Sam and I needed a man around the house to keep us from thinking all people behaved as badly as Janie Maines Girlie, whom she considered an example of motherhood at its worst, my grandmother often sat Sam and me down on either side of the divan and promoted conversations about masculine subjects, such as professional wrestling, Mack trucks, coon dogs, chewing tobacco, country and western music and fighter pilots. She cursed recklessly and sucked her teeth like some horny redneck looking for trouble on an empty Saturday night.

I suspect Marie Girlie worried that her grandsons would become homosexuals as a result of their living arrangement, and she would be forever plagued by guilt, knowing it was her son who was responsible. On every visit she inquired as to our romantic doings with the little girls in the neighborhood. Had Sam, who was only nine, kissed anyone yet? Had Johnny? And if so, had anything strange and wonderful bubbled in their young-man parts? Whatever happened to May Gloria Fuchs with her precious crown of pigtails? she wanted to know. And Barry Neighbor's child with the pouty movie-star lips? I once overheard my grandmother tell my mother that the boys, meaning Sam and me, needed to know the musky odor and ways of a man, day and night. It was time my mother found herself a fellow, Marie said.

"May I remind you of something?" my mother said.

"And what is that, dear?"

"I'm still married to your son, and the no-good sonofabitch is still married to me."

Butch Perles, my mother later said, looked like the sort of fellow who would stand on a bench on a busy street corner, say something about Satan being a hairy, large-nosed bear, douse himself with several gallons of gasoline and set a large kitchen match to his trousers. Sam said he was built like a garbage dumpster loaded with trash but that, I argued, was much too kind. Mr. Perles, who was husky and confined to an area closer to five than six feet above the ground, had large pale eyes, spoke with a clipped, Cajun accent and owned an amazing nest of crinkly red hair that rained flakes of dandruff onto the shoulders of his white tuxedo jacket. This was the prospective mate my grandmother had chosen for her orphaned daughter-in-law, who, dressed in a red satin gown and a sparkling white veil of baby's breath, would be one of the most attractive women at the ball.

Marie no doubt was of the school that thought only desperate, unattractive men considered the possibility of marrying a woman with children. In conversation with my mother, Marie once referred to divorced and abandoned women as used cars. "Some men pick up a new car every two years," she said. "They think nothing of trading in a perfectly fine, clean-smelling car with little mileage on it for one that is even finer and more clean-smelling and altogether without wear and tear. Used cars, as you may know, tend to sit in the lot longer. But they can be, lest we forget, a real bargain."

Accepting a date to a Mardi Gras ball probably broke one of the rules my mother had made for herself, because when Mr. Perles arrived at our door, holding a corsage of pink carnations, she said she had just vomited from nervousness and was simply not fit for dancing. He said she might feel better if she took a little swallow from the bottle of Jim Beam he kept stashed under the seat of his car, but she said not even whiskey would make her feel up to it. She apologized and said one day she would feel horribly guilty for standing him up this way, but as of this minute all she could think about was running to the bathroom one more time, leaning over the open toilet bowl and relieving the enormous fluttering weight stuck in her craw.

A dejected Mr. Perles limped back to his car, roared his engine and left two steaming planks of rubber on our front drive. Later I discovered that my mother, who had learned her dirty trick in school, had greeted Mr. Perles with a mouthful of the cinnamon and banana oatmeal she had eaten just before his arrival. A man, she said, watches a woman's mouth when she speaks, while a woman looks at a man's eyes. What Mr. Perles saw in my mother's mouth as she described her condition worked to convince him that the night was without promise. There was, as I tried to explain to Sam, no pleasure in kissing a mouth full of oatmeal flavored with cinnamon and banana.

"Pretty gross," Sam said.

"Really gross," I said.

That was, as far as I know, the closest my mother ever came to going out with a man after my father left, and it was her one great revenge against the rival sex. Those mornings my grandmother dared come by with gifts of pastries and cold milk and resurrect the subject of men, my mother cut her off gamely by asking, "Remember Butch Perles, Marie?" and removing a box of oatmeal from the cupboard shelf. In time Marie came to see my mother as not only a used car but one that had already been junked and left to the horrors of oxidation.

"Your rust is showing," Marie would say, only to hear my mother respond, "Then somebody call a mechanic, for heaven's sake. Get a tow truck over here."

My mother would never again wear that red satin gown. When I close my eyes, it's not at all difficult for me to see her in it, standing in a narrow corridor of light at the open door of my room. The gown was cut low to reveal her large bosom—Sam called her breasts fat pillows—and fixed as tight as a girdle around her waist and hips. She wore white ribbed stockings and her shoes were red and shiny and sported clever little bows the size of dimes. It later seemed to me that when she put the gown away in her closet, she also put away her femininity; she resigned from a life filled with wonderful sexual possibility for one in which she could eat as much as she wanted and make jokes about the beauty she once had been. But on the night she spurned Butch Perles, she was still extraordinary to behold, and on the verge of sleep I saw her standing at my bedroom door as a welcome friend, an apparition, a dream. She floated toward me and sat on the edge of my bed.

"You awake, John? You awake?"

"I'm awake," I said, and reached and held her hand.

"Unzip me, John." she said, and I sat up and unzipped her and watched the top of the gown peel away like a layer of red satin skin. She reached first with her right hand and removed her left breast from its cup, then with her left hand held the right breast and lifted it too, and sighed with her sudden freedom. Then, letting her gown fall, she walked out of the red satin skin and into the light and away from me.

"Good night," she said. "Sleep tight."

"Good night," I said. "Good night."

It still hurts me to think that my mother then was the same age as Emma Groves when first I touched and loved her, clumsy and wrong, down by the river. At thirty-three, my mother rejected the possibility of ever holding a man again, although I know she was less repulsed by the idea than she made out to be. She wanted something physical, and to be kissed. How else can one understand her lonely visits to the beds of her children, her constant requests for a hug and a kiss, her need, as Sam once said, to always be "bothered with"?

Butch Perles had come to her door and she had turned him upside down and belittled him. She had, as I overheard her tell my grandmother some days later, cut into his scrotum without using a knife. And he had acted as any man would when removed of his balls by a woman without a knife—he'd peeled out in his automobile, stormed through downtown Old Field and run red lights. But what an example Janie Maines Girlie had made of him! In one brilliant performance, she showed everyone, including herself, that her decision to carry on alone, with only her boys, was noble and strong and full of character, and she showed that she was qualified to go it alone, and that no one, not even her mother-in-law and best friend, would convince her otherwise.

She had defeated all contenders in one short round.

"I worry for you, Janie," my grandmother said.

"Don't," my mother said. "I'm perfectly fine."

"You'll be perfectly lonely. Aren't you lonely?"

"I've got the boys."

"But they're boys," Marie said.

"They're my boys," my mother said.

Good character, Janie Maines Girlie liked to say, speaking of every last member of the animal kingdom, made up for a lot of things, including a fine pedigree. "It's a lie that good character has anything to do with breeding," she said. "So don't count on what I've got to have carried over into you. And lest I forget the other person who played a part in your being here, don't worry that his cowardice will make you weak."

When I said, "You're talking about Daddy," she said, "I'm talking about character, baby. No one's talking about anyone named Daddy."

Was it because Emma Groves was almost ten years older than me and more experienced in the matters of love and sex that my mother insisted I never see her again? Or was it because Emma Groves was weird and ruined by her grief—"that spooky woman," as Terrence said. Was it bad character to lose a man and hope to find another, and finding another, to give of yourself so openly and freely, as Emma had? And knowing Emma's roster of failed and easy romance, did my mother worry that her son, her John Girlie, the boss of the house, would be just another quick kill, a whimpering fool for love? Why Emma, I wondered, and why me?

One thing I understood was that I could no more help or stop myself than a starved beast at the trough could help or stop itself. My appetite for Emma quickly became greater and more compelling than my promise and need to please my mother. Another thing I knew was that if I hoped to continue seeing Emma, my mother better not know about it. In her house being twenty-three years old and college educated did not entitle you to live as you chose or love as you chose or even sleep as late as you chose.

Sam once tried to argue his way into a Florida vacation—he was seventeen and the proud new owner of a high school diploma—and she remarked, "I will always be older than you, son. I will always know better. I will always be your mother."

"You use the word *son* like a knife, Ma. The only time you call Johnny and me son is when you want to cut us down."

"Would you rather I called you child?"

"I'm not a child," he said.

"You'll always be a child. You're my child, you and Johnny both. And when you're fifty and I'm seventy-four you'll still be my child."

Early in the morning after my first night with Emma—after I'd showered and had breakfast with my mother and lied about working hard on the job—I called the superintendent of operations at Texas Eastern, apologized for missing my shift and told him I wanted to resign immediately.

"All you did," he said, "was clean two toilets, mop the floor some and sit on a bucket reading dirty magazines. I'd say this word resign is a little strong, John. What you're doing, and I congratulate you by the way, is quitting this shit. I hope you'll consider getting back into football, which is where you belong."

Then there was a second night with Emma, as fine and improbable as the first, and filled with the same strange magic. On the second night I waited near the back gate of Saint Jude and watched her kneel by the grave and touch the stone. She walked to me and said nothing, and riding through town with the wind in our hair and the radio on and a sky like iron, she said nothing. That night we stopped in Thomasburg and danced to Cajun zydeco music on a floor powdered with sawdust and drank dark German beer from cold glass mugs. Jeffery's Friendly Lounge stood by a railroad track, and when the 12:05 headed north to West Jacobs came through, we danced to its squeal and thunder and laughed and shouted with our heads held back but were not heard. I knew we had not drunk too freely, for when we returned to the river and parked and found each other again on the hard ground, there was nothing clumsy and wrong about it. On the second night, I said I was hers and meant it.

Another thing I said was, "How do you live, Emma?"

"That's an interesting question," she said. "How does anyone live? How do you live?"

"You have a job, I mean? You work?"

"Sometimes," she said. "I'm a private-duty nurse. I only work part-time. I work when the hospital calls and needs me. And even then sometimes I don't work. I tell them I have another patient. It's the easiest lie to tell when you start thinking that all the world is sick and messing the bed. Did you ever know a private-duty nurse?"

"Never. Or if I did, I didn't know it."

"Then I'm your first?"

"You're my first," I said.

It was also on our second night together that I first saw her naked in the light. After leaving the Samms River, we rented a room in a hotel near Lafayette, and she insisted we leave the bedside lamp on. She said, "I want to show you something," and she showed me the cesarean scar that ran down her lower belly, from her navel into her bed of pubic hair. The scar was thick and purple, and she took my hand and made me touch it. "It's ugly," she said, "isn't it, John?"

And I said, "No, I don't think it's ugly."

"Do you think it spoiled me? I'll never wear a bikini again."

"Doesn't matter," I said. "I like those one-piece jobs better anyway. The less you see, the more you want to."

To show her I wasn't repulsed, I moved down her belly and kissed the scar, ran my tongue along the thick line. "I like it," I said. "It's soft. It feels good."

"It's Dorsey's scar," she said and felt for my face and mouth. She held me as I licked the scar. "That scar's the one thing his dying will never take away."

On the third night I told her she was the most beautiful girl I ever knew and meant it, and on the fourth I said I was very happy and had never felt so alive and meant it. On the fourth night it started to rain, and she directed me away from the river and back to her apartment building, the Seville Arms, and into the uncluttered one-bedroom apartment she rented on the top floor. She opened the window to the clean smell of rain as we stripped off our wet clothes in the dark and waited for the lightning.

When the lightning flashed, I saw the pale blue walls dressed with framed photographs and small watercolors of the sea and country, the smooth brass tubular frame of her bed and in one corner a baker's rack crowded with plants and white baskets of flowers and some of the toys I'd left on her son's grave. The lightning flashed again and I saw her move to the bed and lie across it with her arms overhead and her legs held together. Her legs were the color of the walls when the lightning came and between her legs was a dark red mound of hair that appeared and disappeared and appeared again. We were serious that night. And lying there, washed by what light the night gave us, she told me about her boy buried in the yard at Saint Jude.

"His father insisted I name him Dorsey after his great grandfather Groves killed fighting at Bull Run in Virginia," she said. "It was a name that sounded pretty put next to the Groves. I was a Dupuis before I married, so I had them put on the birth certificate, Dorsey Dupuis Groves. Of course, his father hated the name. His father said it was pretentious. The funny thing was, you could look at Dorsey and call him Hank or Nick or Steven and he wouldn't mind. He'd laugh because he didn't know what a name was. He just liked it when you talked to him. He liked the sound of your voice." She paused, but only for a moment. She sat up in bed and ran her fingers through her hair. "He was so young, John. Not even young really—he was new. He was brand-new. He wasn't two months old when he died. I went to check on him in the crib one afternoon—he'd been taking a little nap—and he was all blue. I knew what it was because I'd read so much about it. I pushed on his little back and tried to get air in him, but I knew he was dead."

She said this quite hurriedly. She probably thought it would hurt less if she got it all out in a rush. And perhaps it did hurt less, because her voice was even and clear and she did not cry. It was such a painful memory that I wondered at her strength to continue with the telling. "His father and I were living in a place out in the country by Grand Coteau, a beautiful little cottage out by the girls' school, but after it happened and we buried him here, I moved in close. I was lucky to find this apartment, you know. There was a waiting list."

I said something—"How'd you get it?" or something equally benign—and she looked at me reproachfully, as if she thought I was questioning all that she was saying. "You don't have to tell me," I said. "If it's too hard, you don't have to tell me."

She studied the ends of her hair, ignoring me, and then began again. "I told the resident manager about Dorsey is how I got the apartment. She was wonderful, John. She said she had a sister who went through the same kind of thing—cut off from her baby right at the start, right before she could even get used to having him. She gave me the first place that came open, ahead of everyone else. She's always up here, looking in on me. She calls me Daughter and says I'm like the daughter she never had. I like the place because I can see everything I need to see from the window. I especially like wintertime because there aren't any leaves on the trees blocking the view."

I wanted to know everything there was to know about Emma and Dorsey Groves without having to hear her say it. I wanted simply to wake up one morning and discover that the story of her days was neatly stored someplace within me—in my head, my heart, someplace. I heard myself say, "With a name as pretty as Dorsey Dupuis Groves, Emma, you should've cut it on the stone."

"I didn't want to," she said sharply. "It didn't matter as long as I knew it was him. What does it matter if everyone in the whole world knew it was him? You'd think they'd come and pray for him, or talk to him, or worry for him?" She lowered her voice. "As long as I know, John. That's all. As long as I know."

I moved from the bed to the window and looked out at the

night. A flatbed truck with only one headlight was moving down the boulevard, followed by a Greyhound bus and two black boys on bicycles close behind, trailing in its exhaust. "I've got family buried at Queen of Heaven," I said. "My great uncle, three great aunts, second cousins, my grandfather. My grandfather's the one with that sleeping lion statue on his tomb. It cost almost ten thousand dollars to have that lion made, and the stonecutter did it with a finger missing. I told my grandmother that the lion had only nine fingers on its hands, and she said, 'Claws and toes, Johnny. Claws and toes.' "

Emma laughed and said, "Its bigness makes up for its missing toe. It absolutely broods, doesn't it, John? It always looks like it wants to cry. When I see it, it makes me want to cry, too."

"My grandfather killed himself. It would've been wrong to put a happy lion on his tomb. He shot himself in the head with a shotgun."

"People die," she said. "Big people, little people. It's how they live that counts. I learned that from the priest at the memorial service. He said Dorsey lived without sin. He was an angel on this earth. Not everyone can say that. For the time he had, he was sweet and warm and he loved me. It almost makes you proud."

On the fifth night we were serious again, and she said, "You never asked me about Dorsey's father."

"You want me to?" I said. "I won't if you don't want me to."

"Ask me now and get it over with," she said. "If a man's going to love a woman, I figure he's got a right. Go ahead and ask me."

"Tell me about your husband," I said.

"He was so depressed after Dorsey died. He wouldn't talk. He wouldn't eat either, and he cried, he cried in his sleep. His mother, she's extremely religious, always going to church—well, she came over with this minister from First Baptist, and they all talked. And I guess it was the minister who came up with the suggestion that we send him to the hospital in Pineville for a rest. I know now that it was right to let him leave me. But still, going to a hospital to rest? It wasn't like he'd lost his mind and needed one of those straitjackets and a cell with pads on the walls. He went in an ambulance, though, can you believe it? And that's when I moved here."

"That was last year?"

"Sometime last year," she said. "Or more like two years now. His mother told me he still goes to the hospital but only on an outpatient basis. He became a Roman Catholic, which I already was, and he pushed to get our marriage annulled. I went along with it because I knew he wanted it so badly and thought it was important to clean the slate and start all over. And now when I call him—and I don't want you to think I call him very often—he acts like he hardly knows me. I told him I see to it that Dorsey's grave is kept up, but talking to him you would think there never was a Dorsey."

"And that's why you go to the yard every night?"

She pressed her body against mine, and I kissed her wide soft mouth. "Oh, baby," she said. "I knew you'd know why."

On the sixth night I worked my face across her breasts and her soft brown belly, down the warm raised scar and into her bed of hair. "It's okay," I said. "Everything's okay. Let me show you, show you how, this is how," and I showed her how.

"What does it taste like?" she said when we were done. "A good taste or a bad taste? I think you're a good taste."

It tasted like the smell of her but I didn't tell her that. I felt empty and didn't want to talk. "Good taste," I said. "The best."

"It tastes like me when I kiss you," she said. "I don't mind the taste. In fact, I kind of like the taste now that you like it."

I felt suddenly mad at her, and not knowing why knew better than to say anything more. I dressed and watched her through the crack in the door of the bathroom standing before the wide, unadorned mirror with her hair falling in front of her face and breasts, and I told her as I had on the third night that she was the most beautiful girl I ever knew. "Oh hush," she said, and I said, "Oh you hush. You hush, Emma." Then I kissed her again and left and drove out of Old Field on the road to the marsh. I drove not caring where I was going and, tasting her, knew that where I was going was not important; I would come back. I would always come back. I was afraid that sixth night, and angry with myself for being afraid. I knew there was no end to what I would do for her. I tasted how she was on my tongue and saw the dark red mound of hair and the place below like a warm silk wet blossom. I smoked a cigarette and stopped for beer at a bait shop and felt a hard violent shudder run through my body. Outside thunderheads sat above the fields of rice cut by barbed-wire fences and dirt and blacktop roads, and the wind blew. My jaw was tense and the muscles in my chest and shoulders tightened and I thought my heart would explode.

Why me, I wondered. And why this girl, why Emma?

I smoked a second cigarette and the beer and the smoke washed the taste of her smell off my tongue. That was on the sixth night. When at dawn I drove back to Old Field, all the traffic signals were flashing yellow and I made it down Union and through town without stopping once. The shrimpers were out in their white and blue converted bread trucks, parked on the lot near the five-and-dime and advertising special sales on ten-pound purchases of jumbos and redfish and flounder. The milkmen were out, and two old women in hair rollers and housecoats were sweeping the sidewalk by the library, and down by the high school I saw the principal, Mr. Delroy Ortego, raising the flag with one hand and holding an enormous cigar with the other. I drove down the boulevard past the Seville Arms, with its side yard of mimosas and dress privet and the long canvas awning at the front door bucked by the wind, and I knew she was in there. I saw where I knew her room was and, seeing no light on in the window, decided she was asleep and dreaming a dream of me.

On the seventh night I waited for her at the graveyard. She walked through the back gate looking away from me, at my mother's Pontiac parked down by the curb. I grabbed her arm and pulled her to me. I told her I loved her and meant it. "Oh, John, hush. Hush," she said. "Oh you hush," I said. "You hush." She was laughing but I was serious. I was so serious I started to shake, and she did too.

I said I'd never told a woman I loved her before and meant it and then, thinking of my mother, said, "I did tell my mother I loved her but that's different. She's my mother. It's not like she's a girl."

Emma said, "Your mother doesn't count. It's a different kind of love. It's not the same."

"That's what I mean," I told her. "That's exactly what I mean."

In those days, some people of Old Field still lived under the illusion that their town was the yam capital of the world, a title that might've been true at the early and middle parts of the century but was no more. Soybeans was the money crop, and the majority of the farmers in de Laussat Parish ashamedly abandoned sweet potatoes for the most ridiculed staple in the history of agriculture, but the only one that promised to spare them the awful humiliation of foreclosure proceedings at the parish courthouse.

"Men are scared to lose the farms their daddies gave them," my grandfather declared at the celebration kicking off the thirty-third annual Yam Festival. He was standing on the poorly lighted stage of Yam Hall, speaking to a crowd of no more than fifty.

"Soybeans be damned!" he shouted. "To hell with soybeans!"

Experienced public speaker that he was, Jason waited for a response from his audience. He wiped his sweating brow with a dirty handkerchief pulled from the pocket of his seersucker suit. When no applause came, he continued on the same ridiculous course: "Soybeans are pretend food, friends. They end up in pretend hamburgers, trying to taste like beef. Do I, as your humble statesman, have to remind you that there is no beef in today's hamburgers? And that there is no ham in these so-called hamburgers either?

"Every way you choose to look at them, soybeans are phony. But what—and this is the point I want you to think about tonight when you're riding that roller coaster or shooting to win a stuffed dog—what in heaven was ever phony about a yam?"

A few people in the audience—farmers and their women—walked out as Jason spoke, and still others stewed in their seats. Afraid that he was losing votes, my grandfather surrendered to the will of the populace, or at least to those members of the populace present in Yam Hall. Now was the time for compromise. "Of course, what a yam does is give me heartburn. I belch and belch. It's got this funny aftertaste, too. Tastes like paint." I headed for the door, following the rest of the crowd. "It's a fricking root, friends, a mere protuberance! That's what's phony about a yam!"

Old Field then was just another stop on your way south to the Coast or east to the statehouse or west to Texas; on your way north it was an unkind, unsynchronized stretch of traffic lights on an asphalt highway bearing the number 2. It was a little number for a little road, and it ran straight into the primordial head of Bigger's Swamp. At that point the road forked east and west, skirting the wide, dark basin, and rejoined some twenty miles up country, where for some unknown reason it became Highway 3. This confused many travelers, but to the locals it was a natural progression, no more illogical than the increase in a person's age as he grows up. When Sam was a kid, he asked me something about that road I never forgot. He wanted to know if the number of the highway continued to climb as you continued to head north; way up in Canada, he asked, did the number of the road reach into the thousands?

"You'll have to go up there and see," I remember telling him.

"I will," he had said.

Few people who grew up in Old Field ever left to live someplace else, or so declared my grandfather in one of his least memorable campaign speeches, discounting the masses who moved away looking for work whenever the oil industry was down. It could be argued more successfully that few people who ever came to Old Field to visit relatives or tour the old homeplace of Jim Bowie ever decided to stay and live. Jim Bowie was the brave and handsome frontiersman who invented the bowie knife and fought and died at the Alamo, but some of the locals confused him with a fellow named Joseph Bowie, who went on to star on the basketball team at Grambling and die, at age nineteen, of a rare heart disease. It was not uncommon to see mournful groups of black kids standing in the yard in front of the old Jim Bowie place, talking in hushed, reverential tones about the time Jumpin' Joe scored fifty-three points and blocked eight shots in the state high school championship game.

"You got the wrong Bowie house," I told a black man and his two young sons one afternoon. "Jim Bowie lived there, not Joe Bowie."

"Who was this Jim Bowie?" the man said.

"He was no relation to Joe, I can tell you that much."

"Joe had a jump shot from the key, didn't he now?"

"Yes, he did," I said. "Joe Bowie could shoot it."

I'd been running the streets drinking beer. And now with nothing better to do, I decided to stand with the man and his boys and watch the front door of the house, and wait for the ghost of Joe to come racing out and pump a few imaginary shots into the twilight.

"Joe Bowie sure died young," the man said.

"Jim Bowie died young, too," I said. "It was tragic."

"Must be in their blood," he said.

I did not correct the man; he had created his own picture of how things were and he was living in it. "Must be something that goes way back," I said. "I'm just glad I'm not a Bowie."

"Me neither," the man said. "Me neither."

Those few outsiders who came to live in Old Field generally took jobs working the rigs in the oil fields of the Gulf of Mexico, and they lived in the trailer park on the edge of town. Their lives, my grandmother once said, were rough and insignificant—their talent was to give birth to more white trash, keep them dirty and full of fleas and ticks and send them off to stink up the public schools. I argued that she was too hard on these people. When she only shrugged in reply, my mother took up the assault.

"Isn't it funny how some people simply don't count?" she said.

"In God's eyes, we all count," my grandmother said. "But I know exactly what you mean. I even know who you're talking about."

"I wonder if God has ever seen those poor lowlifes living out by the dump," my mother said.

"He's probably just shut his eyes to them," Marie said.

"I wonder if he's shut his nose, too," my mother said.

The townspeople—and I don't mean them and me as much as I do them and them alone, those who took most of their pride from where they came from—liked to think that outsiders talked about who we were and the things we did and didn't do. Jason Girlie, long before he died, answered an editorial in the capital city press by driving sixty miles to Baton Rouge and the offices of the *Morning Standard*, parking in the front lot, climbing onto the hood of his big burgundy Olds 98 and shouting into a megaphone that "good talk or bad talk didn't matter as long as people were talking."

"So talk," he shouted. "Talk about me, goddamnit! Talk all you dumb sonsobitches want to talk! Jason Girlie ain't going nowhere! And Old Field ain't going nowhere either!"

I remember the time my grandmother told one of her friends visiting from Baton Rouge, "I often wonder what they say about us around the statehouse now that Jason's out of office and no longer there to speak his mind. I can almost hear them whispering about us poor little people in poor little Old Field."

Her friend, the wife of a congressman, said, "I haven't heard anyone ever say anything about you, Marie."

"I don't believe it," my grandmother said.

And then her friend, as if reciting a line from a book of familiar quotations, said, "Perhaps by never talking about you one may conclude that a very definite opinion has been expressed."

Booboo Raymond's brother Tree, the salutatorian of Sam's senior class at Old Field High, was of a strange but not untypical local mind. He once told me that he never for a minute considered packing up his belongings and leaving the town of his birth, even after learning from the school guidance counselor that the University of Southwestern Louisiana in Lafayette was prepared to offer him a full academic scholarship. I didn't find this difficult to believe. Tree, like Booboo, was local white trash who spent a lot of time shooting pool at Black Fred's, eating hamburgers and making fun of Sandra Boulier. Handsome and built low to the ground, he kept a comb in his back pocket and reached for it only when an equally handsome and low-built young woman happened to catch his eye. All of Tree's ambition in life, I told him time and again, was inexorably tied to the fine teeth of his pocket comb.

"Refusing to come back to where he come from just ain't like Sam Girlie," Tree said from where he sat on a stool at the New Pool Hall bar. He was watching Charley Harwood make a run for the eight ball on the front table. "This ain't the Sam I knew."

"He'll come home," I said.

"In high school I remember he used to read all the championship pennants in the gym and get the shivers," Tree said. "When he got to his daddy's name and then over to your name, Johnny, he'd get all choked up like he wanted to cry. He'd put his hand over his heart like it was the stars and stripes he was looking at. And the boy would shake. It made everybody else shake so hard you thought it was cold outside."

"Sam was weak," Booboo said. "Anybody who shakes looking at one of them pennants is weak."

"Sam wasn't weak," I said.

"I say it's this fraternity boy bullshit," Charley said. "It clouded his mind. They taught him some Greek letters, gave him a paddle with all these autographs on it, showed him how to drink rum and punch and now Sam thinks he's entitled."

"He was weak and got brainwashed like they do those Jesus people," Booboo said. "Next he'll be on TV some Sunday morning talking about the healing power of the Lord and trying to dissolve the goiter in some asshole's neck. Don't tell me Sam ain't weak."

"Booboo," I said, "Sam wasn't weak. You hear what I'm saying?"

"My brother stayed put," he said. "Didn't you, Tree?"

"I'm here, ain't I?"

"He got a big job with a shitload of responsibility."

"He helps keep books at the courthouse," I said. "There's nothing big and responsible about helping keep books at the courthouse."

"But it just ain't any books he keeps," Booboo said.

"The books they keep in Shreveport just aren't any books

either," I said. "They've got books to keep up in Cleveland, Ohio, and in Baltimore and in Chicago and in Washington, D.C. They've got books to keep wherever you go, Booboo."

"I bet they got a pile of books in Washington, D.C.," Tree said.

"Yeah, but they're not these books," Booboo said. "They're not the Old Field books. Something should be said for that."

"I'll say it," Tree said, and then he said it. "Something should be said for the Old Field books."

Charley said, "While you're saying things, say something nice about Johnny Girlie's little brother so as not to get Johnny Girlie all pissed off. Say something, Boo. Say Sam wasn't weak."

"I already said all I got to say for one day," Booboo said.

"Then you say something, Tree."

"I'm all talked out," Tree said.

"Well," Charley said, then cornered the eight ball. "That's true."

Old Field was also where people from out of town stopped for gas and to use the bathroom and get directions. When a carload pulled up to the two-pump island at Jackie Eagle's Gulf station, the first thing Jackie heard was someone asking for a free road map. The second was a complaint about the smashed bugs on the windshield— "like cream cheese with mold growing on it," said a woman from California. The third was something ugly about the weather or the unwholesome look and smell of the ladies room.

Jackie Eagle hated visitors with out-of-state plates because they never flushed his toilets or thanked him for checking their oil. They bought no-return bottles of soft drinks, bags of corn chips and pistachio nuts, then dropped the paper wrappings in the lot behind the building. Jackie owned that lot and used it every third weekend to slaughter a hog or a goat and to raffle off the meat for the Young Jaycees. On Sunday mornings you sometimes saw him in the lot working a broomstick with a nail sticking out of the bottom end, poking the candy and potato chip wrappers with the nail and slipping them into the burlap sack hanging from his shoulders. Jackie was as big a man as there was in Old Field, and as fat. He was known to have heart disease, high blood pressure and a quick temper. He was also thought to be one free road map away from being buried in a pine box.

Charley Harwood said Jackie Eagle would be hard to bury, considering his width and height and breadth, and the size of the coffin he'd require. But this was the kind of challenge he looked forward to.

"You make do with what they give you," Charley said. "Fat or skinny, short or tall. A dead man is a dead man, and the same goes for women. A real artist, such as myself, learns how to deal with it."

Old Field then was just a place, but it was the place where Emma Groves lived, and it was my place. In time I stopped asking myself questions I could not answer, and began living the way my mother had long ago suggested everybody live. At last I took her advice and quit thinking so much and I started to do. "Don't think," I told myself time and again. "Tonight you do. You're a doer tonight."

At about ten o'clock every night, my mother prepared a ham and cheese or roast beef sandwich and wrapped it in wax paper, poured a kettle of coffee and milk into a thermos and dropped a couple of hot sweet potato or pumpkin turnovers into a paper bag, then saw me off with a kiss. The occasion of my leaving for work, or what she assumed was work, never lacked for touches of grand theater. On a typical night, she would sit on the edge of the bathtub and watch me shave and brush my teeth and wash my mouth with Listerine and water. Then she would walk with me to the door and stand on the front porch in one of her boxy housedresses and wave frantically as I crossed the lawn to the car. She would wave as if I were a poor sailor leaving on a doomed vessel destined for a violent, distant port and she were the pathetic loved one left behind to survive this cruel world on her own. I would salute and click my heels or bow and tip my baseball cap, then back the car down the drive and drive slowly into the night.

Down White Avenue on the edge of the Dupart golf course, I usually dumped my sandwich and turnover in a wire trash basket, took a healthy swallow of coffee milk from the plastic bottle and poured what remained out the window. The taste of the coffee was flat and brown mixed with the taste of toothpaste and mouthwash, and I wondered what Emma would say when she opened the door and put her arms around me and pressed her soft cool mouth against mine.

"You taste like a blade of grass," she said once.

"Like what?" I said.

"Don't worry," she said. "You could taste like dead insects. When I was a little girl my uncle Benny would visit from Rayville and kiss me on the lips and complain if I didn't. He tasted just like dead insects."

"How'd you know how dead insects taste?"

"From tasting him," she said.

"He liked eating dead insects?"

"You'd have to ask him that. But he's dead now, John. He's dead and gone, just like all those insects he used to eat."

When we were done doing what I had willed myself not to think about, I always tasted the smell of her, but we never talked about it. Talking about it that first night had put it behind us and freed us to never talk about it again. We talked about the new things but never with embarrassment, and sometimes talking about the new things gave us the feeling that we must make them seem old and routine that very second or else die. When it was new the pleasure was so intense I thought I would die; I thought she would kill me. You can die from love, but that was just a part of it.

"Will there always be something new about it," she asked.

"Always," I answered.

"You'll get tired of me."

"Never. I'll never get tired of you."

When we were done we sometimes sat in the dark in her little kitchen and drank tall glasses of gin and tonic and ate slices of hard red apples and from wheels of Gouda and Edam cheese. We listened to the sounds and felt the breeze that blew through the window. After it rained there was little traffic on the boulevard, and you could see the many colored lights reflected in the standing pools of water.

On wet humid nights, steam rushed from the drains at both ends of the boulevard, and Emma said it looked like devil's breath. In late winter, when there were no leaves on the trees, you could see the stone Jesus on the cross in the graveyard and, near the back door of Saint Jude Church, the angel Gabriel in the statue garden lording over his family of animals. Gabriel's stone wings were almost the length of his body, and his head was bent at a strange angle of repose. He was silent and beautiful. You could see the tablets at the heads of the graves, white dots on a black field. When the fog moved in they were light gray lines on a dark gray field, and the color of the lamps along the boulevard looked more green than yellow. On exceptionally clear nights, I liked to watch from the window as Emma walked through the graveyard and visited the grave of Dorsey Groves. I could see the red of her hair, and the ribbons in it; sometimes I thought I could almost read her lips as she prayed.

"What did you pray for tonight?" I asked her one night in spring.

"We talk. We talked about how nice the day was."

"Does he hear you?"

"I wouldn't talk to him if he didn't," she said.

This was important to her; I wanted to be gentle. "You think you'll make that walk forever? I worry that there's so much sadness in that place. I don't want you to be sad, Emma."

"I can laugh there. You and that gravedigger get drunk there. What sadness there is, it's inside of me. It's not in that yard."

"I realize that," I said.

"No, you don't," she snapped. "You're just patronizing me. You know nothing, John. You realize nothing."

"I know—" I began, "I realize that twenty years from now you'll still be making that same walk and talking to Dorsey as if he were there and understood what you were saying. Twenty years from now, wherever Dorsey is, and I suspect he's in heaven, he'll be grown. He'll be twenty-two . . . he'll be twenty-three years old, my age, and he won't appreciate his mother talking to him like a child. A grown man doesn't want to be talked to like a child."

She was standing by the window, gazing forlornly at the place she'd just been. "He was a warm pink bundle of joy," she said.

"I'm sure he was," I said.

In the kitchen a blue light stole through the open door from the bedstand lamp with the frilly shade, and bathed in it Emma looked like a figure in a dream. "You're not real," I told her, putting my arms around her. "You can't be."

"If I'm not real," she said, "can I be a ghost?"

"My ghost. You can be my ghost."

"Okay, I'll be your ghost."

Once it was new and different on the floor of the kitchen. The linoleum was cool when I lay back and she straddled me and leaned over with both hands holding one breast. With both hands she guided her nipple into my mouth, and I kissed and sucked hard on the small brown point as she thrust and rocked against me. "If you play with this one," she said, "the other gets jealous." With both hands she gave me the other, and it was like a pebble in my mouth. She sat up tall and flush against me, not rocking now, and I could feel the syrupy wetness move down the sides of my hips and between my legs. Holding her breasts in her hands, she lifted one high enough against her chest that she could reach down and lick the small brown point with her tongue.

"Do you like to see me do this," she asked.

"Yes."

"I should be ashamed doing this."

"No," I said. "I like it."

There was nothing wrong with any of it when it was new. "I've never done this before," she said. "I can't believe I'm doing this."

"I don't believe you," I said.

"What?"

"I don't believe you haven't done it."

"As long as you like it," she said and lifted the other breast, "then I haven't. I haven't done it."

Always we made love a second time and tried for a third but failed to finish. I would collapse on the floor or on the bed and she came close to me and lay on her side with her breasts against my back, her free outside arm around me and her bent legs pressed up against mine. She called this spooning because we were so close "we're like two pieces of silver cuddling in a drawer," she said. "You're the big spoon and I'm the little spoon."

When I was too tired to leave her bed, I lay there and watched the lights move on the ceiling and thought how it was the smell of the woman that made you whole. She smelled prettiest when we were done, and it was not only the sex smell but the smell of her hair and skin and the clean green smell of plants in the bedroom and the soft detergent smell of the white cotton sheets. The sheets never stayed tucked at the corners of the mattress and always we pulled them off our bodies to lay bare and sweating with nothing to dry us but the cool air. We sometimes balled up the sheets and used them as pillows and felt the cold wet spot where we had been.

"Tell me again why I can't see you during the day," she said one night. "I need to hear again."

"We could," I said, "but we can't." ·

"You're saying we'd better not."

"That's what I'm saying."

"On account of your mother," she said.

"Now you tell me you won't make it hard. Just please, Emma, don't make it hard. Tell me you won't."

"I just want to see you. What's wrong with wanting to see you? I want to see you when it's light outside. The only time I see you is when it's dark. I never see you in clothes. You come here in that dumb khaki shirt and those dumb khaki pants and those boots. And you take them off as soon as you're through the door."

"Khaki is clothes," I said. "Boots, too. They're my work clothes. Boss says I have to wear them on the job or get fired. Besides, sometimes it's you who takes them off. You take them off as soon as I'm through the door—before I even say hello and catch my breath."

"You already quit your job, Johnny. There is no boss."

"I thought you said you wouldn't make it hard, so why do you?

You said you wouldn't and now look at what you've done. Sometimes you have no word, Emma."

"Let's talk about what your mother must think seeing how clean your clothes are every morning. Don't tell me she doesn't suspect you're not working. She has to suspect something."

"Most of the time the maid does the wash."

"And the other times? What about the other times?"

"Did I ever tell you how much I love you? Do you know how much I love you, Emma?"

"There are twenty-four hours in a day, Johnny," she said.

"I always knew that," I said. "That's one thing I always knew."

When she was feeling sorry for herself she said I treated her like a harlot at night and a leper during the day. She wanted to know how long I would go on hiding her from my mother, and I told her however long it took. I told her my mother would come around in time. Of course, it did not escape me that the only time she ever talked about these things was after we were done with each other and there was new light outside. The new light gave us both a deep feeling of sadness because it meant I would soon have to leave.

"My graveyard shift's about done," I told her in the morning and pantomimed my final clean-up detail. "This is the time I mop up. All the bugs that came through the windows are now dead on the floor. They're like dust and weightless and blow away from the push broom when I work down the aisles between the compressors. The compressors are hot and spit oil on the floor, and the bugs that fell in the oil and drowned look like chocolate raisins. You like chocolate raisins, Emma? I always liked them."

"Why do you have to make a joke of everything?"

"I'm trying to make you laugh."

"You're trying to make a joke of me."

Because we had stayed up all night, my head ached, and I could hardly keep my eyes open. "All right," I said, "I'm trying to make a joke of you."

She was quiet and then she said, "Chocolate raisins hurt my stomach, John. They hurt your stomach like they hurt mine?"

"They do," I said. "They hurt me here," and I touched the spot on her flat brown belly where they hurt. The spot was just above the purple rope scar. I ran my fingers along the scar.

"Kiss me there and make it stop," she said. "Make it stop hurting. Please, John. Make it stop."

I kissed her there. I made it stop.

11

After leaving Emma, I didn't always drive directly to the house on Ducharme Road. Some days, fighting off sleep, I drove by the graveyards in search of Charley Harwood.

In the early morning light, the Queen of Heaven cemetery, with its ancient white and gray stone tombs standing above ground and the tired cedar trees twisting in the fog, looked to me like a sleeping city in miniature. This wasn't like any real city I knew, because the population never decreased with changing or hard financial times. People here couldn't move to another part of the country when offshore oil production skidded into recession. And people such as Marie and Janie Maines Girlie, not yet included here but certain to be one day, would eventually have no choice but to tolerate a selection of white trash neighbors residing only a few feet away. Each tomb was a private residence, home to one or more persons, either a modest rambler or a multiple-storied dwelling. Some were upstart condominiums, and others were fantastic antebellum mansions spared the ravages of both Yankee pyromania and modern urban development. There were dilapidated shotgun trailers standing next to plantation homes, and lightning rods and television antennae, disguised as crucifixes and obelisks, rose from the rooftops. Creatures either drowsed or kept guard at their masters' beds—dogs, sheep, doves, one quiet nine-toed lion and a magnificent pride of angels. The angels were saintly beings with wings, glorious white phantoms who could fly and converse with the Lord.

It was Harwood who first suggested that the angels were bolder, if less smart than the other creatures in the yard. A couple of them stood poised with swords in hand, he said, as if to protect their masters from bodily harm—yes, from death.

"Somebody ought to tell that angel looking out for Ronny Bloom to lighten up," he said that morning.

"Why's that," I asked, innocently enough.

"Because Ronny Bloom's been dead for ten years, John. No angel can help him now, not even that big muscular sonofabitch with the saber he's got. To my eyes the whole arrangement is pretty damned arrogant."

"Yeah, but if Bloom wanted it—"

"To hell with Bloom," he said. "Nobody bothered with that cocky bastard while he was living. What I want to know is who on earth would want to bother with him now that he's dead?"

At Saint Jude, visitors waiting for the church doors to open sat on the wooden benches that lined the boulevard and fed the pigeons stale popcorn and sunflower seeds and bits of breakfast pastries. The visitors sat thinking of nothing in particular, of everything at once— one moment oblivious to the dead in the crowded yard at their backs, the next frightened of their proximity to such a varied gathering of lost souls.

In the morning at Bellevue, the sun spilled across the ground and the dew shone. The aroma of plowed earth and manure from the adjacent farms was rich in the air. "Smells like shit out here," Charley said. "You like the smell of shit, John?"

I took in a lungful of air. "Yeah. I suppose I do," I said, exhaling. "I like it all right."

"I knew you would," Charley said.

Another reason I went calling on Charley Paul Harwood at the cemeteries in the morning was because I liked the warm taste of whiskey before my mother's breakfast. I liked the way it sent my head reeling and gave me the idea that I was strong and wonderful and would live forever. After loving Emma, the idea that I was strong and wonderful was always in me. But only after so much whiskey did I know for sure I'd live forever.

If I didn't find Charley seated on his tractor, working a concrete vault chained to his front-end loader into the new pit he had dug, he'd be sitting on the floor of the grave smoking a fat, overstuffed stick of marijuana or taking thirsty swallows from a fruit jar filled with bourbon and water. He liked expensive aged whiskeys, but that wasn't all he drank. He also liked champagne and peppermint and peach schnapps. A few times he had cocaine waiting for me in the hole, arranged in crooked lines on a fragment of the tractor's broken rearview mirror.

"Want some?" he said in a voice as thin and fragile as tissue paper. "Got some if you want some."

When I refused, he said, "Be that way then, goddamnit," and inhaled the powder with a rolled-up dollar bill.

Sometimes, seeing me approach from where he sat on the tractor, he would leap into the latest hole he'd dug and emerge firing clods of dirt and rocks the size of a clenched fist. He had a good strong arm and was often on target, hitting me in the chest and once directly in the crotch, which left me howling and clutching my wounded man parts on the grave of Molly Pear Haas. The rocks and dirt stung like pellet fire when I ran in the opposite direction and caught the attack square in the back, and when I tried to charge him and dodge the assault, I risked a large painful serving in the mouth.

At Bellevue one morning, after a fine night with Emma, I arrived feeling strong and wonderful and spotted his tractor parked near a green tarpaulin tent. The engine of the tractor was still running, an empty quart of beer on its hood. Under the tent was a polished oak casket on a metal platform waiting to be lowered into the ground, and it was surrounded by wreaths and great bouquets of flowers, some set on tall metal stands with legs that looked not much thicker than pipe cleaner. Knowing he was nearby, perhaps waiting for the last stragglers mourning at the graveside to leave him alone with his work, I called out his name. Hearing no answer I turned and started back to where I had left the car idling on a gravel side road.

Then I realized that the coffin had remained on the platform through the night. It was too early for a funeral, and there were no lingering mourners. Charley Harwood had neglected to do his job.

I was nearing the side road when I heard him behind me, running across the lawn. I walked with my head down reading the names on the stones and the flat bronze plaques bolted into cement foundations at the heads of the graves. I heard him breathing heavily through his open mouth and pictured him hurdling one gravestone after another with all the poise and form of the competitive sprinter he once had been. His breathing grew louder and I heard the fall of his feet and the rustle of the dry azaleas standing in his way. Then I heard the quick and thunderous rush of air from my lungs, heard it before I felt it, a sound like that of a hammer slamming against a hard side of beef, and I felt the point in my back where he buried his horrible twisted face. How was it that I heard the blow before I felt it? He wrapped his arms around my chest, thrust against me with his hips as I struggled for balance and pushed me screaming to the ground.

"Maybe they were wrong about you," he said after a minute, rubbing the smear of blood off his nose and lips with the dirty cuff of his shirt-sleeve. "Maybe you wouldn't have made such a good pro. I hit you easy. I took you down. I took your goddamned head off."

Hardly able to breathe, I didn't own the strength to strike back. I lay flat on my back and heaved for air and felt a swimming darkness fill the space behind my eyes. I thought I had never been hit so hard, then I knew I hadn't. No one had ever hit me that hard.

"I was like a deer," he said. His nose continued to spit blood, a thick pulsing run he seemed not to notice or, if he did notice, care about. "In my head I was taking the two-twenty high hurdles in the state meet, pulling away from the black boys at my heels. My feet were soft as leaves falling on the top of a pond. It was fucking fabulous. *I* was fucking fabulous."

After I caught my breath, I got up and walked to the car, thinking I would leave without saying a single word. It wasn't fun anymore; none of it was fun. I ordered myself to walk and so I walked, though not without difficulty. My chest burned with every breath and burned even more when I coughed, trying to force the thick wet heaviness out of my lungs. I walked down the side road and turned and saw him sitting there on the cemetery lawn, not far from the tent supported by long lines of rope tied to pegs driven into the ground. He stood up, walked over to the bank of flowers and kicked and missed one of the basket bouquets, then kicked again and hit a white wire stand, knocking over an orange fan of chrysanthemums. He forearmed a wreath of carnations and then, grunting and spitting a feather of blood from his nose, upset several sprays of gladiolas and stomped them with his feet.

"Who the fuck do you think you are?" I heard him say to the coffin. "Well, fuck you then." His fists were clenched and held chest-high, his feet staggered and planted firmly on the green artificial turf that lay stretched beneath the rows of folding chairs. I'd never seen him look so threatening. He began to shadowbox, throwing wild roundhouse punches over the casket, then directed his blows at the flower arrangements, toppling every one. He sent hard quick fists into the backs of the chairs, all of them bearing the name of the funeral home, Lafond and Lansom. The chairs clattered to the ground. "So you got a problem!" he shouted at the coffin. "So you got a fucking problem!"

"The problem," I said, "is that he's dead." Then I shouted, "The problem is that he's dead!"

"Dumb shit," he laughed back. "This ain't even a he. This is a she. This is a goddamned old woman!"

I grabbed a handful of gravel and threw it as hard and far as I could. The gravel rained on the canvas tent and dropped him to his knees. He covered his head with his arms and started shouting, "So what's the fucking problem! What! What is it!"

"Dead people can't talk," I said after him. "You're going to learn that firsthand if you don't quit this shit."

"Quit what shit," he shouted back. "Quit what shit."

"You know," I said. "You know what shit."

At first, seeing the angle he took, I thought he would run past the last line of graves, across the side road and head for the jack pines bordering the pasture of the neighboring farm. But I was wrong. When he reached the road he turned right and came my way, sprinting and leaping invisible hurdles, pulling away from the invisible pack at his heels. His stride was long and regular, his form better than what I remembered of his blue-ribbon days on the high school track team. I braced myself, thinking he was planning to tackle me head-on this time. I lowered my shoulder and tightened the muscles in my neck and chest, resolved to take whatever shot he gave me, take it and give nothing back. It just wasn't fun anymore. His eyes were fixed not on me but on some distant point, the Old Field water tower across the highway or the grain elevator standing just to the east, and I smelled the tired odor of liquor on his breath and the sweat on his clothes as he raced past me, his stride still good. I watched him pick up speed heading down the knoll the side road climbed. I saw only the thick blond top of his head as he turned onto the old Sunset Highway and headed toward town.

I knew running after him would do no good. I wouldn't have been able to catch him, and once his performance was complete he'd tire and need a ride back to the graveyard. It would be my job to help him lower the coffin into the ground, set right the confusion of chairs and dispose of the trampled flowers. I wondered how he had gained the trust of funeral directors to drop coffins and seal the vaults without their overseeing the work; I wondered at the other weird crimes against the dead his drunkenness and perversion had led him to. "You sick freak," I called behind him. "You dumb, sick freak."

I followed behind him in the tractor, bouncing along and having the best time of it, and kept a distance of about twenty feet. I feared that when he dropped I wouldn't be quick enough to keep from running him over. I'd never operated a tractor and kept confusing the clutch pedal with the brake, pressing one instead of the other. On the panel I discovered the button for the horn and blew it; but he continued past the John Deere repair shop and the new feed mill and the U-Haul rental place. He ran hurdling down the yellow divider in the middle of the road and shouted at the drivers of those cars moving down the opposite lane who shot him the bird and shouted obscenities. He was trying to keep his head up and his elbows close in, pumping at a rate equal to the one he had begun in the graveyard, but he wasn't up to it. His drugged or drunken body failed him; he lost his form and then his balance and finally his footing. When at last he collapsed in front of the Fidelity branch bank, in the middle of the road, I jumped down from the driver's cradle, assumed an authoritative pose in the middle of the road and directed the traffic that had lined up behind me onto the blacktop shoulder. When the road cleared, I knelt down beside him and saw the cloud of blood and mucous on his lower face and neck. His shirt was wet with sweat and his pants, torn at the knee from the fall, revealed a glistening red wound. Gravel and bits of dried grass stuck to the bloody cut. I grabbed his shoulder and pulled him toward me, but he fought to turn his face skyward, to the new sun of that early morning.

"An easy hit," he said. "Easy. You ain't such a goddamned man after all, Johnny Girlie."

After about five minutes of lying flat on his back in the road, he hopped to his feet unassisted and started back to the graveyard. His form and stride were good again and he was running faster than he had before. Every ten steps he leaped over an invisible hurdle. When finally he turned up on the gravel side road of the graveyard, he extended his face and chest and thrust his outstretched arms behind him. At this point he was crossing the invisible finish line; he was completing the race. I parked the tractor near the tent and walked to where he knelt fighting for breath under a pink mimosa. His nose had stopped bleeding, but there was a crusty black ring of old dried blood around each nostril. The blood and mucous had dried on the curly hair of his chest that poked out of his wet and wrinkled madras shirt. When he smiled I saw blood in the spaces between his teeth.

"You win?" I said.

He put his arms around me, hugged me close and pressed his sweating face against mine. The smell of liquor was stronger now. I felt the roughness of his whiskers and the beating of his chest. I embraced him. I clutched his shirt and felt his heart thumping against my hands. "Did you win?" I said again. "Did you win your stupid goddamned race?"

He put his lips to my ear and I felt a coarse dryness. "It wasn't even close," he whispered. "I took it going away."

Of course, I knew then that the time was near when I would have to help Charley Harwood, and that this was one of his ways of asking me for help. I also knew that he was telling me that he was not feeling so strong and wonderful and that, unlike me, he was not convinced he would never die. What I didn't know was what I would do about it.

"You know you can't keep this up," I said.

"You can't keep this up."

"You can't, Charley. You're going to kill yourself."

"You can't, Charley. You're going to kill yourself," he said.

As we stood there holding each other, a procession of cars appeared in the bend of the old highway, headed this way, but we didn't move at the sight. If anything, we held each other closer. It was a funeral march, led by a policeman on a motorcycle and a long, obscenely black hearse. All the cars burned headlights, and traffic moving against the procession slowed and pulled over and parked on the shoulder. Soon I heard tires on the gravel and watched the procession of perhaps twenty cars move up the drive. The policeman on the bike glared through his frosted glass visor at Charley and me, but didn't wave us away. The driver of the hearse stared at Charley and me, as did the drivers of all the cars in the procession. I saw a woman in one car make the sign of the cross, and it was clear, then, that these people were moved by the sight of us, that they saw us standing under that pink mimosa near that unmoved coffin, and in the chaos of flowers and chairs, recognized us as members of the family of death. They recognized their bereaved brethren and were filled with pity.

"I never see you anymore," Charley said. "Why don't I ever see you anymore, Johnny?"

"You see me," I said and felt more of the coarse dryness. "It's just not the same as it was."

"When I see you you've just seen that woman and there's nothing left of you. She takes all there is."

"No, she doesn't," I said.

"It's not that I blame you, John. It's not that. It's other things. It's everything."

"I know it is," I said. "I know the hell it is."

The policeman led the line of cars to another canvas tent in the rear of the cemetery. The blue strobe light on his bike continued to turn even after he parked and all the other cars had parked and turned out their lights. "That dig," Charley said and pulled away from me. He pointed across the yard. "I worked all night on that dig, trying to make it perfect. The ground was like stone last night, but I never had a better one, I don't think. When I finished at dusk I wanted to take a ballpoint pen and autograph the carpet. People should know what I do. Did I tell you I'm an artist?"

"You told me," I said.

We picked up some of the flower arrangements and set them upright in their flimsy white stands. I made a stack of all the metal folding chairs and then sat down in the shade of the tent. Charley limped over to the tractor and pulled a bottle of Sambuca from under the seat, and we drank and said not a word. The liqueur was warm and sweet and it hurt my teeth; taking his first hard swallow, Charley coughed and spat a gob of phlegm and blood.

We watched six men in dark suits make two even lines behind the hearse and another man, wearing a white suit, busy himself opening the back door. I recognized him as the funeral director, Theodore Lansom. The six men strained against the weight of the coffin; the women cried; the children looked away. Handkerchiefs flashed like mirrors in the sun.

"Is she good?" Charley said after a while.

"If you mean Emma and does she treat me good," I said, knowing exactly who and what he meant, "she's very good."

"I really did mean Emma, not the other thing, the sex thing."

"I know you didn't mean the sex thing," I said.

"About the sex thing," he said. "When a woman has a baby, does it get stretched out? Is it any different?"

"It's probably different," I said, knowing better than to tell him about the cesarean. "But not by much."

He lit a cigarette and let it hang from his bloody lip. He passed it to me and I took a long hit and gave it back to him. The filter of the cigarette was stained red and looked as if a woman with lipstick had been smoking it. "Will you let me meet her?" he said.

"Only if you promise not to tackle her the way you did me."

"I promise," he said.

"And promise not to use foul language. She hates foul language."

"Foul language?" he said. "What is foul language?"

"Curse words," I said. "She hates curse words."

"I thought foul was birds and chickens and shit."

Across the way I saw the priest in dark red garments swing a smoking silver censer in the middle of the crowd of mourners, and when I turned my nose away from the bottle of Sambuca I could smell the spicy fragrance of incense burning. It smelled red and hot and was pretty nice, though Charley said it smelled like the cinnamon rose candles his woman burned in Mabel's rooming house, and they in turn smelled a lot like the candles they burned in a black whorehouse.

"Ever been to a black whorehouse?" he said.

"Not a black one," I said.

"You been to a white one?"

"Once, a few years ago. I was with my grandfather."

"Old Jason took you to a whorehouse?"

I don't know why he didn't believe me. He usually believed my grandfather was capable of anything. "No," I said, "I took him. I was the one who drove. We parked by the door of the place but never got out of the car. He was too crippled and too old, and he probably couldn't have done it anyway."

"Do dicks die?"

"I think they do," I said, and saw him smile. It was a big, lazy smile, the first of the morning, and a bloody one, too.

"What happens if the person dies before the dick? Or if the dick was hard when he died?" he said. "They'd have to saw it off to close the door of the coffin."

"Either that or build a bigger coffin."

"Or drill a hole in the lid."

"That might work," I said.

When the burial service ended, the policeman drove away on his motorcycle, the blue light no longer spinning. The funeral director drove the hearse down the side road and out of the cemetery, and several cars followed. There remained, I would guess, ten or twelve people who drifted away from the tent at the rear of the yard and walked toward Charley Harwood and me. The women wore veils with intricate weblike designs and knee-length dresses in somber shades of blue and gray and carried white beaded purses. The men, all of whom seemed uncomfortable in their loose-fitting Sunday suits, kept their hands in their coat pockets and removed them only to pat down their hair mussed by the wind or to pick a stray weed growing in their path. The men strolled over the graves as if unmindful of where they were, but the women—stepping carefully to avoid getting their high heels stuck in the soft earth and tripping—veered around the gravesites. These were ordinary people, the people of Old Field, and they came and stood before Charley and me and nodded their heads and bit their lower lips and hitched their shoulders.

It was because they understood the meaning of grief that they had come, and they wanted us to know it. Charley said "Glad you're here" in a peculiar voice, and placed the bottle of Sambuca at his feet. "Glad to be here," a man said, patting me on the shoulder as he walked to the coffin under the tent.

"That's John Girlie," Charley said to one man, and the man said, "I recognize his face from those pictures in the paper. How you feeling, John? You feeling all right?"

"Fine," I said.

Charley and I remained seated. He stamped out his cigarette and I lit another and we lowered our heads in qualified shame. The people surrounded the polished oak coffin and prayed. I saw how their lips moved. The few children in the group who had joined their parents made steeples with their little brown hands. The men were quiet and kept their eyes closed. Some of the women reached out and touched the lid as if to feel for warmth or to let the body know they had come. Others pulled single blossoms from the arrangements, mementos, I guessed, of their having lived this day and seen it through, losing less than what they had gained and giving more than they had taken.

They did not stay long. And when they left it was along the gravel side road, in pairs or clusters of threes and fours; no one walked alone. They walked with their arms around each other, swaying as they moved and moving with no more hurry than the wind in the fields. Then their car engines roared and the gravel popped under their wheels. I saw the clouds of dust lift and dissipate. I watched them go. I watched them drive away.

owever accomplished I became at not thinking and just doing, I always felt empty upon returning to my mother's house after visiting Emma and running by the graveyards for a word and a warm snort with Charley Harwood. It was not a feeling of hunger but of loneliness, and I could not lose it. At the breakfast table, my mother sat with me and watched me eat and drink; I insisted on it. If my mother, who twice a week busied herself with the ladies' altar society at Saint Jude, couldn't stay to see me finish my plate, I asked Sylvie to pour herself a cup of coffee and pull up a chair. I wanted company. Sylvie rolled her huge brown eyes at me even when I was serious, or trying to be, and kept her hands moving, curling, torturing her black flaxen hair. Anyone could see she was nervous around me and had no idea why a man my age and size, a person with a college education and a name of some local consequence, would need to be stroked and babied so. Perhaps I'm reading too much into how she behaved around me when my mother was away. I know that she liked me and found me curious, almost weird. She liked to laugh at me the way a child laughs at a monkey in a cage. The reason the child laughs, I suspect, is not because the monkey is comic but because the monkey is wild and obscene yet familiar. In me, Sylvie saw a creature who owned and deserved a place equal to hers on this earth but who was so different and incomprehensible that walls of steel bars ought to have been placed around him.

"You're trouble," she said one morning.

I had said nothing to bring this on. I was sitting at the head of the table spreading apple butter on half a biscuit.

"You're trouble." she said again. "I never knew nobody so much trouble as you." She laughed a nervous laugh.

"Tell me why I'm trouble, Sylvie. You can't say something like that without an explanation. It's rude and unfair."

"You're asking the wrong person," she said.

"Then who should I ask?"

When she pointed at me, it was like looking down the barrel of a gun. Her left eye closed as her right focused. "Do I have to tell you?" she said. "You may be trouble but you ain't dumb."

Some mornings, if my mother was out, I called Emma on the phone in the outdoor kitchen and, hearing her voice, wanted to have her again. Knowing that I couldn't have her made me want her even more, and wanting her even more really did give me trouble. Emma's ripe husky voice, lumbering through the simplest conversation about the weather or what someone said on the radio, had in it the power to make me feel that if she didn't touch me right away I'd wither and fade away until nothing remained of me but a dim, unexcellent memory. How was it that one moment, drinking with Charley Harwood in a place of death, I was so certain of eternal life, and the next, in a house warm and secure, convinced that my time was up?

"I leave you and I feel all the hell alone," I told her. "It's like I can't bear to think of the day."

She was quiet, then said, "I think you're beautiful."

"No you don't," I said. "If you did, you'd have said it louder." I needed to hear it again. Hearing it made me feel sleepy and good, and relieved some of the loneliness.

"I think you're beautiful," she said, louder this time. "I love you more than anything under the sun."

"And the moon?"

"It too," she said, "the sun and the moon."

It is true that I slept little and ate only what I pleased, which was sometimes nothing for stretches of twenty-four and thirty hours, and this no doubt had something to do with my strange, silly thinking. I was always tired and hungry but never too tired and hungry to think that I could not keep awake and without food forever, or as long as there was Emma to love. I would eat and sleep only when she needed to eat and sleep. How could food and rest matter when the bodies we lived in seemed hardly real? I wanted, I told her, to strip away our prisons of flesh and be done with them. And she laughed. "Now wouldn't that be something," she said. "Our prisons of flesh?" Then she said, "I sort of like your prison, Johnny."

When I woke late in the afternoon and found no one in the house for company, I dressed in a gray pair of sweat pants and a white LSU sweat top and turf shoes and ran my regular course— down Ducharme to Dunbar, up the sidewalk along Dunbar to White Avenue and the Dupart Country Club, across the freshly mowed fairways and then back again, back as hard and furiously as my body could take me. On one of these runs I decided this town of mine was no longer just one place but a place of two separate and distinct parts: the part where Emma lived, and the part where everyone else lived. And of the two, the part where Emma lived was the better because I was never lonely in it. This was the part of dreams and of night and of everything new. When I was in Emma's part I sometimes thought of the other. I imagined myself running as fast as I could, through the bright and terrible day, going absolutely nowhere. Why couldn't I build a bridge from the place where Emma lived clear across to the other side?

I once tried to explain how I felt to Charley and he said, "John, this bitch is problems. She's got you all fucked up." We were in the yard at Queen of Heaven, sitting on a stone shelf not far from my grandfather's tomb. "You think this bitch is problems now, just wait a while. Give it a few years and see what problems this bitch is."

"Her name's Emma," I said. "Don't call her bitch."

"So how old is this Emma bitch?"

"I said don't call her bitch."

"How old?" he said. "Forget her damn name."

"Nine years older than me," I said, thinking I should punch him.

"I didn't say how many years older, what I said is how old is she, meaning how many years has she been on the planet. Tell me how old she is, her age in the number of years since she was born."

"I said she was older than me. She's nine years older than me."

"This bitch is thirty-two," he said.

"She's thirty-two, going on thirty-three. What's wrong with thirty-two?"

"She'll be forty-one when you're her age now. And how old is your mother? Is your mother forty-one yet?"

"My mother was twenty when I was born."

"Your mother's forty-three, then."

"It doesn't matter how old she is. She's my mother. She's got nothing to do with Emma."

"Your mother is two years older than this Emma bitch will be when you're her age now. Your mother went through that nasty menopause shit, right? I know she has."

"She hasn't that I know of."

"Well, she will. Because that's life, John. Men get better looking and women dry up. They're like a tomato you buy all pretty and put on the sill of the window over the kitchen sink and watch go bad. When you're how old this bitch is now, which is thirty-two, and you, John, are like one gigantic ripe and luscious tomato, and juicy to be had, good either sliced into steaks or boiled for stew or whatever, this bitch'll be like your mother. Can you imagine fucking your mother, John? Can you imagine that shit?"

"You're sick, you know that?"

"Me sick?" he said. "You're the one fucking your mother."

I shook my head, unbelieving. He was serious. "Charley, you just compared a woman to a tomato."

"That's right," he said, "I did. I love a good tomato. But can you imagine trying to fuck one?"

In time, wanting her always, I began to feel worried and confused during the half-hour or so each night when Emma left the apartment and crossed the boulevard to visit the grave. I told myself not to, but selfishly I'd come to see Dorsey Groves as my rival. He owned something of Emma that I could never have or touch or know, and I envied his possession. Through the trees I saw her move like the shadow of a great-winged bird, smooth and pure. And watching her stop to kneel and pray, I marveled at the strength of their bond, mother and son.

How long would she grieve for that lost boy? How long would she cry? And what would I have to do to end her sorrow?

"You feel guilt over what happened to Dorsey, Emma?" I asked one night. "I hope you don't. Because you shouldn't, you know. Sometimes things just happen."

"Don't tell me things just happen, John," she said. "I know all about it. I've seen what happens."

I looked for the right words to say. And she knew I was looking. "I wish I'd known him," I said.

"He was a tiny pink bundle of joy," she said. "And Jesus in one proud wave of his hand took him away from me."

"Jesus did that?"

"He did," she said, nodding her head as if she had just spoken an irrefutable fact.

"I don't think it was Jesus who took him, Emma."

"Who then?" she said. "Are you blaming me? I think it's been hard enough without hearing you blame me, John."

"I didn't blame you," I said, raising my hands in defense. "All I said was that things happen."

"Dorsey wasn't even a real person yet, John. He was just a warm little pink bundle of joy and in one proud wave Jesus took him."

Some nights Emma had to work and left the apartment at around midnight to care for some poor sick person who every half hour soiled his bed and screamed for a mother and father buried fifty years ago or more. She left me dozing in her great brass bed but I rarely stayed, choosing instead to catch up with Charley at one of the graveyards and give him a hand. I enjoyed working a shovel once his backhoe had scooped away the stubborn Johnson grass and top layer of soil, and all I had to do was square the corners and level the floor. At Bellevue, he always excused himself at first light, walked to a spot under a magnolia tree and pissed on the grave of Harbold Winn, the Old Field High physics teacher who gave Charley the only failing grade he ever made in his life and who died of a massive coronary while drinking coffee one afternoon in the faculty lounge. Charley spelled his name on Mr. Winn's grave, and rejoiced whenever he had enough ink to write the letter F as a postscript. "Van Gogh!" he shouted. "You demented, one-eyed bastard!" He then ran across the highway and stole the morning paper from one of the boxes at the head of the asphalt drive leading to the Scenic Gardens subdivision. He liked to join me in the grave and read the obituary page, looking to see who died the night before and which family would need to commission yet another work by the town's best line artist.

"Sensitive as I am," Charley said one morning, "I may burn out. A person of my talent, the Michelangelo, the Rodin, the Van Gogh of graveyards—one has to guard against that kind of thing.

"But I'm happiest when they're dropping like flies, John. I want the whole world to stop breathing."

Convinced that someone's financial ruin would lead to stress, heart attacks, death, Charley scoured the front page for local economic catastrophes. He cheered when Abe Dorr, president of the land bank, filed for bankruptcy and was heard to complain of fatigue and ill health. He pounded the ground with his fists and shouted with glee having read that a certain oil company had laid off three twenty-man crews of roughnecks from the Old Field area. He checked the society page to see which social clubs were planning vacations and chartering airplanes to Mexico City, Las Vegas and Miami Beach, certain that the odds were in his favor and that soon now he would be commissioned to make over a hundred digs to accommodate the membership, wives and invited guests of, say, the Old Field Knights of Columbus, killed in a fiery crash off Padre Island, Texas.

"What do you want on your grave?" he said one night. We were sitting on a bench, sharing his famous bottle of booze and a few lines of coke arranged on a square of aluminum foil.

"What do you mean, what do I want on my grave?" I said.

"I mean what do you want. I know what I want."

"And what's that?"

"I want one of those great obelisks like the Washington Monument," he said. "It may look crazy out there on the farm, but I want this great stone monolith set at the head of the grave, and I want it to rise above the willow trees. I want it to look like the earth has a humongous hard-on, like this incredible rod is trying to pierce and impregnate the clouds in heaven. I want it to have blinking lights on the top to warn planes to keep the hell away. And incised on its base I want the words 'Charles Paul Harwood, Son of Malcolm and June: What a manly damn man this young man was.' "

"A stone angel would do me fine," I said. "But not a swordsman. I want a lady angel—tall and slim with wings out to here." I gestured how far I meant, then said, "I want her beautiful."

"You always did want sexual intercourse with the angels," he said. "But what you don't know, John, is that angels are men—all of 'em. I always knew you were a little queer person."

"Not all angels are men," I said defensively. "They're women or they're men or they're androgynous, which is neither."

"Since when?"

"Not since any time, Charley. That's the way it always was."

"They're androgynous, are they? You're saying they're half one thing on one side and half one thing on the other?"

"No, Charley, I'm not saying that at all."

"But if they're half-man and half-woman," he said, "is the right side man and the left side woman? Or is it the other way around?"

"That's not it at all, Charley."

"If that's not it, then what you're saying is that the top half is man and the bottom half is woman, or is it the other way around?"

"Now that I think about it," I said, playing along, "I'm almost certain it's the other way around."

"So Johnny Girlie, who went to college and got a diploma, is telling me angels have breasts but no vagina. You're telling me angels have mammory glands and a penis."

"I don't think we should be talking like this," I said.

"You think I'm being sacrilegious, don't you?" he said. "You always think I'm being sacrilegious. If I really am being sacrilegious then think of the God who made angels with breasts and penises. When you have sexual intercourse with your angel, John, are you going to spend all your time playing with its breasts or what? You going to give this angel a hand job, tweak its nipples or what?"

"All I said was that a stone angel at the head of my grave would do me fine," I said.

"Okay," he said. "I take it back. Johnny Girlie never said he wanted to have sexual intercourse with an angel. He did, however, say angels were men on the bottom and women on the top."

"What I meant," I said, "was that the being of the angel was both male and female."

"Oh," he said, taking another hard swallow. "You mean the *being*. You were talking about its *being*." He was laughing so hard he had to spit out the whiskey and take another shot. "The very *being* at the very essence of this very confused piece of ass."

"All I'm saying is that I want an angel at the head of my grave, okay? Is that so hard for you to imagine?"

"You want one with a penis and breasts or just a vagina?"

"I hate that word."

"You hate vagina?" he said.

"If I say I hate vagina," I said, "you'll say I hate women, and that I really am a little queer person and that I want an angel with a penis and breasts."

"Just tell me," he said. "Do you hate vagina, do you hate the very being of vagina?"

"I hate the word," I said. "I happen to like its very being."

Later we drove in the Jeep to the statue garden at Saint Jude to settle our discussion of angels. I call it a discussion though it really was an argument, tightened by booze and rambling to no easy conclusion. As Charley climbed the marble foundation of the statue of the angel Gabriel, I looked in the direction of the Seville Arms but saw little for the run of trees blocking the way. I had hoped to see some light in her top-floor window, a rustle of curtains, her face through the glass. The yard was crowded with tupelos; more than once Charley had explained that their roots climbed through cracks in the sealed crypts, entered the closed caskets and fed on the dead. He made this claim because he couldn't always maneuver his tractor through the riot of trees and tombs and tablets to set up for a dig and because shoveling through the roots by hand was hard, painful work. Charley was lazy, an artist, and this night he was a drunk and lazy artist talking to a statue named Gabriel.

"You're always mooning about," he said. "You stand here with these gigantic stone wings, looking over these gay little creeps—Mr. Chipmunk and Mr. Toad and Mr. Deer here and Mr. Rabbit—and what they all wonder, as I've been wondering for years now, is what kind of pistol you pack. Or do you pack a pistol at all, friend?"

"Sometimes when nobody's around," I said, "he gets off that perch, walks down to the gutter and takes a leak."

Charley put his hand on the statue Gabriel's groin. "What are you anyway, friend?" he said. "How am I to interpret this stone?"

"That's sacrilegious talk again," I said. "Get down from there before you do something stupid."

"Oh, I'm sorry, everybody," Charley said and pulled his hand away from the statue. "Mr. Toad, Mr. Blue Jay, Mr. Groundhog. Please forgive me, Mr. Deer here and Mr. Rabbit. I'm being sacrilegious."

"I'd feel a whole lot better if you hopped down from there."

"He's smiling," Charley said, smiling himself. He then shouted to wake the neighborhood, "Look at him smiling that smile, John! I swear this angel's starting to smile! I say he's loving this! I can feel it in my palm, John. He's a happy damn angel of the Lord, John."

I stepped on the platform and pulled Charley's hand away and felt the sandy hardness. I pressed my palm against the stone robe covering the angel's middle, but Charley knocked my hand away and covered it again with his own hand. I put my hand over his and tried to determine what was there, but all I felt was the back of Charley's hand pushing against my palm as he figured the erect penis of an angel might.

After a moment of wriggling his hand under mine, Charley said, "How did it happen that we ever came to this—two grown men not only playing with a statue's thing, but fighting with each other for the privilege?"

We both threw up in the privet under the great stained-glass Window of Judgment at the rear of the church, and I announced

143

that doing so would make us feel better, though in reality it only made me feel worse. It seemed nearly miraculous to me that both of our bodies rejected all that our stomachs held at the same time, but when I tried to say so the words wouldn't come. I lay on the ground and stared at the sky and laughed, and the sky laughed back. I threw up again, and then Charley threw up, and the Window of Judgment shone down on us with brilliant panes of red and green and blue light. The window depicted a neatly groomed Jesus and his pride of angels leading the dead to their proper eternal home, and Charley attempted to delay their journey with a fist of pebbles he grabbed from the statue garden. The glass didn't break and the fistful of pebbles rained in heavenly retribution on both of us. Charley covered his head and collapsed on top of me, and we rolled and struggled like two young puppies until the wall of the church stopped us. Lying with my old friend under the privet hedge, I noticed the thin trickle of blood leaking from his right nostril. The blood ran into the corner of his mouth, curved back onto his cheek and formed a red stain on his jaw. He swiped at his face as if bothered by a gnat or tickled by a blade of grass, and in so doing, smudged the blood into the shape of a feathery blossom. "You know you're bleeding?" I said.

"Fucka buncha bleeding," he said.

"You're bleeding out of your nose," I said. "Why are you always bleeding out of your nose?"

"Fucka buncha nose," he said.

"I'll get a napkin or something."

"Fucka buncha something."

I started for the Jeep, thinking there might be a towel or handkerchief in the glove compartment; but he ran by me, leaped into the driver's seat and started down the boulevard, moving slowly enough that I might try to catch up. In the middle of the boulevard, about twenty feet ahead of me, he braked the Jeep and waved me over. When I was almost close enough to climb in, he sped off in a smear of smoking rubber. I jogged down the road after him and heard him shout, "That there tree is a great tree," and looked up in time to see him pointing at a giant oak at the edge of the cemetery. I kept running, harder now as the Jeep picked up speed. "That there house is a great house," he shouted, pointing at the old Victorian where the Dubissons lived. When he turned the corner, he raced down Sanduval, turned right on Darbonne, right again on Braddock and completed the block with a final quick, two-wheeled right onto Beverly Boulevard. I was too drunk to run any further and stood in the middle of the road trying to talk myself out of throwing up again. The more talking I did, the more I felt like throwing up, so I tried to stop talking to myself altogether. "Don't talk," I said aloud. "Don't you talk."

The lights of the Jeep brightened and dimmed and brightened again, then I saw that he was standing in the seat, braced against the roll bar and guiding the vehicle with one of his feet. He moved slowly toward me, looming spectral and huge above the burning heads of light. He stopped a few feet from me and revved the engine. "That there mailbox is a great mailbox," he said. "That there trash can is a great trash can."

As Charley himself had in the Sunset Highway only a few weeks before, I now sat in the middle of the road. And looked up at the Seville Arms to the window at the top of the building. For a moment I thought I saw Emma's face through the glass and curtains, but the moment was brief. Charley moved closer in the Jeep, close enough for me to feel the heat of the engine and smell its terrible fumes. When finally he stopped, I could've leaned forward a few inches and touched the hot grill with my nose. "That there road is a great one," he said and pointed at the ground where I sat. "But that there Johnny Girlie is for shit. You hear me? Johnny Girlie is for shit."

I leaned back to see over the hood. The blood on his face, blown by the wind, fanned out to each cheek like a scruffy red mustache, and his hair was as distressed as a fright wig. My insides hurt so badly that it seemed not to matter that he might have slipped and hit the gas pedal and run me over. The truth is, I almost hoped he would. I thought that if he ran me over I'd at least be done with the night and the drunkenness and the enormous emptiness. I was feeling too sorry for myself to think that if he ran me over I would also be done with myself and done with Emma Groves, which meant done with all the strange and wonderful possibilities of this life. "Go ahead and kill me," I said in a weak, pitiful voice. "Run my sorry ass over."

He didn't say anything.

"Kill me. Go ahead and kill me, Charles. Run me into the pavement."

"You want to die?" he said.

"I do."

"Me, too," he said. "I want to die, too."

"You go first, then. You go first and I'll be right behind you. We'll go one right after the other."

"If I go first, then who'll dig your grave?" he said. "I'm the only person in town with the talent and skills to do it right, the only artist. I can't go first, John. You'll have to go first."

"If I go first who'll be around to build the monument at the head of your grave? You can't forget about the phallus in the clouds and its blinking little lights."

"Phallus," he said after a moment, "that's a great word. Phallus is so great a word I could cry." He moved down in the seat where I could no longer see him, and cut off the engine. He left the bright lights on, and when I listened beyond the clicking and popping noises the engine made, I could hear him crying. It was sad but I didn't know what to do about it. "You're right," I said, trying to make him laugh again. "Phallus is one of the great words. But what I wonder is how it can be so great and penis so bad."

"Penis is for shit," he said. He was sobbing. "Penis is a word for shit. Fucka buncha penis." Then he shouted, "Fucka buncha penis! Listen to me, John. Fucka buncha penis!"

"And vagina," I yelled after him.

"Now, John," he said in quick dissent, "I don't have no problems with vagina. I never for a day had no problems with vagina."

After the road became too hard and uncomfortable, as any road used as bedding should, I stood up and walked over to the cemetery and the white painted bench not far from the grave of Dorsey Groves. The back of the bench advertised Trudy's Yam Bar and said RELAX, MAN, RELAX. I leaned against the bench and looked at Charley slumped in the seat of his Jeep, heard him talking to it. "What

I'll get for you come light," he said, "is a good hot wash-down, some wax on that chrome, some wax on that paint, some cleaner on those windows, some vacuum on those floors . . ."

I listened to Charley's voice and promised I would never forget it, the good familiar sound of it, although the words he spoke were not at all important. I lay back on the bench and stared through the tupelos and saw the stars beating like a million lost hearts. The stars beat like something far-off and unknown in a dream. I heard the wind in the trees, the same wind I always heard when I listened for it, and it became a part of me. I knew I would never forget it. "You won't," I said, and felt myself drifting into sleep. And then hearing Charley start the engine of his Jeep and drive off, I knew I was no longer drifting but sleeping now and there was no coming back.

"For shit!" I seemed to hear him shouting in my dream. "Pecker, rod, wong. Pulsating python! Penis! Penis is for shit, John! Penis is for shit! Do you hear me?"

In the morning when I woke, Emma Groves was standing in a wet gold splash of light, looking and laughing at me.

"Where's Charley?" I said.

"There's only me," she said.

"Only you?"

"Only me," she said.

She helped me off the bench and across the boulevard to her apartment building. She helped me into her apartment and off with my clothes. She was wearing a white dress and white shoes with white rubber soles and white stockings and white underwear, and she helped me help her undress. The bed groaned beneath us and, naked and warm upon it, we groaned too. She helped me and I helped myself and there was nothing wrong with that. There was not a thing wrong with that.

Every summer, the public pool at South City Park attracted Old Field's prettiest girls, many of whom worked as lifeguards and swimming instructors and as ticket takers at the front gate. To work each day they carried floppy straw bags filled with keys, spare tampons, romance novels, tubes of cocoa butter and huge blue jars of Noxema skin cream, and under their loose-fitting shorts and polo shirts they wore sheer one-piece bathing suits that probably weighed less than a piece of paper. Some of the girls removed their shirts and shorts at poolside, I suspect without imagining what effect their undressing might have on the young male bodies splashing around in deep water. After the top suit of clothes was removed, almost every girl then checked to make sure the seat of her bathing suit had not slipped into the crack of her rear end. Anyone who didn't make sure to pull the bathing suit over the whole of her butt quickly developed a reputation as a tease, and Jodie Marx was one such girl. I dated her the summer after my freshman year at LSU, and because she worked at the park pool I went swimming and sunbathing almost every day and spent many long, dangerous hours admiring her fleshy and darkly tanned buttocks.

Jodie was a white-haired beauty. She climbed the wooden guard tower with small bare feet, her silver whistle hanging by a nylon rope around her neck and flashing like a jewel in the sun, and once situated she didn't move or make a sound for fifty minutes. When her ten-minute break came on the hour, she barked an order at some undisciplined child splashing water in the baby pool and descended the tower as quietly and carefully as she had climbed it. She liked to play football in the game room, and at night we shot pool at Black Fred's and went parking near the Samms. Her brown skin was tough and as scaly as a fish, and she smelled of sweat and tanning lotion. We kissed and fumbled for hours in the front seat of my mother's car, but she never let me go all the way. "John," she said, "it's gross and overrated," and only twice did she touch and feel me long enough to make me come. When I touched her she was slick and warm and tight, and the odor stayed on my fingers for hours. At night in bed, I put my fingers against my nose and smelled her and fell asleep smelling her. It was a ripe, earthy odor that led to dreams of sun and clear blue water and pretty girls in tight one-piece bathing suits performing jackknives and cannonballs in the chlorine mist.

My mother never met Jodie Marx. When I told her I had a girlfriend, she said, "You're too young to get tied down with just one person," and leaned over and pressed her lips against my forehead. "You need to live more, John. Shop around."

After Jodie I dated the girl from Rougon, Sissy Sanford. When I called my mother and said there was someone I wanted to bring home over Easter break, she said, "He's more than welcome as long as he doesn't eat us out of house and home," then I told her the someone was a girl. "I don't think it'll be a good time, baby," she said. "Your mother's not feeling up to entertaining guests."

Sissy was a student of modern dance, small-boned and muscular. Her thick mouth never opened when I kissed her, but she compensated by letting me do whatever I pleased with the rest of her body. Making love, she was loud and bossy, and it frightened and thrilled me all at once. Every other weekend, we rented a room at the Prince Murat Inn near campus and acted like a married couple. We made love, went to a movie, ate oysters at a downtown raw bar, danced at a club by the river, attended mass in the morning. It was good with Sissy because it was familiar, but I didn't love her or think I ever could. The Easter week I brought her home to Old Field against my mother's wishes, my mother pretended to be Sissy's best friend, though her face remained fixed in an expression of wild disbelief. That she was quietly questioning my choice in women was plain.

"Your mother looks like she's smelling something stinky," Sissy said. "You don't think it's me, do you, John?"

Once I told my mother she'd better be nice, she lost the funny look, apologized and went out of her way to make Sissy comfortable. She prepared meals using difficult French recipes she claimed to have memorized as a young girl, invited the ladies of the altar society over for tea and cookies, took Sissy on long drives through town and showed her the sights. But when the holidays were over and Sissy and I returned to Baton Rouge, my mother called me on the phone. "You can do so much better, John. She's such a trite little thing. And Sissy—is that short for Sister or what?"

I loved Emma, and knew better than to push her on my mother and threaten the life I'd made for myself. Although there were problems, I had come to feel the most peculiar joy with that world of nights Emma and I had invented for ourselves, and was resolved not to let my mother violate it. Always, after we made love, I watched Emma move in the dark from the bed to the bathroom, awed by this movement and made to wonder how someone so elegant and rich might choose me. From the bed I could see through the doorway when she sat naked on the toilet to pee. She never closed the door. And if she saw that my eyes were open to her, or that I was squinting and pretending not to look, she asked me politely to either cover my face with the sheets or wait in the kitchen. Even before moving into the bathroom she would switch on the radio to drown out the sound of her urine trickling in the toilet bowl, and it all seemed very honest to me and modest and something a lady would do.

Watching from behind a huddle of pillows, I saw that she was done; she moved to the dressing mirror and looked at herself, no doubt pleased. I never saw her brush or comb her hair after we made love, or press a lipstick to her mouth, or spray herself with perfume, or shower or wipe the stuff of me off of her with a towel, and for these reasons I knew she was happy with who she was at this moment. I wondered if she knew, as I did, what a lady she was. When she moved back to bed, she moved from one quiet little dream I held of her to another. She moved without making a sound and was like a light in the dark room, felt and seen but not heard.

What did we talk about? Did we do anything other than make love and lie in a naked drowsy embrace listening to music and talk shows on her radio and the sound of our own regular breathing?

"I want to go into your home," she said.

"Let's not start," I said. "You always start this."

"I want to meet your mother. I want to meet Sam and this Sylvie woman. I want to meet your grandmother. I want them to like me. Am I so bad they won't like me?"

"I like you. That should be enough."

"Well," she said, "it's not."

"It should be," I said. "I'm the one you say you're in love with."

When she pressed to see me during the day or demanded an invitation to my mother's house, I generally got around her insistence by asking her to name every man she'd ever slept with. After she named four and said they all came into her life before she met and married the fifth, the father of her little boy, I told her she was leaving some out just to seem pure in my eyes. I called her a liar and a couple other bad names. And I said her five old lovers were assholes and I hated having them parade about in our bedroom, watching us when we were together. They were ghosts who kept putting their hands on me, I said, intruding on my life and preventing her from being with me always. It was not *our* bedroom when all her old men were around, I said.

"You're a shit," she said. "You're such a shit."

I dressed and danced around the apartment swatting at the faces of five absent assholes, and she wanted to know what I was doing. I named them all, and called the fifth Dorsey Senior the Dumbfuck for no reason except that I thought it sounded good and funny. Then I slammed a right-left combination, throwing hard punches at the five men she had held and loved before me, hoping to beat them out of her life and mine. These five, I told her, were the reasons why she couldn't come into my home. She said they had nothing to do with it, that I was the reason.

"You talk about football and what a hero you were. You tell me you were such a big man out there. Why can't you be a big man out here? You're a mama's boy, Johnny."

"You should've waited for me," I said. "If you were such a lady and if I really am the only man you've ever been in love with—not counting those other five assholes, lest we forget—you should've waited. And don't get on me with this mama's boy baloney."

"You didn't wait."

"It's different."

"It's not different. It's not different at all."

"If it's not different, then why did my mother get so upset when she learned I wanted to see you?"

She was sitting against the bed frame in the blue lamplight, smiling and probably not believing we were having this conversation. Hers was a wicked smile. "Mama's boy can't handle it," she said.

By swatting at the faces of those five absent assholes, I made a sixth of myself.

One other issue was even more difficult to put behind us, the one that made Emma cry and accuse me of not understanding her. "One day," I said, "you'll have to let go of Dorsey. This just can't continue every night."

"Who says it can't?" she said.

"Ah, Emma. Please."

"Do you say it can't? Johnny Girlie says it can't?"

"Come on, Emma."

"You make all the rules then, do you? John Girlie holding court." She shook her head and her hair covered her face. I couldn't see her eyes, but I imagined them as tiny sparks of fire that saw right through me. "You don't have the courage to admit to your mother that you're seeing me and love me and want to marry me, and yet you come and try to tell me to stop seeing my son. I am *not* going to stop seeing my son."

"You're not even seeing your son, Emma."

"You don't know what I see."

"You talk to the goddamned ground. You just talk."

"And now God has damned the ground, has he? God has

damned the ground where Dorsey lay? Isn't that nice to know? In John Girlie's court, God has damned the ground where Dorsey lay."

"Emma, come on. Stop. Please."

"No," she said. "I won't. I won't stop."

We were not always so moody. Some nights we sang dumb children's songs and read from an old faded book of English verse. We bathed and showered together, and I sat on an unfinished stool and watched her make pies and cakes in her little kitchen. We went for long walks that took us to parts of town I hadn't visited since childhood. One night we climbed the hurricane fence at Donald Grange Stadium and threw passes with an imaginary football, dodged imaginary tacklers and scored imaginary touchdowns; then we made love on the painted grass of the end zone and went home with orange and black stains on our backs.

Another night, not bothering to ask permission, we swam naked in a neighbor's pool until first light, then dressed and walked barefoot back to her apartment. With one hand she held her shoes and with the other she held me. Often we danced in her apartment, holding each other the way lovers do and without even listening to the music on the radio. We didn't care about music, and dancing was just an excuse to touch each other standing up.

Once we went to Toussaint's Grill and sat at the counter, and I wondered if anyone could tell we'd been fucking. When I asked her what she thought, she called Bubba over. "Can you see it in our faces, Mr. Toussaint? Don't be afraid to look closely. Look as closely as you like."

"What is that, Miss?" Bubba said.

"How I love him," she said. "Can't you see it?"

Bubba leaned over and studied both of us, and squinted as if gazing into the sun. "Only when I look, Miss."

I was never at ease with Emma out in the town. And she knew it. Or worse, felt it. I hated to think I was making her feel not pretty or wanted or good enough but worried that word of our steady companionship would reach my mother and make things impossible at home. When I gave her lame excuses why it was a bad idea to shoot pool at Black Fred's until closing, she saw the truth in my face. One Saturday night she asked to go to a midnight movie at the Delta Theater, and I told her I'd seen it twice and that I didn't think I could tolerate a third viewing. "Does Clark Gable die in the end," she asked. And I said, "Blown away."

"He isn't even in it," she said.

Walking down the street at three or four in the morning, I was relieved when there was little or no traffic. I shielded my face from approaching cars or turned around and walked backward. "You *are* ashamed of me," she said. "You can't bear being seen with me."

"It's not that," I said. "If people see me out they'll stop and want to talk about football. I hate talking about football."

"I don't believe you."

"They'll pester the crap out of me."

"Johnny, you're not talking to an idiot."

"They'll run me down for an autograph."

"They'll run you down?" she said and laughed.

I nodded. "For an autograph."

She thought about it a moment and said, "Mama's boy," and I closed my eyes and tried to shut the words out of my head. "Mama's boy's afraid mama's going to be mad."

"Shut up," I said.

"You shut up," she said, and I did. But a few hundred yards down the road she said, "You really are a mama's boy. If you weren't one, you wouldn't have shut up."

I tried to keep quiet, but in no time I heard myself say, "You can really be a bitch. You know that, Emma? A real bitch."

"I know." She put her arms around me. "I'm sorry."

At home there were days when I thought my mother suspected me of being up to no good. I'd grown tired of wearing the same suit of khaki to Emma's every night, and she too complained about "the same old Boy Scout uniform, minus the merit badges and Tenderfoot medal," so I started putting a pair of jeans and a plain white T-shirt in the trunk of the car early in the evening, and changing in the rest room at Jackie Eagle's Gulf station once I'd made it downtown. One of the living room windows faced the front drive, and I was afraid my mother would look out and see me depositing the change of clothes in the car, then find them soiled in the laundry bin the next day and conclude that something out of the ordinary was going on.

Almost every morning at breakfast she asked how my night was.

"Fine," I'd say.

"Anything happen?"

"Nope," I'd answer, trying to detect any sign of doubt in her face. "Nothing happened that didn't happen the night before."

One morning she said she'd run into Ham Viviano, a mechanic's helper at Texas Eastern, while shopping for crates of sweet potatoes at the farmers' market off Jennifer Lane, and he'd asked about me.

"Ham asked about me?" I said. "Ham Viviano?"

"He did," she said. "It must be a big place, this compressor station, if you two never run into each other."

"I work nights, remember. Ham works the day shift."

"But is it a big place?" she said.

"Pretty big," I said. "A person could get lost in it."

"You should invite me out for a visit sometime. I'd love to see it. I haven't been out to Prairie Ronde in years."

"Really nothing to see," I said. "But if you want to, I don't think there'd be any problem arranging it."

"No," she said. "I was just thinking it might be nice. I suppose I'd end up getting in everybody's way."

Sometimes in the rest room at Jackie's station I rubbed motor oil on my khaki shirt and pants, then dropped them on the floor near the toilet. I'd told my mother that part of my job consisted of cleaning the johns and thought an occasional spot of grime and urine might be compelling evidence.

"What do these men aim at?" Sylvie said one morning, holding up a pair of khakis wet with piss. She was loading the pants into the washing machine. "There must be a whole Pacific Ocean of tee to wash out of these pants."

"Tee?" I said.

"Tee tee," she said. "Urinate."

"Oh," I said. "That kind of tee."

As I went along lying to my mother, I worried that a bank teller would report to her that I'd quit making deposits into my savings account but was withdrawing small sums of money every two weeks or so. If that wasn't enough to set me on edge, I worried about the day when I'd run out of money. When I told Charley I'd soon be hurting for cash, he said, "Why do you need money? Your mother buys the food, she pays Sylvie, she keeps up the house. The only money you spend is on beer and betting pool at Black Fred's. Besides, you never lose. I'm the one who should be asking you for money."

Then he said, "Oh, what a tangled web we weave," and left it at that. My growing anxiety annoyed the hell out of him, and even when drunk or stoned he showed little patience listening to me rattle on about my fear of being found out.

"Should I feel guilty," I asked, feeling perfectly guilty.

"You should," he said. "But do you feel like shit?"

"Like a whole sack of it." Then I said, "Go ahead and hit me as hard as you can."

"You want me to hit you as hard as I can?"

"Just knock the living shit out of me," I said.

"The whole entire sack?" he said.

"That's right," I said. "All of it." He tapped my shoulder with a clenched fist, but I hardly felt it. "Thank you," I said, feigning injury. "Thanks so very much."

"You're welcome," he said. "But you're still full of shit."

"Must be a pretty big sack," I said, "if you couldn't knock it out of me."

One evening my mother asked why I never dated and, before I could come up with an answer, said it made sense to her that no girls in town appealed to me. In my paranoia I wondered if she had heard something and was trying to draw me into a confession. But then she said, "You're every girl's dream of what a man should be. I think that must be difficult to live up to."

"I'm only your son," I said. "If anything, I'm one mother's dream of what her son should be."

It was early summer, and we were sitting at the patio table, drinking beer over shaved ice and waiting for Sylvie to finish cooking dinner. My mother wasn't as close to being drunk as she pretended to be, she just wanted to talk everything out and feel good about herself. "Did I ever tell you that I carried you for nine months?" she said. "Did I ever tell you that?"

"You did," I said.

"I carried you right here," she said and rubbed her belly. "Did I ever tell you that?"

"You told me."

"I used to sing to you in the bathtub and you weren't even born yet. Did I ever tell you how your feet kicked and kicked against my insides like drums?"

"You did," I said. "You told me."

When we were done with our beer, she picked up the glasses and moved toward the back door, and I watched how she moved. She didn't move like Emma. She was overweight and seemed to be carrying two small melons in her back pockets. I recalled having heard Charley once say of a fat woman, "You could've set a can of Coke on her butt and not spilled a drop."

"One day it'll be just me," she said at dinner. "You'll leave me, and Sam will never come back. Sam hates it here."

"Sam doesn't hate it here," I said. "And I don't have anywhere to go."

"You'll find someone and she'll take you. She won't want to share even the smallest part of you."

"Where will she take me?" I said. "And she won't take me anywhere if I don't want to go."

"She'll take you wherever she wants," she said. "But not the way I did twenty-three years ago. I carried you. For nine whole months I carried you here. And it wasn't easy." She rubbed her belly again.

"You did good," I said. "You did damn good."

14

When I was a freshman at LSU and home for the Mardi Gras holidays, Jason Girlie phoned my mother from the store on Union Street and asked for somebody to drive him to Bean's Grocery for a pack of cigarettes. Because Sam was still too young to drive, she gave me the car keys and told me to go help my grandfather or else head back to Baton Rouge by the next morning. Every time she said something like that, she was as sad and pathetic as a young calf on its way to the sale barn. She didn't mean it, of course, and didn't expect you to believe that she did. What she meant was, you'd failed her in some way and she was giving you a chance to make up. She let her eyes glaze over and might've moaned had it not shown Sam and me that she wasn't a calf after all but a woman who loved her sons and hated to see them drift away from their grandfather.

"When did he start smoking cigarettes?" I asked on my way out. "I thought it was those cigars he liked."

"It's not cigarettes he wants," she said. "It's to be with you."

When I arrived at Girlie's Men's-and-Boy's, the old man was waiting outside under the green-and-white awning, inspecting the mannequins in his show window and making an appeal to one of the clerks inside the store. He was moving his lips and dancing around in a grand theatrical manner, not making a sound. I rolled down my window and called out his name from where I had parked across the street, but he kept on and I knew better than to ask what he was doing. He moved from one side of the store to the other, pounding the air with his elbows and puckering his face into what resembled, as I later told Sam, a chewed-up dog bone. His body was surprisingly agile for one so afflicted with arthritis and terribly hunchbacked. He moved like an athlete. People were watching through the glass doors of the laundry and from down by Old Lady Hazzard's antique shop, shielding the sun with the flats of their hands as they walked toward him. It wasn't a man's dance my grandfather was dancing, but one I would later see performed by the women who made their livings at the strip joints along Highway 2. He was bumping and grinding the way those women do when they want you to like them and give them something to prove it.

I stepped out of the car and started across the street, but he motioned for me to stop. When I kept walking, he quit dancing and words came out of his mouth. His face no longer resembled a chewed-up dog bone. He was Jason Girlie again, and I was his grandson. "What took you so long, you helpless little fuck," he said. "I said ten minutes not twenty."

My mother was right about my grandfather—he hadn't wanted cigarettes. I followed him up the back stairs to his apartment and sat next to him on the edge of his unmade bed. "You ever get your thing wet?" he said directly and pointed at my crotch.

"What thing," I asked.

He reached into his pocket, withdrew a roll of cash and tossed two twenty-dollar bills on the floor at my feet. "Go get your dick wet," he said. "And don't ever say I never did nothing for you."

I stared at the money, not knowing whether to pick it up and thank him or bolt for the door. "I might not have been much, but I was more than nothing." He chuckled.

Much later, when I was living at home again, and living for the nights with Emma, my mother walked into the outdoor kitchen. I saw by the dark smudges of mascara on her cheeks that she'd been crying. "Ben Mawry just called from Baton Rouge," she said. "You remember Ben Mawry?"

"Ben Mawry the lawyer?" I said. "He worked with Jason."

She nodded. "Sam went to see him about changing his name."

"Not our Sam," I said.

She nodded again. "Sam Girlie your brother and Sam Girlie my son. He wants to be called Sam Goodman or Goodwin. Sam Good-something. Ben said he hates Sam Girlie. I mean, Ben doesn't hate him. He said Sam hates his name. It disgusts him."

"I don't believe it," I said.

She threw a set of car keys at my feet. "You're his brother," she said. "Go talk to him."

From the kitchen I made a pretend call to my pretend boss at Texas Eastern and told him I needed a day of sick leave and thanked him—"You really are quite a guy"—before hanging up. Then I called Emma and pretended to be talking to the engineer with whom I used to work the graveyard shift. "Well, Rodney," I said, "I'm afraid I've got to take a day off work. I've got to go to Baton Rouge. My brother wants to change his name and I've got to try to talk him out of it." My mother, crying on the stool next to me, suddenly grabbed for the receiver and tried to wrestle it away from me. When I wouldn't give it up, she mouthed the words *don't tell him* and started to cry even harder.

On the other end, Emma was saying, "I'm always riding in the back seat, Johnny Girlie. If you really cared you wouldn't be so embarrassed to be seen with me."

"Goddamnit, Rodney!" I shouted, and nearly sent my mother spinning off her chair. "My brother Sam's threatening to change his name to Good-something and you're acting like a spoiled child. This is a serious, extremely volatile family matter, Rodney. Extremely volatile."

"Johnny!" my mother begged. "Please. Please, don't tell him."

"It's a dumb name!" Emma shouted back. "Girlie's a dumb name. I always thought it was dumb. It's dumb and you're dumb. Dumb and selfish." She was either laughing or crying, I couldn't tell which over my mother's own noisy display of emotion. In a weird gutteral voice, Emma said, "It's a girl's name, Girlie's a girl's name."

"It is not," I said. "Girlie is not a girl's name."

"Girl, girl, girl," Emma said. "Girlie's a girl's name."

"You're the girl, Rodney," I said. "You're the one acting like a spoiled little girl."

"Johnny," my mother pleaded. "Oh, Johnny, please. Please don't argue. Girlie is a very fine name. It is not a girl's name."

"If I'm a girl," Emma said, "then you're a mama's boy. You're a mama's boy, Mr. Girlie. Hello, Mr. Girlie. Good-bye, Mr. Girlie. Have a nice life, Mr. Girlie. What a dumb, stupid name!"

"Rodney," I said, "Rodney," and she hung up.

My mother, while she whimpered, had Sylvie get her a cold washcloth to place on her forehead. I went to the cupboard for a bottle of whiskey but, after withdrawing a pint of Old Crow, put it back.

"I can't say I approved of how you addressed this Rodney person," my mother said, smiling now and daubing her tears with the washcloth. "But a fellow must stand up for his family, musn't he? I'm very proud of you, Johnny."

"Johnny did good," Sylvie said. "Johnny did real good."

"May the name Girlie live forever," I said and kissed my mother on the cheek. Then I went back to the cupboard, removed the same Old Crow and took a shot straight from the bottle. No shot ever tasted better. "May it live in infamy. May the name Girlie forever grace this great land of ours. May it never perish."

"Amen!" declared Sylvie.

"Oh, John," my mother said. "Oh, baby. Oh, John."

It was Sunday noon, and church bells rang across town as I drove to Charley Harwood's house to see if he might like to ride along to Baton Rouge. I was feeling awfully alive and giddy and no one would break this mood—not Emma, who was probably only upset because I would not be coming over for the night, and not even my brother, who I decided had put Ben Mawry up to the call in consideration of some future promise. Sam was broke, I figured, and needed some of my mother's money, and this was his best attempt at blackmail. After I pulled him out of bed and explained our mission, Harwood said, "What man or boy in his right mind would want to be called Girlie anyway?"

"Just get dressed," I said. "I don't want to talk about it."

"Suppose his initials were I. B. Girlie or I. M. Girlie. Or suppose your mother had called you Hurley Girlie and Sam Burley Girlie."

"Suppose you shut up," I said.

"I'm just glad my name ain't Dick. Just think if your name was I. B. Dick or I. M. Dick. Or if it was Dick Dick or Peter Dick."

"That's enough," I said.

"Or Hymen," he said. "If my name was Hymen I'd change it and if they wouldn't let me change it, I'd walk out into one of my old man's soybean lots and blow my fucking brains out."

Because I was in no hurry to confront Sam, I drove with Charley to the Seville Arms and asked him to wait in the car for about five minutes while I ran up to Emma's apartment and apologized. When she refused to undo the chain lock, I spoke through the crack in the door. "I hope you'll forgive me, Emma." And I could tell by what I saw of her face that she already had.

She was wearing a green terry cloth robe tied with an unmatching maroon-colored sash at the waist, and I could see the lovely brown cluster of freckles on her chest and how tight and full her breasts were. I could see enough to know that Charley Paul Harwood might be waiting out on the boulevard longer than five minutes. "I've decided that the way I've been treating you is wrong," I said. "After I talk to Sam, I'm going to tell my mother it's time she invited you over for dinner. I know she'll like you."

"She'll never like me," Emma said. "She hates me. But that's okay. I like me. I know I'm not a bad person. Tell me I'm not a bad person, Johnny."

"You're wonderful," I said.

"Maybe not wonderful," she said, "but I try. I try to be wonderful and good to you, and sometimes I just feel as though you hardly care. You put me in a closet, Johnny. You won't be seen with me. You always look to see who's on the boulevard in the morning before walking down to your car. How do you think that makes me feel?"

"I said I was wrong. I said you were wonderful."

"Just be a man, John," she said and moved to close the door. "Just be a man with me. Will you promise me that one thing?"

I had been wrong about my mood. It was broken now and there was no fixing it. "I am a man," I said. Then I almost shouted, "Why do you always say I'm not a man? Why do you do that to me, Emma?"

"I don't always," she said. "But I do sometimes."

"You make me want to hit things. I feel like driving my hand into the wall and kicking in the door and gobbling at the world. I want to gobble at the world sometimes, Emma."

She was smiling and looking happy again. And I wondered if she had some secret wisdom, some way of knowing that Charley Harwood had been the first to speak of such a wanton hunger for the world and that I was simply borrowing from his dream. How many young men had she known who claimed such a prodigious appetite?

"Gobble," she said, "gobble, gobble."

"Go ahead then," I said. "Turn it into a joke."

She reached to touch me through the crack in the door, but I pulled away. If she'd really wanted to touch me, she would've unfastened the chain lock. But she didn't. "It must be hard being Johnny Girlie," she said. "I know it's hard being Emma Groves, but when I think how hard it must be being Johnny Girlie, I get so sad. I could cry. I want to take your little heart away on clouds of joy."

She meant it pretty and it was, but I was still thinking I should hit something. "I've never seen one of those clouds," I said. "I've seen clouds full of rain and fury and some with lightning but none of joy. I've never seen one of those clouds you're talking about. What does a cloud with joy in it look like, Emma?"

She closed the door. "You wouldn't see it if I pointed it out to you." Her words through the wood were muffled, but to me no less dear. "You won't let yourself see it, John. You have to let yourself and you won't."

I pressed my head against the door and felt its coolness. "I'd die for you, Emma," I said. "I'd die for you. I swear to God I'd die for you."

"Gobble, gobble," she said, then, "I'd die for you, too, John."

Charley and I took the old two-lane highway out of town, driving past bait shops and dance halls made of cinder blocks and set high off the ground on wooden pilings. Near Wide Springs, we saw the bleached stone statues of Jesus and Joseph and the Virgin Mary standing in the rock gardens of trailers in a mobile home park. We drove over the little wooden bridge at Bayou Claire, where my father once took me fishing for bull bream. Claire was never good for fishing, but it was pretty in the spring when the water was high and muddy and the banks green with weeds. In the fall, Claire was soupy and slow moving and no one fished from the sides of the bridge. We drove past the Domineaux's cattle farm and its handsome red barns and grain silos shining in the sun and, after a few more miles, skirted the eastern edge of Bigger's Swamp and saw where the bald cypress and water tupelo had been cut back to accommodate a bustle of hunting camps and aluminum storage sheds. Deep in the swamp a black man in hip boots was crawfishing with a single hand line fashioned out of what looked like kite string, and you could see the white chunk of lard clipped to the end. We drove over other dark streams named for long-dead Frenchmen and saw people catfishing with cane poles leaned against the cement pilings of the bridges, and at D'Arbanville Run I watched a speedboat pulling somebody in an inner tube. In the boat's wake, whoever was on the tube dribbled from side to side and kicked up a brown feather of water. D'Arbanville Run was the color of rust, white and foaming along the banks. I told Harwood I thought it looked like a fat snake rolled over on its back, trying to squirm away from something.

He said, "Since when are you the goddamned poet?"

The road was a familiar one. There was a place near Port Allen, just across the river from Baton Rouge, where at night you could stop on the gravel shoulder and see the climbing squares of office lights at the state capitol. Once my grandfather had stopped at that high spot in the road and, pointing to the capitol building, said, "There, that light. Eighth floor, four windows from the left. See that, John, Samuel. See it? That's my light and my window. That's my office, boys. That's where I run things from."

Closer in, there was a place where state troopers hid behind shrub cover and were most likely to stop you for speeding, and just a quarter-mile beyond their post was the hard curve where, every few months, somebody lost control and died. The field in which the car and the dead body generally came to rest ran strong for miles, and there were few things finer to see than how this field looked some mornings with the dew on it and the dark green spread of beans pulling up from the rich black earth.

From the top of the bridge crossing the Mississippi River, I saw how Tiger Stadium rose above a cluster of buildings and dormitories and the student assembly center with its great white dome. It was the first time I'd seen the stadium since leaving Baton Rouge the year before, and it was as huge and beautiful as I had ever seen it.

Charley said, "There she is, John."

We drove through campus and parked in the lot behind the Kappa Sigma fraternity house, where a boy in knee-ripped jeans and a sweatshirt was sitting on the back stoop with a dark-haired girl. They were making out and not giving a care if anybody saw them. It was broad daylight, and the boy was trying to put his left hand through a crack in the girl's buttoned shirt and feel her breasts. She kissed him with her eyes closed and with an open, red and deliciously wet mouth. He kissed her, his flat brown eyes on the bridge of her nose and his tongue exploring the lower half of her face. Charley, who hadn't said a word since Tiger Stadium, walked over, cleared his throat and said hello, but neither seemed aware of his presence. Then he said, "Where's Sam Girlie?"

The boy pulled his face and hands away from the girl and answered, "Who?"

And Charley said, "Sam Girlie. Where's Sam Girlie?" When the boy shrugged, Charley said, "Tell me where Sam is, you little skunk fucker."

The girl muttered something about a skunk, then said quite

loudly, "Just who do you think you are?" The boy stood up and acted like he was ready to tell Charley to take it back. Because fraternity boys are supposed to be gentlemen, they are known, at least in Baton Rouge, to first politely ask of their challengers to retract the insult before resorting to blows. This boy, scowling and still hard in the crotch, took in a big breath and moved off the stoop. He was a finely built fellow, but there was nothing polite about him. He was cocked and about to throw a right hand when I stepped in front of Charley and grabbed him by the neck. It was a thin neck and against my palm his Adam's apple, bouncing up and down, felt like a bug trying to escape through the hole at the upper end of his throat. "Please," I told him. "Do you know Sam Girlie?"

He wanted to nod but I wouldn't let him; instead, he blinked his eyes and I took this as meaning yes.

"Run and get him," I said pleasantly. I wanted to keep calm and let him know that there was no reason to hurt him. "Tell him his brother wants to talk to him about something."

I released my grip on the boy's neck and he said, "His brother Johnny? You're Johnny Girlie?"

"That's him," Charley said. "The one, the only."

"I didn't mean to cause problems," I said. "Neither did my friend Charley here. We just don't feel very good today. We'd appreciate it if you ran up and got my brother for us."

I figured the boy was confused—not knowing whether to be mad at Charley and me for giving him trouble or ashamed of himself for being caught making out with his girlfriend in the middle of the afternoon. His hands hung limp by his side, and his eyes met mine. "Sam changed his name, Johnny," he said. "I'm sorry. It's too late."

"No," I said. "He didn't. Not yet he didn't."

"He did," the girl said. "We had a party for him."

"You had a party," Charley said. "What kind of dumb-ass reason is that to throw a party?"

"He's Sam Goodwin now," the boy said. "We tried to stop him but he wouldn't listen. He wouldn't listen to anybody."

Charley moved over to the car, and I stood there looking at the boy and the girl. I could see a red shadow in the shape of four fingers where I had gripped the boy's neck. The girl's lips were white and chapped from kissing. Through the hole in her blouse where the boy had worked his hand, I saw how her small pink breast sat in the cup of her brassiere and how part of the flat of her nipple was exposed. "When did he do it," I asked.

"Two weeks ago," the boy said. "Or maybe three. All I know is he did it. The fraternity threatened to fine him, but he did it anyway. I never thought Girlie was such a bad name."

"He hated it," the girl said. "He's the one whose idea it was to have the party. We made jungle juice in the bathtub upstairs and everybody got shit-faced. You should've seen Sam."

"You really had a party?" I said.

"And Sam danced with everyone," the girl said, "including the guys. They gatored and then he passed out outside in the bushes. Whenever you tried to wake him he sat up and threw clods of dirt at you and yelled 'Girlie, goddamn. Girlie, goddamn.' He was a riot. He was so proud."

"Little girls shouldn't use words like shit-faced," Charley said. He was sitting on the hood of the car. "Especially on Sundays. God hears everything you say on Sundays."

"It's just a word," she said.

Charley said, "Fucka buncha shit-faced."

When the girl laughed, I said, "You think that's funny?"

"It's just a word," she said.

"Fucka buncha Goodwin," Charley said. "Fuck it. Fucka buncha Goodwin. Fucka buncha Sam Goodwin."

I pointed at the girl, but I was talking to her boyfriend, who now was sitting back down on the stoop. "My brother changes his name, and your girlfriend thinks it's funny. She says it's just a word."

"She meant shit-faced was just a word," he said. "She didn't say anything about Girlie being just a word or being funny. You ought not blame us, Johnny. Sam's the one. I told him he was wrong to do it."

"And tell him what he said to that," the girl said.

"He said the only thing wrong was that he had to live with it. He said he was born a Girlie, but he wouldn't die one."

Charley and I walked to Dalrymple Drive at the front of the fraternity house and sat at the foot of a magnolia tree, waiting for Sam to show up. Although Sam was several inches shorter and about thirty pounds lighter than me, whoever saw us together knew we were brothers. He had brown wavy hair that he kept cut short and blue eyes that were slanted and almond-shaped and looked vaguely Oriental if he slept too long or off-kilter with the blood rushing to his head. Sam had always been a handsome boy, and he was tough, too. "Where'd you get those Chink eyes?" a junior high school physical education teacher had once asked. "None of your Chink fucking business," Sam had said, and then swung at him with an aluminum baseball bat.

When out of laziness or plain hatred of razors he let his beard grow for more than a few days and I saw that he was a man, I felt terrible thinking of how we had grown apart, and how time would only pull him farther away. Sam with whiskers? Sam old enough to grow a beard? Sitting under the tree with Charley Harwood, I closed my eyes and saw his perfect little face in the shadows of the bedroom tent he had made of sheets and blankets, lamps and desk chairs, and I saw him in the fluorescent light of the bathroom—the perfect little boy sitting on the cool floor of the bathtub, pretending to read the newspaper. It was so easy to see him in all the ways I knew and loved him and counted him as mine. And in all the pictures he was still Sam my brother, Samuel Daniel Girlie, and not the least bit ashamed to announce it to the world.

"I'm going to stomp his dick in," Charley said.

"You won't touch him," I said.

"I'm going to bite a chunk off his ass."

"You won't move unless I tell you to."

It was autumn, and the girls strolling across the lawn between the clock tower and the Christ the King Catholic Church wore wool and cashmere sweaters that burned as many different colors as the changing leaves on the trees. Their boyfriends, dressed for church, danced behind them like frisky puppies new to their feet and the miracle of locomotion, and everyone seemed at peace and full of life. Charley watched the girls walking down the sidewalk in front of the

Kappa Sigma house and rated them from one to ten, ten being an absolute beauty. The lowest score he gave was a seven, and that was to a girl with pink sponge-rollers in her hair. Every time he saw a nine—and he saw scores of nines—he said, "Could you fuck that, John?" When I didn't answer, he said, "Well, I sure the hell could. I'd even fuck her with your dick."

Sam was walking with a young woman Charley rated a seven. Had I been in a better mood, and not so wounded and so mad at Sam, Charley might've given her a ten. She really was beautiful. Because she was with my brother, and because my brother had changed his name, she would score no higher and be judged no more becoming than the tragic little person with rollers in her hair. Charley said, "I couldn't fuck that one, John. Could you?"

When I didn't answer, he said, "I don't think you could. Not even with my dick I don't think you could."

Charley stood up and started to cross Dalrymple, but walked back when he saw that I hadn't moved. "Sam's here," he said. "Let's go talk to Sam, John."

I was leaning back against the trunk of the tree, looking through the branches and the dry autumn leaves at the dark sky coming on and feeling how cool and ripe the late afternoon had become. Lights were showing in almost all of the windows of the fraternity house, and you could see shadows move on the closed curtains. Where the curtains were open, you could see the white walls crowded with calendars and girly-magazine pinups and LSU football posters, and an occasional bare-chested boy looking at himself in a full-length mirror, picking at a pimple on his face or playing an invisible guitar and shaking his body to music I couldn't hear. I looked for Sam in the open windows, but didn't see him. Finally Charley sat down next to me.

"You think Goodwin's a bad name," I asked him. "You think Sam Goodwin is a bad name?"

"Not really," he said. "But I don't like it on Sam."

"It's really not on Sam," I said. "It's just what he wants other people to know him by."

"He'll always be Sam Girlie to me," Charley said. "He can be a hundred years old and Sam Goodwin for eighty-one years and I'll still call him Sam Girlie."

"It's how he started out," I said.

After a while night fell and the street lights came on and fewer students walked past us down Dalrymple. Charley lit a joint but I waved it away. I was watching the fraternity house. I was watching when the front door opened and my brother appeared, standing in front of the boy we had seen kissing the girl on the back stoop earlier in the day. Sam was just a dark figure wrapped in the gold light that poured through the open door behind him. You couldn't tell how short his hair was cut or even its color. You couldn't tell anything about his eyes or what happened to them when he slept wrong. You couldn't tell that he looked like me.

"I'm not changing it," he shouted. "And you can tell Ma that, Johnny. I ain't changing it back."

I pulled the keys out of my pocket and gave them to Charley, who headed back to the car.

"Harwood!" Sam called. "Harwood? Who are you calling little skunk-fucker, Harwood?"

Standing behind Sam were more dark figures wrapped in gold light, and a few others leaning against the railing and columns of the covered porch.

Charley pulled the car up to the curb and opened the door for me. I got in, leaving the door open so Sam could see my face in the overhead light. I wanted him to see Charley Harwood's face, too, and I wanted him never to forget what he saw. I wanted him never to forget that his brother had driven from Old Field to Baton Rouge to see him, and why he had come to see him, and why he had left without saying a word. "Johnny!" Sam shouted. "Come back here, Johnny!"

He started across the porch and down to the steps, and those behind him followed. "You don't know anything," he said. "You don't know the half of it. Johnny, you don't know."

I closed the door, and Charley pulled away as if we had all the time in the world. Neither of us bothered to look back. We crossed the river and took the old familiar two-lane highway home. At Bayou

Claire, Charley stopped in the middle of the road and we both got out and pissed from the bridge into the dark, muddy water. Charley said he was getting tired and wanted to give up the wheel, and I drove the rest of the way to Old Field. In the Phil-a-Sack parking lot, Charley cut a couple of lines on the arm of the vinyl seat and we each took a hit with a rolled-up dollar bill. The pretty, young Vietnamese woman I had thought about and wanted so often was working the register, watching a John Wayne movie on a portable black-and-white television set up on a stool by the Icee machine. I went in and bought a pack of Camels, and she laughed and said, "Girlie. Hi, Girlie."

"That's right," I said. "You remembered."

I dropped Charley off and, when at last I reached the house on Ducharme Road, waited a long time before leaving the warmth of the car. I turned off the engine and listened to the radio. I smoked a cigarette, and then another. I wet my fingers and ran them over the arm of the seat where Charley had cut the lines. I rubbed the tip of my fingers against my gums, hoping to feel something. But there was nothing. Then I went into the house and woke her up and told her what I knew about Sam.

15

For more than a week after she learned that my brother had changed his name, my mother refused to leave the house. She returned to her days of sleeping sixteen and eighteen hours at a stretch and waking only to fall asleep again. When I went into her bedroom after lunch, to see how she was doing, she sometimes opened her eyes and smiled and offered a cool, limp hand to hold: the hand of a woman who for too long had been in the dark, waiting for what she long ago had called the underestimated good in her life to equal the overestimated bad, and you could feel the proud suffering in her fingertips. We talked, but never about anything important. Was I eating and feeling well, she wanted to know, and had I been getting along at work. I told her everything was as it had always been and not to worry. She wanted to know—and never in our twenty-three years together had she asked this question—if my bowel movements were regular and was I comfortable. I told her I was perfectly comfortable and she, in her weird dream sleep, said, "When a person has his health and is comfortable, God is near."

Some days she didn't move or offer me a cool, limp hand, and I checked the pulse in her neck to make sure she was still alive. One afternoon I placed my hand on the side of her neck and she said, without moving or opening her eyes, "Do you think I would kill myself over Sam, Johnny?"

I was quiet, then said, "No, Ma. I don't think you would kill yourself over Sam. I was just worried."

"Will you tell me you love me?" She sat up and hugged me. "Will you please tell me that, John."

"I do," I said. "I promise I do."

"Say the words," she said. "Not just I do. Tell me you love me."

"I love you," I said. "I love you."

She started feeling better and sleeping less after Marie came by and told her I'd paid a visit to the editor of the Old Field *Times* asking him to consider not running a story on Sam. Marie said I'd threatened to sue for violation of privacy, and that the man had respected my request and agreed to spare the Girlie family further embarrassment. "I didn't talk to anyone about anything," I told Marie as she was leaving.

"Maybe you didn't," she said, "but I sure as hell did."

Later my mother offered me a bit of unqualified praise. "Sam came into this world a baby, John. But you were born a man."

Though I tried not to think about my brother, it wasn't easy. In the whole world I was the only person I knew who had a brother who'd changed his name, and I did not much care for the distinction. "You're the one who should have done it," Emma joked one night. "When we get married, I'd rather be called Mrs. Goodwin."

The way I looked at her, she probably thought I was going to hit her or walk out and slam the door behind me, but by then she was probably getting used to that look of mine that said I was going to hit her or walk out and slam the door behind me. I ground my teeth and my jaw quivered. "You don't mean it?" I said. "I love my name and I'm proud of it. Girlie's a good name."

"I love it, too," she said. "It fits."

I thought about my name fitting and how it might fit. "It fits? What does Girlie fit? That's a lousy thing to say."

"Right. Absolutely. What's wrong with Girlie?" she said.

"You're the person suggesting something's wrong with it. You said it fits. What does Girlie fit? Tell me. Tell me what it fits."

She was about to laugh but I wouldn't let her. When she started to say something, I said, "Fit my ass, Emma. Fit my ass," and threw her down onto the bed. I put my mouth on her mouth, and it was cool. She had the coolest mouth I ever knew, but after I had pressed my lips to hers and felt her tongue, and the dense wet softness of it and how it moved along my teeth, her mouth was warm. I thought that for such a cool mouth, hers was pretty warm. "You wanted to say Girlie fits because you think I'm a mama's boy."

"I didn't want to say that, and you should stop trying to read my mind. You're a Girlie through and through, Johnny Girlie. You're all Girlie."

"Is that good or is that bad?"

"It's neither," she said. "It's what you are."

When my mother went from feeling better to feeling well, she came back to the outdoor kitchen with a pitcher of cold milk. "I'm well," she announced. "I'm myself again."

"You're well?" I said.

She lowered the toilet lid and placed the pitcher on the flat surface and started a bath. "I am," she said above the flow of the water. "Your mother's well again." With the flat of her hand, she touched the water pouring out of the faucet and adjusted the spigots to make sure the temperature was how I liked it. Then she dropped a fresh bar of soap on the floor of the tub. I knew she was running the bath for me, so I took off my shirt and she moved over and sat on the bed and watched me. I took off my pants and socks but left my underwear on, though I wasn't ever self-conscious when she saw me. Was she not, after all, the same woman who brought me into this world and lived to remind me of the event? She sat there watching me with her mouth half-open, and her eyes danced in the wet uncertain light that fell through the window by the bed. I knew she was feeling like herself again because she was suddenly unable to believe that she had carried me in her womb for nine months. "You were a much better little one than Sam, John," she said. "You never cried at night. When you messed your diapers you cried, but you never cried at night."

After I removed my underwear and settled into the bath, she sat on a stool next to the tub and held the pitcher of milk in her long, thin hands. Beads of moisture dripped down the big tin pitcher and left a ring where she had rested it on the lap of her dress. She held the pitcher up with both hands and guided the spout to her mouth and, without pressing the spout to her lips, tilted the pitcher and waited for the flow of milk. I leaned back in the hot soapy water and watched as the milk splashed against her nose and mouth and ran down her chin. She said, "Oh, John. It's cold," feeling the milk run down her neck and chest, and she laughed a soft, little girl's laugh. On the front of her dress was a dark spreading cloud. "I've made a mess," she said, and sat on the edge of the tub with her back to me. "Baby, please," she said. "Unzip me."

I unzipped her. "You don't even like milk."

"Not to wash with."

"Not to drink with either," I said.

After a long moment she said, "Not to drink with? Or simply not to drink? That word *with* has no place in what you just said."

After an even longer moment I said, "That word *simply* has no place in what you just said either," and she laughed her beautiful little girl's laugh.

She let the dress drop to her ankles, then she bent down and picked it up off the floor. It was the kind of formless cotton dress women wear to conceal their fat, boxy figures, the kind she always wore. My mother had big, strong legs, as thick as those of a long-distance runner, but the backs of her thighs were a dimpled mosaic. There was a full ring of flesh over her middle, but her figure, for years a point of self-ridicule, was not so bad for a woman who'd been locked away in a house most of her adult life. In those billowy housedresses she appeared much bigger and heavier than she actually was. Her breasts, heavy and white with talcum powder, spilled over the cups of her brassiere. She draped her dress over the shower curtain rod and sat back down on the edge of the tub. "Undo me," she said, and I undid the clasp at the back of her brassiere. When she turned to face me, I could see the streaks on her chest where the milk had run. The streaks had muddied some of her powder and ended at the fleshy top of her breasts. Around her large, flat nipples the milk looked soapy, like suds from the bath. "Am I a pig," she asked.

"What?" I said, having heard her perfectly.

"Do you think your mother's a pig?"

"No," I said. "I don't."

She leaned over the bath and put her left hand against the tiled wall, then with her right hand scooped cups of the hot soapy lavender-scented water and splashed them against her chest. There were stretch marks, barely visible, running the length of her breasts, the same color as her nipples.

"I'm glad you don't think your mother's a pig," she said.

"You're glad?"

"I'm glad," she said.

She dried herself, and with the same towel wiped up the spilled milk. She handed me the pitcher, and I put the spout against my lips and took a swallow. The milk was so cold it made my teeth ache and my gums tingle. The second time I drank, some of the milk dripped down my chin and into the water, which by then was iron blue, tepid and gritty. I handed the pitcher back to her, unplugged the drain and stood up. Again she sat on the edge of the tub and placed her left hand against the wall. She held the pitcher with her right hand and poured what milk remained into the funnel of dirty bathwater moving down the drain. Then, standing up, she started to dry me off with a clean towel, first kneading my back and arms through the thick cloth and then my chest and belly. The towel was mauve-colored and made of combed cotton on one side and a rugged cloth on the other, and it was almost as long as I was tall. She moved down my legs and up again, kneading harder it seemed, and before she reached my middle I stopped her. I said one word, "No," and pulled the towel out of her hands and covered myself with it.

"Oh, baby," she said, and I said, "No, Ma."

"John," she said, and I said, "Ma. Please." Then I said, "No."

She sat on the toilet seat, holding the pitcher close to her naked breast. The coldness of the tin made her nipples contract and tighten, and her skin turned to gooseflesh. I dried the rest of my body, and when I was done she said, "You are born and then you live and then you die. It's as simple as that."

She said it as plainly as someone else might say ginger comes before egg whites in a recipe, and there was a smile on her lips.

"You're right," I said. "But I wouldn't say it's as simple as that. It can be pretty hard."

"If it's not simple it's because the living part lasts longer than the being born part and the dying part, though your being born part, John, was just under ten months of my living part. And for me, that seemed to go on forever. You were a late baby. I always say I carried you for nine months, but it was closer to ten."

"I didn't know I was late."

"Two whole weeks," she said, "and part of a third."

I dressed in the same clothes I was wearing before the bath, and she asked me to run into the house and tell Sylvie to please hurry and iron her favorite chicken dress and to bring it out to her in the outdoor kitchen. I asked what this dress was, and she said, "It's the one with little red roosters along the hemline."

When I gave Sylvie my mother's instructions, she said, "The chicken dress is in the washer. Go back and tell her I can iron the dog dress or the tree dress, and the alphabet dress is hanging in the closet. It's too tight for her, though. If she wants the chicken dress, she's gonna have to wait a good twenty minutes."

When I returned with the message, my mother said, "It's because she's a fat pig that your mother wears the clothes that she wears. I'm a fat pig, aren't I, John?"

She was still sitting on the toilet hugging the tin pitcher. Against the fluorescent lights over the sink, her skin was a strange color, blue with a wash of pink mixed in it, and thinly marbled.

"You're not fat," I said. "And you're not a pig. You're just a little overweight."

"Is it because she's fat that you don't love your mother?"

"That's not true. I do love my mother. I do love you, Ma."

She had been looking away, but now she turned to face me. "You don't love me. You love you. You only love yourself, John."

If I was quiet, it wasn't for very long. I groaned and stammered before saying, "I'm sorry you think that, but it's not true. I love a lot of people."

"It's because your mother's fat, isn't it?" she said. "That's why you don't love me. You don't like fat girls."

"I told you you weren't fat."

"She starts her fast this very minute," she said. "Your mother won't eat until her sons love her again." I didn't say anything, so she said, "Well, she actually started her fast last night. Supper was the last time she ate. And all she ate was a slice of zucchini pie."

"You had boiled carrots, too," I said. "And French bread. And after all that you were in the freezer looking for a chocolate bar."

"Your mother won't eat until Sam changes his name back to what it was, to what it should be, and until her first born learns the meaning of respect. I'm talking about you, John."

"I know the meaning of respect," I said. "And I know who you're talking about."

"She won't eat until he starts loving other people."

"You don't mean what you're saying."

She pinched the roll of flesh around her middle. "Good-bye this." Then she patted the backs of her thighs. "Good-bye that."

I started for the door. She was still sitting on the toilet seat and rocking gently with the pitcher, emptied of milk but wet with beads of moisture on its silver belly. She held the pitcher with all the care and tenderness one could ever expect to offer something made entirely of tin. She held it like a baby, as if she were out to convince the pitcher that living a life was not so bad a thing. The hard edge of the pitcher's mouth left a scarlet indentation high on her chest, and I thought it looked like the reluctant smile of a person who did not much feel like smiling.

"The one son changes his name," she said behind me, "and the other won't have anything to do with his poor fat mother."

"I need some air," I said. "I don't feel up to talking about this anymore. I'll be back later."

"The one son changes his name, and the other goes riding in his mother's car, burns his mother's gas and fills his mother's ashtrays with cigarette butts."

"Bye, Ma," I said. "I'm leaving now."

"The one son changes his name," she said, "and the other son

178

runs the streets. But where is their mother? Their mother's at home getting old and fat and sleeping the prime of her life away. She's fasting, too. She won't even drink water." Then, after I'd closed the door, she shouted so that I could hear her from the back patio, "And she did not eat French bread! And she did not eat carrots! And she would never—do you hear me, John—she would never rummage through the freezer looking for a chocolate bar!"

There is never any reason to carry on a conversation with a person who speaks of herself as if she were not herself at all, but my mother was not the first to teach me this lesson. Jason Girlie had also referred to himself in the third person, though only on occasions of extreme drunkenness or when he was out politicking with a couple of speakers on the roof of his car. Jason never spoke of himself as someone else, a stranger, when there was something to be happy about or proud of. And I suppose my mother had learned what she knew of self-mockery from him.

When drunk, Jason said, "The old man will have your ass, boy," and, "He was a leader of the people, but it was the people who, in the ignominious end, just didn't want to be led." When running for office, he steered his Olds through town with one hand on the wheel, and with the other he held a microphone to his lips. "He will keep integrity in the statehouse," he said, knowing it was a lie and that he hadn't the strength of character to keep integrity in his own house much less the statehouse. "He will make you glad to say you know him. He will make your vote count."

Looking for answers, I decided that what my mother was doing was not all that different from what Jason had done before her. She was politicking to win Sam and me back to her side, and like her alcoholic father-in-law she was trying to do so by means of fear or pity. She wasn't running for office, but she worried that she was losing something that was rightly hers. One son had changed his name, and the other, confused yet knowing better, had not reached out and held her in the way she most wanted to be reached for and held.

It was not easy being twenty-three and loved by two women,

especially when one was my mother and the other a woman my mother forbade me to see. My grandmother had long ago traced her fingers over the picture of Janie Maines as a young woman in a wedding gown, Jay Beauregard Girlie's bride, and I had thought, "So this is why he loved you." That same girl became a woman wearing a red silk Mardi Gras gown, and she had stood in the light of an open door, on the edge of the darkness that filled my room. The woman in the gown had become a woman in a large boxy dress who cleaved to her son. But what I wondered, being twenty-three and loved by two women, was what had become of me and how I had let it happen.

I drove to the Seville Arms and felt none of the self-hatred or revulsion or sadness a person who had almost made love to his mother should have felt. I was happy. I was happy because I believed everything would soon be made right and simple and I would be the reason for it being made right and simple. I drove along, and the radio played. The windows were down, and I could smell the autumnal smell of old leaves and earth and of wood fires going. I drove through a fine day when gold and green light danced in the trees and on the roads, and the sun seemed less interested in warming the earth than in giving it light to see by. As I turned on to Beverly Boulevard, I knew why it was that I was happy. It was not yet noon, and I was crossing the bridge that joined the world of Emma Groves to the world of everyone else. The bridge was imaginary except to those who crossed it, and those who crossed it amounted only to Emma and me.

To say that she was more beautiful at such an hour would be a lie; she was just as beautiful as she had ever been, no more. But there was something in her eagerness to see me come through her door that said she had never been so proud of me and so pleased with herself. She was triumphant in the way of someone unaccustomed to triumph, and seeing the light in her eyes made me feel good. "John, baby, it's not yet dark," she said less as a matter of fact than of bewilderment. "It's not even close to midnight."

"No," I said. "It's not. It's broad daylight." I checked my

watch. "And it's not even lunchtime. Nothing in town is closed. Nobody's asleep. The street lamps aren't on. The moon is down."

"So what are you doing here?"

"I came to see my girl," I said.

"Would you like to stay awhile? Take your shoes off?"

"I'd love to stay awhile. And take my shoes off."

We did what we always did when alone in her apartment, but this time we did it with the windows open and the shades pulled back and the light of the world upon us. In the light she moved as she had in the dark, but the difference was in my being able to see her better. It was better loving Emma with the chilly day breeze moving through the window screens and the murmur of traffic on the boulevard and the shrill, incessant birdsong. When, after the second time, I fell upon her hot and sweating, I could not move. And I couldn't keep awake. I felt the largeness leave and the tightness of where I had been close in and hold me like a grip. She was wet and felt like home. There was the smell of me and the smell of her and together there was one smell, and together there was no smell better. I slept on top of her, and the smallness of me remained in the place of her slick and incredible warmth, and for a time before I was entirely gone and dreaming my sweet dream of her, I felt the gentle pull and the gentle suckling of Emma trying to keep me deep within her.

"Don't leave me. Don't," she said, but I couldn't help it. "Don't sleep," she said, but I slept.

When I woke it was to the time when light and dark merge into something neither light nor dark, when the day is gone but night has not yet found its place, and I was hard again but not where I had been hours before or where I wanted to be. I felt neither warmth nor wetness. Everything was dry and cold, and I shivered against it. Emma lay beside me, beneath white sheets and a blue quilted blanket. There was no sound of traffic. I listened for the song of the birds, but it too had left us.

As I made my way across the room to the open windows, I said, "Good Lord, it's cold—it's so cold." The lamps had come on outside, high above the boulevard, and far down the way I saw the pink and green glow of the neon at Bubba Toussaint's Grill. I saw the painted glass of Judgment on the back wall of Saint Jude, and the stone angel Gabriel and the stone animals in the rock garden and the spread of stone tablets beneath the tupelo trees. In the middle of the trees and markers and monuments of stone, a single white Jesus hung on a red cross, a few pigeons sitting on its head. And not far away, near the grave with the red, uncut marble stone, the grave where Emma visited each night and would visit again this night, I saw the figure of a man working a shovel into the earth.

He was driving the blade into the ground with his foot, and stacking the soil in a pile that grew larger with each shovelful. He worked furiously, without stopping to catch his breath, never looking up from his labor.

"Harwood," I said, and it was him. It was Charley Harwood.

16

When it came to food, my mother's weakness had always been ice cream, and I don't mean the kind you buy in cardboard tubs and cartons at the drug store. She liked it homemade, churned by hand in a freezer packed with ice and rock salt and holding a sealed metal can full of eggs, cream, sugar and fruit. The ice and rock salt and painful, uninterrupted turning of the freezer's handle conspired to create a silky miracle of the ingredients in the can. My brother, when just a second-grader at Park Place elementary, learned in a science manual that the wheel was man's greatest invention. My mother said, "No, it wasn't, Sammy. Man's greatest invention was the ice-cream freezer. What are they teaching kids in school these days?"

Then she said what she liked to say whenever she detected a twitch in the world's evolution: "What are things coming to? Will someone please tell me what things are coming to."

She rejected electric ice-cream freezers just as she had electric dishwashers. Electric ice-cream freezers and dishwashers were signs of modern man's lazy heart, and they did not, she argued, deserve a place in the kitchen or, for that matter, anywhere else in the home. She and Sylvie washed all the dishes by hand, and she stored her wooden, crank-handled ice-cream tub in the garage, where it belonged. Manly things belonged in the garage: the Pontiac, the fishing tackle, the tool box, the wooden, crank-handled ice-cream tub.

It had always been her job to prepare the cream in the kitchen, in a big plastic bowl that was good for licking once the ingredients had been thoroughly mixed and boiled and transferred to the freezer's metal can. And it had always been my job to turn the handle, and Sam's to sit on top of the tub and keep it steady. The business of turning the handle was a tiresome but not unrewarding one, and the business of sitting on a couple of bath towels placed on top of ice and cold metal was hard on the buttocks and always unappreciated.

"How you doing there, young man?" my mother would ask me.

"I'll make it," was often my heroic reply.

Sam said, "What about me? I'm working too," and my mother said, "Don't flatter yourself, Sam Girlie. I see what you're doing."

After two days of listening to my mother refuse to sample Sylvie's generous offerings, I decided to take it upon myself to make her eat. Whenever I went into the kitchen, I'd shout at the top of my lungs so that she could hear me at the back of the house, "You should taste this cold fried chicken, Ma. I mean fried, Ma, and cold. And my God, Ma, what is this? Boiled carrots! In a plate! Look at all the little boiled carrot chips in this plate, Ma. They're orange and tender, and there's fresh-ground pepper on them. Come over here and look."

Sylvie worked hard at the stove and seemed to relish playing the role of culinary seductress. She prepared enough food for a family of five, arranged each steaming item in my mother's best china and placed the whole mess on a wheeled serving cart. She said, "These are the best biscuits I ever cooked," as loud as she could, but her voice wasn't strong enough to make it down the hall to where my mother slept. "I got homemade fig preserves on these best biscuits I ever cooked, Mrs. Girlie," Sylvie shrieked. "I got butter. I got such flaky crusts you'll want another half-dozen."

Once Sylvie proclaimed her specialty. "Nobody in America never made no bread pudding like my bread pudding," she shouted.

My mother heard her. "But she doesn't like bread pudding," she called. "She doesn't now, and she never has."

"Who don't," Sylvie asked, and her face bunched up like a withered red grape. "Who don't like it?"

"The person you want to eat it. That's who."

I rolled Sylvie's carts of hot food down to the door of my mother's room and parked them in clear view of the bed. In the dark, my mother held a remote control in one hand and a copy of a fashion magazine in the other, and she watched television on her small black-and-white set. Since she refused to acknowledge either me or the food, I told Sylvie to put an oscillating fan behind the cart and blow the smell of dinner at her. Sometimes that worked to stir my mother, but the stirring was never in the direction of the carved roast beef, mashed potatos and white-pepper gravy, drop biscuits, baked acorn squash and red apple pie that sat waiting like a dream in the hall. The stirring usually sent her under the covers or pressing the key on the remote that turned up the sound on the television. It was as if she meant to match the incredible degree of smell she was experiencing with an equally incredible degree of sound.

"She will not surrender until the one son changes his name and the other son proves to his mother that he is not dead to love," was what she said when she said anything.

She was not open to discussion, either. When she wouldn't talk to me, Sylvie tried her best. "I ever tell you about my great aunt's colitis?" Sylvie said.

"She doesn't want to hear about it."

"Well, I want to tell you about it," Sylvie said.

"She's not listening."

"My great aunt couldn't eat. But it was not because she didn't want to eat. She couldn't keep nothing in her stomach. Her insides were like greased pipes that couldn't hold down nothing. Colitis killed her."

"But she doesn't have colitis."

"No. Not anymore she doesn't. She had it so bad it killed her."

My mother was agitated. "She is talking about herself, your employer," she said. "She is talking about the person you are trying to make talk, the one you are looking at."

"You got colitis?" Sylvie said.

"She wants you to know that she is neither listening nor saying anything more. She wants you to leave the room immediately and get back to work. For heaven's sake, Sylvie. Go dust the furniture or something. And take her son with you."

After Sylvie left, mumbling to herself and confused, I sat on the floor at the foot of the bed. "What is this colitis anyway, Ma? Is that a big worm people get in their craw or what?" But she had covered her face with covers and wouldn't answer.

This was not an entirely bad time for me. For one thing, I never ate better, what with all the food Sylvie worked so hard to prepare, and I could come and go as I pleased and not worry that Janie Maines Girlie, wearing a face of white cleansing cream and pink sponge-rollers in her hair, was standing by the kitchen sink, watching through the window for me to leave the outdoor kitchen and appear on the back patio. The best part of it, though, was not having to worry that some blunder of mine would tip my mother off. At last there could be semen stains on the inner front of my underwear, long red strands of hair stuck in the zipper of my khakis and lipstick smudges on the collar of my shirt.

And because the day was no longer divided into two parts, Emma thought it wasn't so bad, either. One night, sitting in the kitchen, she said, "So how long's it been, Johnny?"

"Eleven days," I said. "She drinks juice and water, nothing else."

"Has she left the bed?"

"Only to use the bathroom."

"And that's it?"

"That's it," I said. "Except for the one time she got up to change the battery on the remote control."

"I bet she's been eating. I bet she steals food from the refrigerator when she thinks you're out working and when Sylvie's not there. There's no way she can keep this up without having a happy little nibble of something on the side."

"My mother has never been happy with a little nibble," I said. "She's a big-nibble kind of person. And besides, I count the pieces of fried chicken in the icebox every night before I leave. I count the number of carrot slices and cranberry muffins and I count the number of kernels on every last piece of boiled corn. When I get home the next day, the count's the same. She's not eating."

"Poor woman," Emma said and hugged me. "Poor, sad, pitiful woman."

One morning, much to my delight, I discovered a head of cabbage missing from the produce drawer in the refrigerator, and went into my mother's room. "I'm on to you, Janie Maines Girlie," I said, accusing her of boiling and eating it. But Sylvie, a few steps behind me, said she'd thrown out the cabbage with the trash, and my mother laughed with a certain meanness and nearly coughed her lungs into her fist. It was an awful, obscene racket, and I couldn't bear it. I left the room and headed down the hall, banging my clenched right hand against the heavy oak paneling and adding to the storm of noise, and I heard her shout behind me, "You think if she ate she would eat an old rotten head of cabbage that was sitting in the box for weeks? Why would she eat cabbage? She hates cabbage. She's always hated it. And she always will."

When I told Emma what I'd done, she said, "If not cabbage, what? What does she like? What food can she not resist?"

I didn't even have to think about it.

Sylvie worked from a recipe she discovered in my mother's junk drawer, and the smell of the cream boiling on the stove was everywhere in the house. It smelled like Christmas and the eggnog my grandmother always made, a beautiful, warm smell. I brought the freezer into my mother's room and set it in front of the television on a couple of bath towels. The sides of the tub were worn smooth, and its red painted finish had faded to reveal the white of the wood. "That's one strange piece of furniture," Sylvie said.

"Yes, it is," I said. "But that's one strange woman lying there," and I pointed at my mother. "She's strange and hungry, and it's time she ate. You ready to eat, Ma?"

I was talking like a wild, spirit-filled preacher, and my sudden burst of enthusiasm so inspired Sylvie that she danced around the room pumping her knees, waving her hands over her head and shouting "Amen, John. Amen, John." The faster she danced, the louder my preaching got, and the angrier and more hostile my mother became.

"You ready to eat," I asked.

"Sing it, Lord!" Sylvie rejoiced.

"I said are you ready to eat!"

"Feed me, Jesus!"

My mother stood in bed and waved the remote control. She was wearing a black tattered slip that reached below her knees, and dark shadows of hair grew under her arms and on her legs. "She can't see," she shouted. "Get out of the way. You're blocking the screen."

"That thing ain't no magic wand," I said. "So don't go pointing it at me." Then I turned to Sylvie and wailed, "Eat, child! Eat!"

"Feed me," she said. "Feed me."

My mother pressed a button on the remote and the channel changed, and then she pressed it again and again, and the television screen flashed a succession of different images, each one reflecting for a humble second or two in my mother's eyes. "Does she wish she could change her son the way she changes channels?" I said.

"What she really wishes," she said, sitting down, "is that her son just disappeared," and she turned off the television.

Sylvie settled down, but only after I assured her that my preaching was over and it was time to get serious. Making a good tub of ice cream had never meant so much to another human being in the history of the world, I told her. And with conviction she marched off to the kitchen for her creation and brought it to me in the bedroom. We set the can in the middle of the tub, poured in the hot cream and added the ice and rock salt. Sylvie helped me fix the metal yoke across the top of the freezer, then sat on it as I started turning the handle. The turning was easy at first, but after about ten minutes my right wrist and arm felt sore and I switched to my left. Through it all, my mother watched from behind a shield of magazines—frowning and severe one minute, smiling and enchanted the next. Finally she said, "Did you use fresh or canned peaches? It makes a difference, you know."

"Who wants to know?" Sylvie said. "This ain't for you."

"She never liked it with canned."

"Doesn't matter," I said. "She's not getting any, anyway. It's for Sylvie and me."

"Just tell her—canned or fresh? Come on. Canned or fresh?" Her voice was young and seductive.

I nodded at Sylvie.

"Fresh," Sylvie said. "Picked three giant ones from the pile at Bean's Grocery. They're ripe and soft and sweet, sweet, sweet."

"Sylvie, you're fired," my mother said, waving her remote control. "Leave her room this very minute. Leave it now." When Sylvie didn't rise from the tub, my mother threw a magazine at her, and then another. "Did you hear what she said?" she shouted. "Leave!"

Sylvie said nothing. I saw a wet cloud moving up the seat of her pants, and I imagined how cold that cloud must have felt. Sylvie was sitting up tall with her hands on her knees, facing my mother in the bed, and she was smiling and looked half-mad herself.

"You're fired," my mother said. "Fired! Did you hear me? As of this second you are no longer a working member of this household. You have no place here. You will leave the grounds immediately."

"Work for me then, Sylvie," I said.

"Okay," Sylvie said. "I'm working for Johnny now, Mrs. Girlie."

When the ice cream was ready, Sylvie went into the kitchen and got a couple of spoons, and we tasted and made a fuss over how good it was. My mother leaned back against the headboard and pouted and hung her lower lip as if on the verge of tears; she crossed her arms and set her chin hard against her chest. Sylvie didn't blink when my mother threatened to call the police and report "a certain black worker-woman as a trespasser and thief," as she put it, because she didn't move to pick up the telephone. Sylvie and I sat on the floor by the open ice-cream can and ate as if my mother wasn't in the room. We carried on like children at a birthday party, groaning with pleasure at each bite. When I could eat no more, I said, "Oh. Ma. Where'd you come from? I didn't see you lying there."

And Sylvie said, "We just made the best tub of ice cream there ever was, and we were wondering if you'd like to try some. It's way better than store-bought, ain't it, Johnny?"

"It tastes pretty good," I said.

"So good I could cry," Sylvie said and she started to sob. It was only a fake sob but it was first-rate. "Look at all these crocodile tears, Mrs. Girlie, strolling down my face."

After a while the ice cream began to melt, and Sylvie carried the can into the kitchen and put it in the deep freezer. "Last call for ice cream, Ma," I said. "Peach ice cream, last call." My mother had pulled the covers over her head, and the only exposed part of her body was her right hand holding the remote control. She switched on a public television documentary about sea cows, and turned up the sound as loud as it could go. The noise was frightening and unintelligible, and I reached over and killed it by pressing the on-off button. With her remote, my mother turned the television back on and the enormous sound of sea cows with it, and again I reached over and cut it off, only to see and hear it live again a few seconds later.

"Has she won," she asked. She had to shout to be heard.

"Not yet she hasn't," I said.

"Will he go away now?"

"He'll go. He'll leave and never come back. And then how will you feel about yourself? You want to run me off like you ran off Sam, Ma. I bet you ran off your husband, too. You ran him off, didn't you, Ma?"

"You don't know what you're talking about."

"I'll go and it'll just be you and Marie, and then after Marie it'll be just you. And you'll be stuck all by yourself in this room in this stupid house. It'll be you and you and you, and it'll be you again. And I'll be gone."

The television went quiet, and her voice was a dry angry whisper. "Turn off the patio lights when you leave."

In the outdoor kitchen, I changed into a suit of sweats and ran the familiar route to the Dupart Country Club, through a day that was cold and gray and full of dirty street smells. Hope was such a tenuous thing, as was joy—they were there and then they were gone, and someone you loved had taken them away. The running was hard because my mood was low and my legs felt thick and heavy. I thought about my mother. I thought I'd lost her. Coming back down Dunbar, I stopped and leaned against the trunk of a tall pine and nearly threw up, but the feeling passed. After regaining my breath, I walked the rest of the way home, waving at the drivers of cars who pumped their horns seeing me in the road. At first I thought they were honking because they recognized me, and I imagined them saying, "Why, it's John Girlie. Look, it's John Girlie the ball player. What's he been up to?" But then someone blasted his horn and shouted through an open window. "What are you walking in the middle of the street for? Get outa the fuckin' way!" And I knew better. It no longer mattered who I was.

Back in the outdoor kitchen, I turned on the burners of the small gas range to help break the cold musty dampness. The odor of the gas was nauseating but the heat felt good, and I stripped before the four blue circles of fire and warmed my body against them. Then I moved into the bathroom and sat naked on the dry floor of the tub and drew a hot bath until the water reached close to the rim of the tub. I sat in the water until it turned cool and blue, then stepped out of the tub and unstopped the drain. When the tub was empty, I plugged the drain again and ran a second bath, this one much hotter than the first. I was feeling old and unhappy, and didn't use soap or a wash cloth. I just sat there, leaning forward in the scalding water, my arms crossed against my chest. The hot water burned my testicles and feet, and I felt lousy and ready to throw up again.

"He'll leave and never come back!" I shouted. "He'll leave this house and this town and he'll never come back!" I started to cry and my insides filled my head, and nothing and no one could have stopped me. "He'll leave," I said again. "He'll up and fucking go."

Knowing it would help, I pushed a couple of fingers down my throat and felt the pain and its loud red sound come out of me in a rush. I threw up in the steaming water and all over my legs and groin, and didn't move to clean up the mess for five minutes or more. The bathroom door was locked, and no one would know of this. It seemed not so different from the times in high school when I'd come into this same room and locked the door and entertained myself looking at pictures of naked women in magazines. If no one knew of it, a small and insignificant an act such as this, then it might as well not have happened. I unplugged the drain, but instead of refilling the tub a third time I turned on the shower and stood against the warm spray. I leaned against the tiled wall, and it was cool and smooth on my face. I let myself cry until it began to feel like a dumb sappy thing for a grown man to do, so I stopped.

"Where the hell do you plan to go?" I said. "How will you get there? In your mother's car?"

Thinking of the prospects, the places and ways I might end up, I laughed, and the water soothed and settled me down.

From the phone in the outdoor kitchen, I called Sam at his fraternity house in Baton Rouge. He wasn't long in coming to the phone, although I had to go through three indolent male voices that said "Kappa Sig" before asking how they might help me. Sam said, "Hello. Same here." Hearing his voice made me feel better.

"Sam," I said, "This is Johnny. I don't mean to bother you, but it's pretty important. I think you should come home."

We talked, or rather, I talked and he listened. I told him what our mother was doing to herself, taking my time and trying not to sound upset with him.

"She won't kill herself," Sam said, "will she, John? Let's be real about this."

"Be real? God, Sam, if she keeps refusing to eat, it will come to the same thing. It'll be two weeks this Monday that she last ate."

"She's just fooling around with you, John. It's a game, a ruse. She's not serious."

"I don't know how long a person can go on living without food. If you come home, if you just come home and tell her what she wants to hear, I'm certain she'll eat again."

He was quiet for a moment, and then said, "But what is it she wants to hear? I really can't promise anything I won't later feel up to delivering on. You understand my feelings, John?"

"Yeah," I said, "I understand. All she really wants is for you to change your name back to Girlie."

"Well," he said, "I won't do it."

"You don't have to do it. All you have to do is say you'll do it. Just come home, see her for a few minutes and promise you'll do it. You won't have to put it in writing or anything."

"I won't lie, John. I'm sorry. I'm tired of lies."

"You won't do it, then?"

"I won't do what you're asking. No. I think it's wrong."

"It's only a name, Sam."

"You know it's more than a name," he said. "If it was only a name it wouldn't mean so much."

"Then fuck you, all right? Go fuck yourself."

"You don't know what you're saying, John. Something's happened to you. A person shouldn't talk to anyone that way."

"Fuck you, Sam Girlie."

"Don't talk to me that way, John, and don't call me that," he said. "It's Goodwin now." And he spelled it. "G-o-o-d-w-i-n."

"It's Girlie," I shouted. "It's Samuel Daniel Girlie."

He was quiet again. I could hear people talking behind him, men laughing and music playing, a terrible crowd of sound. He said something, but I couldn't make it out. Then he said it again. "You could have been worth a shit, John. You could have been whoever you wanted to be. And I mean that. People loved you."

"You mean it?" I said. "They loved me?"

"Yeah, they did. You were a hero, Johnny."

"We never understood each other," I said. "You wouldn't tell me those things if we did. You'd know better."

"I know what might've been."

"You know jackshit."

"I know what was."

I said, "You always were a pussy," and hung up. I started for the door but turned back and said to the phone, "You never knew, Sam. You never knew shit for someone so smart." And I called him again. I'd always been impatient with fools who suffered through calls, hung up and called back a few minutes later to argue what had been avoided the first time, but there I was doing it. He was wrong, and I was still four years older, and it was important that he not forget it. Another couple of indolent fraternity boys said "Kappa Sig" before giving up the receiver, and finally Sam answered. He knew who it was; I could tell by his surly, unrepentant tone of voice. But I didn't speak. "All right, who is this? Who's there?" he kept saying. I listened to his voice, so young, so far away from me. "Don't think I don't know who this is," he said. And finally I erupted and said, "Girlie, Girlie, Girlie. Your name's Girlie, Sam," and pulled the phone line out of the wall jack. It was an old rotary dial phone, and Sam's voice was trapped somewhere in it. "Girlie, Girlie, Girlie," I said again. I threw the phone against the floor and watched it break and spill open and go spinning in every direction. I heard the dumb, incessant ringing of the bell, and I saw where the phone had left a black scar on the cheap linoleum. And then I heard myself spell it, "G-i-r-l-i-e. G-i-r-l-i-e. G-i-r-l-i-e."

In the house, my mother had turned down the sound of the television and was sitting up against a huddle of folded pillows, a gardening book open beside her. She didn't look up when I entered her bedroom. "Where's Sylvie?" I said. "She go home?"

"She fired her, didn't you hear?" my mother said.

I waited for her to look at me, but she didn't. She was watching a game show on television, and the silver of the screen filled the wide folds of her face. "I talked to Sam," I said. "He's not coming home and he's not changing his name back to Girlie. He said he can't live a lie anymore, whatever that means."

"She will starve then," she said. "She will die."

"Die then," I said. "See if I give a flying fuck."

"What?" she said, sitting up tall. "What did you say?"

She was trying to stare me down, but I was equal to everything she gave. "See if I care," I said. "See if I give a shit, a flying fuck, a good goddamn. I don't care, Ma. Die if you want to die. I'm going to live. I'm not going to die with you."

I went into the kitchen and opened the top and bottom doors of the refrigerator, then I opened all the cupboard doors and the door to the pantry. I reached into the freezer compartment and grabbed packages of beef and chicken wrapped in white wax paper, stacked them on the counter and then carried them in my arms to my mother's bedroom. I dropped the packages of meat beside her on the bed and returned to the kitchen for the small boxes and cellophane bags of frozen vegetables, the TV dinners and the pudding and gelatin fruit bars. I dumped each load on the bed, although along the way some of the things fell out of my arms and dropped to the floor. Her eyes stayed fixed on the game show, and I laughed during one of my hauls hearing her mutter, "The letter *F*, dummy, not *Y*. The letter *F*." After the refrigerator was empty, I started on the cupboards, holding as many cans of soup, bags of rice and tins of seasoning as I could. By now the pile on her bed was so large that some of the food spilled down the side of the heap and fell against her. Only when a tin of sardines bounced against her uncovered breast did she speak to me, and even then it was nothing that offered any hope. "Sylvie and her damn fish," she said. "They smell so rank and their eyes look at you funny."

"I think you're going through the change of life," I said. "And if you are, it's not your fault. You're not to blame for the way you're acting. Women rot. Charley Harwood says they rot like tomatoes. It's inevitable, this chemical imbalance women get."

"Menopause had nothing to do with chemicals."

"Well, minerals then," I said. "It's a mineral imbalance."

"She's got neither chemicals nor minerals in her, so shut up."

The cupboards took about fifteen minutes to empty, then I started on the pantry. When there was no room left in bed, I dumped the groceries on the floor in front of the television, thinking to block her view of the screen. Although I quickly saw that the heap would cover no more than the bottom half of the set, I was still surprised to see just how much food there was in the house. Placed in uniform rows on the kitchen shelves, and stacked and lined in the compartments of the refrigerator, there seemed so much less than what I'd piled in the two chaotic heaps in the bedroom. "Why would you want to accumulate so much food, Ma? It's waste. Doesn't most of this go bad? Who eats all this?"

She pointed the remote at the television. "That show where

they spin the big wheel is rigged. The host has this pedal back behind the rostrum that he steps on when he sees they're giving too much money away. That's why they call him Mister Sneaky Feet."

"Who calls who Mister Sneaky Feet?" I said.

"That's for her to know and for you to find out."

"Come on, Ma. I want to know."

"And that girl who turns the letters has implants. Nobody's tits sit up tight like that without plastic surgery."

I had left only one thing standing on the table in the kitchen, and when I went for it I believed it would accomplish what it had failed to earlier in the day. The clicking of the serving spoon against the cylindrical walls of the can sounded like the toll of a dinner bell, and in seconds my mother's voice echoed down the long dark hall. "Johnny," she called. "What are you doing, Johnny? Why haven't you left?"

I took my time working through the litter of cans and boxes that stood in the hall, careful not to slip where a large plastic bag of dry white beans had spilled open and spread like a puddle across the floor. In front of the television, I stopped and stood in the purple glow and watched as my mother rose to her feet in the bed. She was staring down at me, her arms reaching way out in front of her. The shoulder straps of her black slip slipped down to her elbows, and her breasts hung heavy and low behind the frilly nylon.

"Sit down," I said. "You're going to eat now. This is ice cream and you're going to eat it."

She lay back down and rested her head against the pillows. Her breath smelled like old newspapers, and the flesh on her neck and face was dry and peeling. I scooped some ice cream and held it in front of her, then moved it toward her mouth. She was staring at the spoon as if it held something poisonous, and she shook her head from side to side. I pushed the end of the spoon against her open lips, but her teeth were clenched. When I tapped her teeth with the spoon, she slapped my wrist and the ice cream fell on her shoulder and eased down her chest, disappearing under the front of her black slip.

"Eat," I said, "please eat," and I tried with a second spoon of ice cream. She hit my wrist again, and the ice cream fell on the bed covers. "Fresh peaches, Ma," I said. "There's not a canned peach in this stuff." She rejected the third spoon, too, and there was ice cream all over her neck and chest. I traced the spoon along her lips and wet them with cream, and they no longer looked so dry and raw. "It's good," I said, "and it's good for you. Eat. Eat it. Please make me happy and eat."

She kept shaking her head, and after a while I saw I couldn't win. I tossed the can on the floor and it rolled under her antique chifforobe, leaving behind a trail of cream, and then I grabbed a couple of soup and vegetable cans from the heap and dropped them on the floor. I pulled the pillows out from under her and threw them in the corner of the room. The pile took less time to tear apart than it took to build, and soon everything was on the floor and there was only Janie Maines Girlie and me in the bed. She was lying on her back now, and both of her breasts had pulled free of the slip and were hanging low against her ribs. The cream on her chest was syrupy and sweet when I put my mouth against her. I was crying again. "You are not going to ruin my life," I said and felt all the pain and fire and thunder come rushing out of me. "You hear me, Ma? You are not. I won't let you. I won't."

Her arms were strong around me. I felt the wetness of her lips on the side of my face, and the sticky cream on my beard. There was a terrible purple brightness in the room. I felt her legs move under mine. She touched me. When I pushed her hand away, she touched me again. She was laughing now, and someone on the television was laughing. First I hit her with a tight fist, then with the back of my hand. When I hit her a third time, it occurred to me that I was not the kind of man who would hit a woman. I watched the blood come out of her mouth like spit. "It's my life," I said. "It's mine. It's my life. And I'm not going to let you kill it."

She let go of me, but she didn't stop laughing. I saw the dark open place between her legs. She pressed her bloody mouth against the sheets and then reached in the space between the mattress and the headboard. She threw something that sailed over my head. "Want to eat, John?" she said. "Hungry? Make me happy and eat, John. Make me happy and eat." She was throwing graham crackers, sticks of beef, sun-dried pieces of fruit. "Eat, eat," she said. "Please eat."

17

When she was six years old, Emma's parents were killed in a car crash out at Gorilla Ridge on Highway 3, and an aunt and uncle, Sally and Harold Dupuis, took her in and raised her as one of their own. The Dupuises had nine children and lived in what Emma called the bunkhouse on Beatrice Avenue, an enormous, run-down wooden structure that looked less like a family dwelling than a livery stable. With her parents Emma had lived in a small brick rambler on a quiet back street near the stockyards, and her most vivid memory was of running through the pastures and the herds of lowing cattle on her way to catch the school bus. She said dodging the salt licks and the soft green pockets of manure was the most difficult part of the run, even more difficult than overcoming the fear that bottle flies of incredible size and appetite were snapping at her heels, waiting for her to stumble and fall so they could feast on her sweet young flesh.

She never felt entirely at home with the Dupuis family, she said, though she loved them and was grateful for all their kindnesses. Her Aunt Sally's insistence that Emma do as the other kids and refer to her as Mee Mom, and to Uncle Harold as Pee Pop, only made the loss of her own mother and father more difficult to bear. On the wall of her apartment was a sepia-toned photograph of her real parents, and I thought them to be unspectacular-looking people. Her father had a glass eye that stared left when the right eye looked straight ahead, and his nostrils and ears were filled with an abundance of hair; her mother had light wavy hair that fell to her shoulders, large irregular ears and a scarred, somewhat masculine complexion. One night when Emma left the apartment and walked down to the cemetery, I turned to that picture of her parents and offered them a quiet moment of praise for having found and loved each other and for producing such a fine daughter. Then, suddenly feeling arrogant and mean, and upset with Emma for leaving me alone in the apartment, I said, "Too bad you never learned how to drive a car."

Emma liked to tell stories about her parents as much as I liked to hear them. Listening, I never saw the people in the picture on the wall; instead, I saw my father and his young wife, and I saw myself. Hearing her tell of the time her father rode a mule bareback in the Yam Festival parade, I saw my own father riding the mule, though he never would have. I saw Jay Beauregard Girlie wearing chaps and brown leather boots and a shirt with pearl buttons, and every few hundred yards he reached over and gave the poor animal an appreciative slap on the neck and a piece of apple. Hearing of the time Emma's mother made a five-layer red velvet cake for her fifth birthday, I saw my mother making that same cake for me, though she either bought our birthday cakes at Sanders' Bakery or had Sylvie make them. I saw Janie Maines Girlie wearing a starched white apron, gold earrings and bracelets and a sweetheart necklace, and she let me lick the smooth red batter off the beaters and help prepare the icing.

"I ate so much of that cake I got sick," Emma said.

"Your stomach hurt so much you had to go to the doctor," I said.

Emma was confused. "Well, John," she said, "I do clearly remember Mama mixing up some seltzer to settle my insides, but I don't remember going to the doctor."

A few weeks after I moved out of my mother's house and into Emma's apartment, the winter rains started in force and brought with them a huge, impenetrable darkness. The tupelo trees in the graveyard bent against the strong wind, and puddles stood inches deep in the streets. The rain fell for seven straight days, eased up for two and then came down even harder, falling in noisy white sheets, and the weather turned cold. Ice formed on the roads overnight, and in the early hours you could hear the graders and sand trucks clearing the way for the morning traffic.

One afternoon I went shopping for fresh apple cider at the market off Jennifer Lane, thinking a hot mug would pick me up and help break the sharp chill, but the place was closed. On the way back to Emma's, I saw a pickup truck skid on the icy road and slam its right front into a parking meter. Phone lines were down in the streets, and the radio reported that the storm had ripped a trailer park into tin parts and scattered it all over the outlying prairie. That night I accompanied Emma to the grave of her little boy, both of us dressed in slick rubber ponchos and rubber hats and shoes wrapped in plastic garbage bags. We held hands crossing the street and struggled to walk against the wind and rain. Kneeling, she said, "Mama's here now, don't you worry." Her knees sunk into the cold sod and she patted the earth with the flat of her hand, smoothing the wet grass as if it were Dorsey's hair. "This storm will pass and everything will be like it was," she said. Her voice was kind and full of love.

"How was everything before the storm, Mama?" I said, acting as if she were talking to me. "Was everything bright pretty sunshine?"

She put her ear to the ground and after a minute said, "I know he's a difficult man, Dorsey, but he's a good man and he's mine."

The lamps on the boulevard cast a pale yellow glow on the stone tablets and figures in the graveyard, and the ghostly murmur of pigeons rose from the eaves of the church, and the wet wind moved in the trees. A few feet from Emma, I saw where Charley Harwood had begun a new hole. The shovelled-out area was hardly large enough to hold a washtub, and some of it had been filled in with soil. The rainwater steamed and seemed to bubble in the hole, and when I stuck a downed branch in the muck I could push it down little farther than two feet before reaching bottom. The shovel Charley had used in digging was still imbedded in the ground, its flat rusty blade shoved several inches in the sod. "You never let me meet your friend the gravedigger," Emma said, walking toward me. "You said you would, but you never did."

"I haven't seen him around to introduce you," I said.

We were both staring at the puddle as if waiting for him to emerge from the muddy pool, and for a moment I believed that he would. When he didn't rise out of the dark water firing rocks and dirt clods and shouting obscenities, I was a little disappointed.

"What was his name?" she said.

"Whose name?"

"The one who made this mess here," she said, pointing at the puddle. "It was Harbaugh, wasn't it?"

"Harwood," I said. "His name is Charles Harwood."

My mood had soured in the rain, and I felt stuffy in the plastic clothes and uncomfortable. My lips were windburned and sore. I scolded her. "Maybe if you stopped worrying about yourself and you-know-who for a minute, Emma, you might remember something about those who are living, and that includes me. I'm surprised you haven't forgotten my name too."

"Who is you-know-who, John?"

I pointed to the ground at her feet. "Him," I said. "Who else?"

She stood there a moment without moving or saying a word. Then she slowly lifted her right hand and placed it against her forehead. Her hand was shaking but not from the cold, and she sniffled to keep her nose from running. She cut her eyes at me. "Why don't you leave me alone if you hate me so much? Why don't you leave . . . leave me alone."

"You know what I said is true," I said lamely and started for the back gate; but she ran ahead of me and crossed the boulevard alone. "Don't say it's not," I called. "It is true. You know it's true, Emma. So don't go acting like it's not." After she disappeared through the front door of the building, I shouted above the rain. "Tell me who's living, Emma, and who's dead! Is that boy Dorsey living or is he dead?"

When I got back into the apartment, she was locked in the bathroom. I pressed my ear to the door and heard her crying. "Quit being such a baby," I said. "I know I'm to blame for a lot of things, but I had nothing to do with you losing that boy, Emma."

When she didn't answer, the quiet was unbearable. "Look, I'm sorry," I said. "I'm sorry. I've got a lot on my mind." I sat on the floor and leaned against the door. My hair was soaking wet from the rain and thick and heavy in my hands. Talking seemed the only way to keep my teeth from chattering. "I think we should leave this place," I said. "I think we should just pack up all our gear and go. But when I start thinking about leaving, I think it's no good because you'll never come with me. I think you won't leave that boy and it makes everything hard. Why does it feel so impossible sometimes, Emma? I wish I was God and could bring Dorsey back. But I'm not God and I can't bring him back."

She opened the door and helped me to my feet. Her hand was small and frail in mine. She led me into the bathroom and closed the door behind us. The bathroom was warm; blue gas flames crackled and flared against the waffled lining of the wall heater. She turned off the overhead light. By the light of the lamps on the boulevard that came in through the window, I watched her unbutton her rain-soaked blouse. She wasn't wearing a brassiere. I saw her nipples, brown and hard in the pale light. She moved her breasts against me and I moved to kiss them. "I wish I could bring him back, too," she said. "Now I have you instead. I'm glad I have you."

"You promise," I said.

"I'm glad I have you," she said.

"Sometimes I'm a mean bastard, Emma. I get things in my head and I get mean and I turn into a bastard."

"No you don't," she said. "You're not mean. You're not a bastard. You're good, John. You're good."

"Sometimes I think we should pack up and leave. Maybe I wouldn't be such a mean bastard someplace else."

She kissed me. Her tongue filled my mouth. "We don't really want to leave, do we, John?" she said. "We don't want to go yet, do we?"

I felt her touch me. I felt her move down on me. "No, we don't," I said. "We don't want to do anything."

During the entire time I lived with Emma, I wore the same suit of clothes—khaki pants and shirt, a raggedy sweater vest, boxer shorts and calf-length athletic tube socks with holes in them—and

I came to refer to it as my uniform. Every few days, I washed the clothes by hand in the bathroom sink and placed them on the radiator to dry. The clothes steamed and hissed when I put them on the radiator, and after a few minutes they were ready to wear again. Emma wanted to wash them in the laundry room in the basement, but I told her I was roughing it.

"Roughing it?" she said. "You're punishing yourself is what you're doing."

One morning I gave her my measurements and some money and sent her to a discount place for jeans, flannel shirts and underwear. But when she returned with the clothes, I told her to take them back. It was cowardly and unmanly of me, I said, not to return home, grab a suitcase full of clothes and confront my mother, and she said I was being too hard on myself. I told her I'd called my mother once but had hung up after the second ring, and she said, "Two rings is better than one, John. You did fine." I took off my clothes and announced that I would wear nothing until I got up the nerve to leave the apartment and go back home. Emma said, "I always liked you in nothing better than I liked you in something."

"But I'll get cold," I said, trying to sound like a weak, frightened child. "I don't want to get cold."

"Oh, baby, you won't," she said. "I won't let you."

In Old Field, the downtown businesses always dressed up for Christmas, and I watched from Emma's window as workers hung giant silver stars and red bells and blinking lights on the storefront lamps and awnings. At night I could see some of the brightly lighted decorations through the bare trees of the graveyard, vivid blurs in the rain and very beautiful. I saw across the way where Bubba and Terrence Toussaint had put cardboard likenesses of Santa Claus and his reindeer on the roof of the Grill and, in their front window, a huge snowman wearing a tuxedo and a stovetop hat looked out on the gravel lot. The snowman held a white poster board announcing the day's special. RED BEANS, it said. RICE. PORK SAUSAGE. CORN-BREAD. ICE TEA. ONLY $2.

Emma bought a fine little evergreen and spent an entire afternoon making scratch paper cutouts and popcorn strings. Because she had done everything else, she had me place the sparkling blue-winged angel at the top of the tree. The sharp green needles of the tree pricked my naked middle, and I howled and danced around the room. "Are you bleeding?" she said. "I'll get the Mercurochrome and some Band-Aids."

She saw I was joking and came over and put her mouth against the spot where I'd pricked my skin. Her mouth made a wet sucking sound, and I could feel myself wanting her again. Through her teeth and soft lips, she managed to say, "You should marry me, John."

When I was quiet, she said, "I'm not so terrible. You're lucky to have me." Her mouth felt larger than it was.

"Did I ever say you were terrible?" I said.

"I'd make you happy. Wouldn't I make you happy?"

"Of course you would."

The sucking sound stopped, and she was holding me now. Her hand was tight and warm. "I know what you're thinking," she said. "You're thinking I've already done that once. And you want no part of a secondhand thing. Well, I am not a secondhand thing. My marriage was annulled. In the eyes of the state of Louisiana, I never was married. In the eyes of God, I don't know what I am. But I'm not bad. I'm not a bad person. I'm good. God made me good and pure, and I'm dear. I want to be dear, John."

"You are dear," I said.

"Will you marry me, then?" she said. Her mouth suddenly was on me again. "Say you'll marry me, John. Promise you'll marry me."

"Marry you," I said. "I'll marry you." And I felt myself push and buck and come against the sucking sound her mouth made.

After three weeks, everything in the apartment smelled of the wet soapy clothes drying on the radiator, and all food tasted the same. Emma's perfume was lost under the ubiquitous cloud of Ivory soap; Emma's surprise chicken supreme tasted no different from Emma's surprise tuna casserole. One morning we started making love hard and strong on the floor but stopped after a few minutes when I complained of fatigue. I simply pulled out of her. In fact, I wasn't tired at all, only lacking in spirit. My mind was elsewhere.

The radio was playing, and I was concentrating on the weather report rather than on the woman beneath me, and the woman beneath me knew it. In the bathroom I handled myself vigorously and tried to restore what had been lost, but it did no good. I returned to her and said I was ready again, but she no longer was willing and I had to prove again that I really wanted her love and surrender. She kept her eyes open as I pushed into her, and she started to hum along to the song on the radio. "Why is it not fun for you all of a sudden?" she said, and I said, "It's fun. It's a lot of fun. I'm just tired. My thing's tired. I swear it."

I moved away and she closed her eyes and began to masturbate. Except in Charley's blue videotapes, I'd never seen a woman play with herself and make herself come. At any other time I probably would've been thrilled, but now she seemed to be telling me she could have fun without me, she could get along well enough by herself. I wondered how she could exclude me from her pleasure, how she could so enjoy herself without me by her side. "Why should I be forced to endure the impotence of a troubled mama's boy," I imagined Emma asking herself, silently mocking me, feeding on my fear and frustration. I remembered the five absent assholes who had so often upset and haunted me in the past, and there they were again, standing along the walls of the room, watching her move her hands over herself as if it was nothing out of the ordinary. My face burned. I wondered how many men before me had known her this way. I wondered why I was not man enough to tolerate it, to enjoy and encourage it.

"So it's okay for you to do it but not for me?" she said.

"I didn't say anything."

"You didn't have to. I can just look at you."

"I'm not condemning it or you or anything. I'm just surprised. I get a little tired of fucking and worried about things and you don't see any point why it should concern you and you just go to work on yourself and have a fine old time."

"Oh, John, it's not hurting anything. I think of you when I do it. I can feel you. I see you on top of me."

"Yeah," I said. "I bet you do."

"I do. I swear I do."

"I bet you do," I said.

When she continued doing it, I said, "You want to marry me and I don't even know you, Emma."

"Just because of this you say you don't know me. That's ridiculous, Johnny. That's so ridiculous."

"You don't need me. Look at you."

"I do need you. I love you. Oh, baby. Johnny, what's wrong with you? What's happened? Why are you so mad all the time?"

"Look at you," I said. "I wish you could see yourself."

The weather cleared and warmed, but after only a few days another front moved in off the Gulf. The large darkness outside the window and the beating of water on the glass overwhelmed me. Each night I sat by the window and watched Emma return to the cemetery; she was always the only person in the yard, kneeling and picking leaves off the grave of her son. I thought she looked less like the shadow of a great-winged bird than something small and unknown. Back in the apartment, she put the leaves in a shoe box in her closet, saving them like letters from a lost lover. "I can't believe you're doing that," I said. "How can you save leaves?"

"They're not just any leaves," she said. "And don't start on me, please. It's not me you're mad at."

Near the end of our fourth week of being shut in together, Emma took a night job nursing an old woman at the doctors' hospital, and I promised to get out more and work up to returning to the place on Ducharme Road. After all that time, I still had my mother's car parked down on the boulevard. I had to get out, get drunk, shoot some pool. I wanted to roll down the windows and let the wind blow in, and I wanted to see Harwood. Emma said, "You shouldn't try to rush things, John," and I detected something peculiar in her voice. "Take it easy," she said. "Relax. You've been through a lot. I love you, John. I don't want you to be so confused about things. I don't want you to get emotional and run off in a fuss and hurt yourself."

"Hurt myself?" I said. "You think I'm crazy enough to hurt myself? What do you mean, hurt myself? You mean kill myself?"

"Oh, baby, why are you so suspicious. Please don't be suspicious of me. I'm your friend."

"Then don't talk to me that way, friend," I said. "Don't do it."

"Oh, John. Oh, baby," she said.

"You're talking to me the same way my damn crazy mother talks to me. 'Oh, baby. Oh, John.' You talk like a regular person when you talk to a dead boy in a grave, but you talk to me like I'm a child. I'm a man, all right? I'm all grown up. And I'm here, right in front of you. I'm not a mama's boy, either. Don't ever say that about me again. Because it isn't true."

"I know you aren't, baby," she said and reached for me. I pushed her away and she said, "Oh, John. Oh, baby. I know you aren't. That's an old fight. Why are you bringing up all the old fights again?"

I was pointing at the window and at the piece of ground that lay beyond the boulevard. And I was saying whatever came to mind, shouting and gesturing wildly. "There's nothing living but dumb old tupelo trees in that place," I said. "That boy you visit every night isn't living and he can't hear a word you're saying. Dead people don't hear when you talk to them, Emma. They don't answer back. They don't do a thing but make it hard for those who aren't dead yet. Well, I'm not dead. Do you hear? I'm a man who's alive and I'm not dead."

She was crying. "John. Oh, John. Baby," she said.

"Sometimes you don't know who the fuck you're talking to," I said.

The Pontiac's battery was too weak to turn the engine over, and I needed a jump start from the wrecker at Jackie Eagle's station to get it going. Dressed in my uniform and rain gear, I took off, riding through town with the windows down and the radio blaring. It was late and there were few cars on the road. Dirty brown rivers of rainwater moved in the gutters, and everything was shiny and black. I stopped at Black Fred's for a beer and one of Cheryl's burgers, and Booboo Raymond said he hadn't seen Charley in weeks. He also said there was a young Hungarian girl with a figure better than Sandra Boulier's who'd come around looking for me. When I told him I had no desire to stick around and listen to the same old line of bullshit, he said, "Bullshit? Boo Raymond bullshit?"

"She wasn't Hungarian, she was one of those Japanese," Sandra said as I walked out. "She wasn't no better than me either, John."

"The woman had a ginger ale," Black Fred shouted from behind the bar. His words, though muffled, reached me in the street. "She was a wild one! She had wild eyes and hair and big wild lips, and she left in Jake Comeaux's cab. And she was wanting Mr. Beauregard Girlie's boy!"

I drove through the yard at Queen of Heaven, but Charley wasn't there. All the monuments looked bigger than usual and were soaked gray with rain. The wind had blown cones from the pine trees onto the road, and they crunched under my tires and popped against the undercarriage. Through the open window a cold mist wet my chest and face, and I tasted the salty Gulf air. I saw the great brooding lion at my grandfather's grave, and I thought I saw it raise its head and crouch as if preparing to leap. I braked and reversed to get a better view of the lion, and as always, it lay on its belly with its chin resting on its front paws, the name SENATOR JOHN JASON GIRLIE incised on the marble tomb beneath it. I sped away, blowing a storm of painted white shell behind me, and raced through the streets headed to the outskirts and Bellevue cemetery, but the place was deserted. There was enough light to see how the ground dipped and rose and how the white stones and bronze head plaques gleamed. There was something moving across the wide ground, and I ran after it in the slow, dark rain. What that lost little hound must have thought of me I can only imagine, for it ran off yipping under the fence at the edge of the yard and disappeared in the night. I was cold and shivering and my stomach was uneasy from the food and beer. I doubled back into town and stopped at the Harwoods' house. The yellow porch light came on when I knocked on the front door, and both Malcolm and June answered. They were wearing nightclothes and slippers. They appeared to have been pulled from sleep.

"Charley home?" I said.

"Why, John, we thought he was with you," June said through the screen. "You mean he's not with you?"

I lied and said, "Well, he was. The weather, you know."

"I figured the rain would run you boys in," Malcolm said. "My idea of camping has always been renting a room in a nice hotel next to the woods. I like a good firm bed under me."

June was laughing. "We thought you'd go for shelter in the barn," she said. "I wanted to bring some dry clothes and blankets out there, but Malcolm said no. He said this would teach you."

"It taught us, all right," I said. "Charley came in for more food. I guess I thought he'd backed out on me. If he comes by and tries to pretend we called everything off, tell him to get back out there."

"We'll do it," Malcolm said.

"You boys take care and keep warm," June said. "And don't think we'll think less of you if you decide to come home and stay in your own beds."

"Nothing like a good firm bed under you," Malcolm said and turned out the porch light. "You keep warm, son."

I took Highway 2 south to Summer's Point and from there drove down a slick blacktop road to the meadow at the front of the Harwoods' farm. The aluminum gate was open wide, held from swinging shut by a cord of cedar, and by the lights of the Pontiac, I saw the long muddy road and the place about fifty yards away where a tree had fallen and blocked the pass. I took a flashlight out of the trunk, locked the car and started down the road. The beam of the flashlight was weak against the rain and hard darkness, and after I had used it to help me cross the downed tree, I turned it off and dropped it in the road. I walked without seeing more than five feet in front of me, but I knew the road ran straight and true for about a mile, ferried across a little wooden bridge to a pasture and a stand of pine and ended at the tumbledown hay barn and the Harwood burial place. I took my time, stopping every now and then and turning my face to the wet black sky. Mud squeaked under my shoes. My heart beat furiously. I was afraid of what that road might lead to.

The grave Charley had dug for himself was about eight feet

deep, fifteen feet long and six feet wide; two cars stacked on top of each other could've fit in it. Walking through the cluster of willow trees, I saw only the glow of the kerosene lantern in the green canvas tent staked at the back of the yard and a great mound of dirt rising from the place of Uncle Joe Wendell Harwood, who, Charley often bragged, had died of heart complications while screwing a Chinese whore in Sanborn Heights. There was a flare sputtering at the top of the dirt mound, and a shovel and tin pail lay at its base. At first I didn't connect the hill of earth with what was beneath the tent; I thought Charley had simply set up camp at the resting place reserved for his mother and father and him. But as I got closer, I saw the levee he had built around the grave to keep out the rain-water, and the clever system of ditches designed to prevent the water from pooling at the site. On one side the ditches drained into the run of willows, and on the other into the bean field. His Jeep was parked at the edge of the field, and I saw that the two rear wheels were bogged in mud, all the way up to the axels. Rays of light danced from the flap of the tent, and the air smelled of fried meat.

At the bottom of the pit, Charley was sitting on a lawn chair and staring at the dying embers of a fire in the opposite corner. The flames had blackened the earthen wall, but the fire now was almost out. He was wearing an insulated overcoat with a fur-lined hood, holding a bottle of whiskey in one hand and a charred hot dog in the other. Egg yoke and what looked like bacon fat had congealed on the paper plate at his feet. He looked at me and said, "I started this hole out at Saint Jude thinking it would be easier for you to visit. You know what I'm saying, John? You know where I'm coming from?"

"I know." I dropped into the grave.

"But do you know what I mean?"

"I do," I said. "I know exactly what you mean."

"I thought you'd have me to visit and your girl would have that young boy, and you two could come out together each night. Wouldn't that be something, John?"

"I don't think I much like that idea, Charley."

"That boy and me would be set up right close together, helping to make the grieving less separate. You could bring out one of those red checkered blankets and a Frisbee and a bucket of chicken and have yourself a picnic. But then I started thinking that I got family, and I can't hurt Malcolm again. Remember how that priest business nearly ruined him? Shit, John. It nearly killed him. I think it's only right that I took it here to die."

"But I don't want you to die, Charley."

He started laughing. He nearly fell over he was laughing so hard. "What a person finds out when he's sitting in his grave, waiting to fill it, is that dying makes a corpse out of you. I never could finish anything, John. You?"

"Me neither," I said. "I come from a long line of quitters."

"You surely do," he said. "I won't argue that point." He took a healthy bite of the wiener and offered what remained to me, but I shook my head. "Your old man, your grandfather, Sam. Look at what Sam's done with his name. He turns twenty years of age and decides to stop being who he is. He doesn't want to be Sam Girlie anymore. And you, John. I know it's football you're talking about. In the end it turned out you didn't have the balls for it anymore. Am I right on that point or am I wrong?"

"I had the balls," I said.

"Then I'm wrong. It wasn't the balls. It was something else." He chewed on the burned meat. "If it wasn't the balls," he said, "what was it then?"

"It was everything."

"Don't start on that shit," he said.

"All right, Charley. I'll tell you what it was. It was nothing."

He was smiling now, the pink meat glistening through his parted lips. "That's what it was, John. It was nothing."

There was no mud or rainwater in the pit. Along the walls, Charley had stacked travel magazines and books, canned coffee and beans, jugs of peanut oil, fruit juice and lighter fluid and sacks of flour and corn meal. His shotgun, its polished wooden stock glistening in the firelight, was leaning in one corner. Next to the gun was his rod and reel and tackle box and a large black cast-iron frying skillet. I opened the lid of the plastic cooler standing in the middle of the floor; it was filled with chipped ice and cold cuts, bottles of generic beer and several uncleaned fish and wild birds. The fish and birds had stained the ice with blood, and they were frozen solid and smelled rank. Their wild black eyes looked out at me.

"Hey, man. How long are you planning to stay out here?" I said. "This your new home?"

"I already told you. It's my grave."

"This isn't your grave, Charley. Come on."

"It's my grave," he said again.

I was afraid to leave him. I sat on the floor and tried to get him to talk, but he was distant and his words, when they came, went right through me. He was trying to make peace, trying to make sense of what it means to live this life. He talked about our town and named his favorite streets and his favorite teachers at Old Field High. He said to remember the good times shooting pool on the old battered tables at Black Fred's and said I could have his Jeep when he checked out. Those were the words he used: checked out. The Catholic Church was not so bad a thing as he made it out to be, he said, and then told me the name of the woman at Mabel's rooming house. "It's Mabel herself," he confessed. "For a woman twenty-some years older than me, I liked her pretty good for a while there. I almost liked her too good."

"Mabel?" I said. "It was Mabel?"

He was nodding his head, happy his secret was finally revealed. "That's right—Mabel Foose. She and Mama went to grade school together. This was bizarre, but she liked to sit naked at her piano bench and play songs I never heard before. Her skin was so warm and soft, John. And she loved Van Gogh. She loved the demented one-eyed bastard. I should say that woman was always good to me, John. And the songs she played were from another day, and they were fine, John. It was nice. Aren't girls nice, John?"

"They're nice," I said. "I always liked girls."

"You know I'm talking about Mabel Foose, don't you?"

"Mabel's a nice person," I said. "I always thought so."

"She wanted to marry me. A woman ain't herself without a man."

"I think you might have something there, Charley."

"Dead men don't lie," he said.

He threw what was left of the hot dog into the fire. It burned blue then turned red and yellow. "You always knew everybody, John," he said. "And when you didn't, they knew you. You were famous."

"Not really."

"No, man. You were famous. Believe me."

He said to remember that I was his best friend and brother. And he told me he loved me. Then he said, "Tell me who taught you Girlies how to get along. Who was the first Girlie to tell you people never to finish what you start? That sonofabitch was smart."

"Come on, Charley," I said. "Cut the crap."

"The trick is dropping out, isn't it, John? Quit while you can. Quit before it makes sense to go on."

"Shut up, Charley. Just shut the fuck up."

"See what I'm saying," he said. "Stop talking. Quit."

I walked over and put my arms around him. He didn't seem to mind how wet and cold I was. He hugged me like a man. On his breath, I could smell the whiskey mingled with the fried pork. "Listen," I said, "Emma and me, we're leaving. And I want you to come. Will you come with me, Charley? I want you to come with me."

"You people need your privacy," he said. "You don't want me drag-assing around, getting in the way of every good thing."

"We'll just drive. Isn't that how it works? Go until you get there. Come with us, Charley."

"Where to?"

"It doesn't matter where. Let's just leave. Come with me now."

"Can't come now," he said. "Can come later on, though. Can come in a day, earliest. Gotta free the Jeep. Jeep got stuck in the mud, John. Gotta free it. Gotta fill up this hole, too."

"Promise you'll come. Promise me, Charley."

"Promise. And I promise it'll be some pioneering sort of shit," he said, but there was nothing in his voice that sounded convinced. He was just excited. "Jim Bowie and the great frontier and shit.

They'll want to know why we left and where it was we went, and we won't say."

"Let's go," I said. "Let's leave and go in the morning and drive out of this place. Run, piss, shit, fuck and dance and sleep in the sun. We can do anything, Charley. Why can't we go? We're young."

He laughed and cried at once. "I like thinking we're young," he said. "I do like thinking we're young."

18

I cannot remember the last time I saw my father. I think it was in the house on Ducharme Road, but I'm not certain. It was probably in the morning before I went off to school; if not, it was the night before, and both of us were getting ready for bed. Because I had no idea he was leaving, I didn't know how important it was to study and memorize the man and to look and see the whole of what was happening around me. That last time, was there music in the house? Were unkind words passed between my mother and father? Was there something in his face that revealed his unhappiness and intention to leave? What was the weather like? He probably studied and memorized me. He probably told me something he thought I would hold onto forever. "Always be good to your mother," he might have said. Or, "In life one must make choices, and those choices are often hard." Or, "Sometimes running away is okay, John." These are my words, of course. I cannot remember what he told me, or if we talked at all. And I use them only because the time of his departure was like a wild, blind dream. Things happened and the world changed. My eyes and ears were open to them, but I just could not see. I was deaf to it all.

My last day in Old Field, I made sure nothing was lost. I felt the cold, wet wind. I saw the rain and heard the water gurgling in the streets. I even imagined a life and time that were not my own but my father's, and for a wonderful fleeting instant I thought I understood why it was he left and how he could have done it. Could it be so difficult to walk out of that place and away from those people and never look back? In inventing Jay Beauregard Girlie's heart, and allowing it to beat as my own, I invented every good reason to go and the strength not to feel guilty about it. My invented heart was not indentured, and there was nothing and no one to keep me from going.

"Should I call and tell Mrs. Rose that I won't be able to work tonight?" Emma said. "You sure this is what you want, John?"

"We're leaving," I said. "Call if you want."

"John, are you sure?" she said. "I'm not sure."

"I'm sure. What's there to be sure of?"

"Money, for one thing. What will we live on?"

"I've got a little left in savings. And I can always call my grandmother from the road and get her to wire us some. I know she'd do it. She'd love to do it. It would give her a reason to preach."

"Do you know any place to go? John, is this smart? Shouldn't we plan this out better?"

"You're scared," I said. "Don't be."

"What about Dorsey, John? I am scared. I'm scared for Dorsey. You don't want me to leave Dorsey, do you, John?"

"Emma, he's dead."

"You don't have to say it that way," she said.

"How did I say it? I just said he was dead."

"You don't know what you said."

In my arms she trembled. She was wearing her white nurse's uniform and her hair was wet and dirty. "Please," I said. "Please let's go." She was shaking her head no. "What do you want me to do? What do you want me to do, Emma?"

"Keep things like they are. Let's keep things like they are."

"I can't."

"I'll take care of you. I'll love you and feed you. I'll be good to you, John. Live with me. You said you were mine. Why can't we keep things the way they are?"

She held my face in her hands and rubbed her mouth against me. She rubbed her face against mine. I felt her shaking in my arms. "We could," I said. "But we can't."

"We can!" she shouted.

"No," I said. "No we can't."

I told her people do it all the time—people leave for no reason, abandon everything and everyone, go to a new place and begin again. I told her to take some clothes and whatever she could carry and couldn't do without. I promised a grand and gorgeous adventure, an odyssey. She lay on her great brass bed and said nothing; she lay on her belly, her face toward the window, gently rubbing the wrinkled sheets with her hand. I opened her closet door and pulled out a suitcase and filled it with shirts and undergarments and the dress skirts she seldom wore. The tricycle and a few of the other toys I had bought for Dorsey were in the corner of the closet, covered by a heavy green wool blanket, but there was no room for any of these things. "I don't know why you kept all this stuff," I said. I dumped the shoe box of leaves on top of the clothes and closed the case, and I took the picture of her mother and father off the wall. The rectangular space on the wall where the picture had been was lighter than the space around it. I started to remove the other pictures, most of which were of Sally and Harold Dupuis and the rest of Emma's adopted family, but I stopped. "You want all this? It's baggage. You can see these people in your mind, can't you?"

"I never even took a Polaroid of Dorsey," she said. "I didn't have him long enough."

"Pictures don't change anything," I said.

"They help you remember."

"Yes, they do. And that's what's wrong with them," I said. "The only thing they're good for is making you lonesome. I don't want to be lonesome, Emma. Why do people keep going back to what they'll never have again anyway? If you had a picture of that boy it still wouldn't matter. It's wrong, don't you see?"

"No, it's not wrong."

"He's dead and gone, Emma."

Suddenly she was angry. "You know everything, don't you? You and your importance. I hate you and your importance."

"You don't hate me," I said.

"I hate you," she said.

I walked to the bed and kissed her wet, dirty hair. I pressed my mouth against her cold face. She struck my chest and face with her fists and fought to get out from under me. She began to scream and I covered her mouth with my hand. I fought with her to pull up her white dress. She was wearing panty hose, and I felt only dryness through the white nylon. I rubbed her, rubbed her there until she stopped struggling, then I felt the power of her arms around me, her hands clutching my shirt. She was trying to tear my shirt off of me, and her legs opened as she closed her eyes. I moved against her. "You love me," she said. "You love me."

"I love you."

"Yes. You love me," she said. "Yes."

"I love you," I said.

It was early morning when I left the Seville Arms and headed through town on my way to the house on Ducharme Road. Rain fell in furious white gusts, and twice standing pools of water slammed against the Pontiac and drowned the engine. Phone and electrical lines were down on Memphis Street and repairmen in orange slicker suits worked under giant flood lights. Their welding torches spit baubles of white fire that bounced and melted on the pavement. Their generators, set on trailers, coughed and screamed. A flagman waved me onto a detour, and he looked at me with laughing eyes when I shouted through the window, "Hey, man, it's raining. Get out of the rain. Don't you see it's raining. Don't you see."

"Cats and dogs!" he yelled above the drumming rain and the roar of the machinery. "Cats and muthafucking dogs."

When I reached Ducharme Road, I stopped before making the turn and stared down the long drive. It was a sad strip of road, a winding ribbon of pea gravel and dirt covered with big brown and red leaves and splintered branches. Small white and pink frame houses lined either side of the road, and all were dark. They seemed to defer to the great old house at the end of the road, which was ablaze with lights. I reached the front circle and, in the side parlor window, saw the aluminum Christmas tree trimmed with plastic red apples and shiny red and green bulbs and strings of popcorn and twinkling white lights. When I knocked on the front door, it occurred to me that I had never before knocked on this or any other door of the house. I had always simply walked in, certain that it was my place and home and that I belonged here. "You coming for trouble, John," Sylvie asked through the screen. "It's good to see you again, but not if you've come looking for trouble."

"I came for clothes and to see Ma, Sylvie. No trouble."

"Sam came home last week," she said.

"Sam? You're kidding."

She rolled a wisp of black hair between her fingers. "He was asking for you. I showed him the mess you made in your mama's bedroom and me and him put everything back in the kitchen. That pork and beef got spoilt, though. You can't just let meat defrost without planning to cook it, John."

"Where's Ma?" I said.

"Bedroom."

"She's still in the bedroom?"

"Still in it," she said. "But she's been out, and that business of talking to herself like somebody else has finally stopped, too."

"Well, that's a relief."

"First time she got out was when Sam said he would change his name back. Then he called from that clubhouse at school and said he'd changed his mind again. He wanted to be a Goodman. And she went back into the room. It didn't last long, though. She got well. I'd say now she's completely healed. I'd say she's almost all the way back to how she used to be."

"If she is, then what's she doing in the bedroom?"

"Dressing. She's been getting dressed every day, wearing new clothes. She shows me these old magazines she was in, and then she gets dressed like she used to. She's been looking like a New York model, John. And the last thing she needs is to go through more of the business with you and Mr. Goodman."

"It's Goodwin, Sylvie, not Goodman," I said. "It's Sam Goodwin."

"Goodwin, Goodman—same difference. He ain't Sam Girlie no more."

She pushed the door open and I walked into the foyer, the air heavy with the smell of lemon furniture polish and Sylvie's cleaning. "Sam grew a beard is another thing," she said.

"Really? I can't picture it."

"It's thick and full, John, a real beard. I teased him and he said it was to hide the pock marks on his chin, but it wasn't that. Sam never had a pimple in his life. Never had a blackhead. Nothing."

"No," I said. "He never did that I knew about."

I followed her into the kitchen, and she pulled up a chair at the table and nodded for me to sit down. When I remained standing and started for the hall and my mother's room, she said, "You won't find clothes there, John. Not in the outdoor kitchen, either. So don't go looking. You said no trouble, remember?"

"What do you mean no clothes, Sylvie?" I followed her eyes to the window. She was looking out on the back lawn.

"I admit I helped her, John. It was me, too."

"Helped her with what?"

"She was too sick to do it all by herself. She was weak and the big things were too heavy for her. I carried those trophies. And it was her idea to put those sheets of plastic on top. She wanted to keep it dry for when she burned everything. But I think the mildew got to some of it. It's been there all of three weeks now. Maybe four."

The pile of my things seemed to be about the same size as my father's had been. The covering failed to provide much protection against the weather, and the transparent sheets didn't even extend all the way across. Water had gathered on the surface, forming puddles on top of the heap. I walked uneasily across the patio and saw my books and clothes, and the trophies I'd won dating back to my years as a player in the Sertoma Little League, and pictures of lost girlfriends and lost boyfriends. It was a great pile. I saw all the lost faces. My LSU letter blanket and jacket were in the heap, lying under the Army-issue woolen blanket. Letters held in bundles by rubber bands were rain-soaked and covered with mildew, and the ink had run and bloomed into purple splotches. There were also birthday and Christmas presents I'd given my mother over the years—green glass vases, cheap jewelry, a set of unused steak knives, a small ceramic statue of the Virgin, crayon-book drawings of farm animals, an elaborate serving bowl for soup. On the top of the pile I recognized the green metal box holding all of my private papers, including my birth certificate, baptismal record, report cards and high school and college diplomas.

I heard the back door slam shut behind me, but I didn't turn around. I knew who it was.

"What do you think of Janie Maines Girlie now?" she chortled. My mother was dressed impeccably, and I suppose the last time she had looked this smart was when she turned away poor Mr. Butch Perles some ten years before. Her dress revealed much of her generous bust while concealing her wide hips. She wore makeup that obliterated the dark folds of her face and gave light and purpose to the angles, and earrings of diamond clusters, calf-leather shoes with spiked heels and rings on her fingers. Her hair was gathered in a delicious, perfectly round bun on the back of her head and held in place by ornate purple combs. She appeared darkly, exotically tanned, and I wondered how she had come by it. She had overstated her perfume.

"Got a date?" I said, and mimicked her wicked chortle. Then I turned back to the pile. "For someone who's got a date I don't know why you'd want to stand in the rain and get all wet."

She was holding a box of kitchen matches, and she walked next to the pile, not five feet from me, and started flicking them one by one onto the wet plastic. The black heads of the sticks issued spinning threads of smoke, and I smelled the burning sulfur. Some of the matches were wet by the rain as soon as she took them out of the box and wouldn't catch no matter how determinedly she scratched them. "I have decided that you are not responsible for who you are," she said. "And I am not responsible for who you are. I tried to be a good mother. I blame your father."

"I came to say good-bye, Ma," I said. "I don't want to hear it."

"You don't want to hear what?"

"It," I said, turning to face her. "I don't want to hear *it.*"

One matchstick succeeded in igniting the sleeve of a dress shirt, but the flame went out quickly. "I'll give you this much," she said. "At least you said good-bye. That's the Maines in you, though. That's not the Girlie. The Girlie in you would be gone by now."

She started flicking the burning matches at me, and they died in the wet air and fell soggy at my feet. I didn't move to stop her. "Now your brother Sam," she continued, "he's the one I haven't quite figured out yet. He's fought being who he is from the day he was born. He never liked the Girlie in him. He never wanted to look like one or talk like one or think or act like one. He came here smoking a pipe and talking like an English country squire." She laughed at the thought and flicked another match at me. "I said, 'Sam, where'd you get those clothes. Where'd you get that beard?' And he said, 'What clothes, Mama? What beard?' You would've thought he'd looked and behaved that way all his life. I can forgive Sam, poor boy. Can you forgive Sam, John? I hope you can."

"No," I said.

"No what?"

"No, I can't forgive him."

"Well of course you can't," she said and her voice trailed off dismally. She was serious now and trying to set the great pile on fire, holding a burning match against the lacquered wooden base of one of my trophies. "Worse than his father running off was having to follow you," she said.

"I said I don't want to hear it."

"No," she said. "You don't. But of course you don't."

I stared off into the gray distance and held my face up to the dark sky. The water felt good and cold on my face, and I rubbed my hands over the heavy stubble of my beard. "I'm leaving," I said. "I'm taking Emma Groves. And I'm going to marry her. You remember Emma Groves, don't you, Ma? I'm taking her with me and I'm going to marry her. Good-bye, all right? I'm leaving. I'm leaving and I wanted you to know how sorry I am for the way things turned out between us. I never meant to hit you that day."

"You only think you're leaving, Johnny," she said. "The Maines in you won't let you leave."

"I'm leaving," I said. "It's not something we can discuss or change. My mind's made up. It's too late." She threw another match at me, and this one hit the back of my hand and I felt a quick, almost electric sting. I put my mouth against the spot and sucked it and I felt a small blister form. "Shit," I said. "Shit that burns."

Beads of dark oily water sat on her brow, and clouds of mascara stained her cheeks. Makeup the color of flesh ran in streaks down her neck and chest, and she shivered against the cold rain. Until then she hadn't touched me, but now she was moving toward me and reaching to hold my hand. She put the burned spot against her open mouth and ran her tongue over the blister. Then she turned away.

"Oh, John," she said, "it's only skin."

She pulled back the plastic covering and tried to light the dry clothes in the middle of the heap, but she was frustrated and kicked a box of camping gear. The tinny clatter of the poles and stakes was not the effect she had hoped for, so in an angry, defiant huff she thrust the heel of her right shoe into the circular dial of my radio. She put the other heel into the screen of my portable television and turned to me for a response.

I shrugged and said, "If it's going to burn, it doesn't matter how much or how long you beat on it."

She was still kicking as I drifted across the patio to the garage and picked up the gasoline can. The ten-gallon metal can was full, and I needed both hands to carry it. I climbed onto the pile, struggling clumsily to reach the top, and emptied the fuel onto the clothes and papers. My mother was holding a single lighted matchstick with one hand and deflecting the rain from the sputtering yellow flame with the other. I stood precariously at the center of the pile, the wash of gasoline on the stuff at my feet, and watched the flame move slowly down the white vein of wood and meet her fingertips. She didn't flinch. Her lips peeled back against her gums and she laughed. "Shit," she said. "Shit that burns."

"Don't mimic me," I said.

"Oh, John, it's only skin," she said.

Long strands of hair had slipped free of the bun on the back of her head, and both combs fell out at once and dropped to the ground. In the grass they looked like shiny purple spiders. She bent over to pick them up, and when she stood up her hair fell across her shoulders and covered her face. She looked less like a wet middle-aged woman than a wet little girl, and I had to fight the urge to reach over and hold her and walk with her out of the rain. "What happens to people?" I said, climbing down from the heap. "Would you please tell me what happens to people?"

She was silent, trying to fit the combs back into her hair.

"What happened to us?" I said. "What the hell happened to us, Ma? Was it me that caused it? Was it my fault? If it's me, I'm sorry. I want you to know that if it's me, I'm sorry."

She tossed the combs on the pile and struck a match on the edge of the box. "It wasn't you, baby," she said, and tears cut her cheeks already cut by the rain. "It was never you."

"Who was it, then? Tell me who it was, Ma."

She protected the burning match from the rain with a framed certificate of excellence she pulled from the pile. I tried to read the lettering on the certificate, but the glass covering had shattered and there was no seeing through it. The fire was slow in starting, but burst into flames when it reached the gasoline. In no time the fire was huge and terrible and moving like a wave. The ashes and embers rose and danced and disappeared into the dark morning, and my mother cried. She put her face in her hands and cried in the hard, cold rain. "It was never you, John," she said.

19

Malcolm and June Harwood were easy people with strangers, and for some reason I always associated their plain kindness and generosity with their devotion to cultivating the land. He was a farmer and she was a farmer's wife, and Charley was what they called "the son of farm people," implying that because they teamed up to create him, he should've been as good and simple as they were.

The Harwood place was situated near the intersection of Sanduval and Pine Log roads, and a red warning light, hanging at the exact center of this dangerous crossways, beat regularly against the dressed-up western side of their small house. Holidays, particularly the late September weekend of the Yam Festival, were a busy time for the Harwoods—a drunk speeding down either Sanduval or Pine Log could be counted on to ignore the stop signs and warning light and slam into some young innocent out for a joy ride in his father's car. It was Malcolm and June Harwood, hearing the crash, who first reached the dead and injured and pulled them from their ruined vehicles. I know that the Harwoods' severe and charismatic faith in the Lord guided them through these times. They reminded survivors of the crash that the souls of good men prospered in death while their bodies joined the dirt of the fields, and I always considered this something only a farmer and a farmer's wife would think to say.

Charley Harwood might have killed himself on any number of occasions—stoned behind the levers of his backhoe, lying hungover in bed watching pornographic videotapes, running screaming down some dark back street—and if he had, I suppose his mother and father would've blamed his death on his long, unreasoning abuse of drugs and alcohol. I also suppose that through prayer and penitence his parents would've campaigned against these demons and come to piece together their own understanding of how their son could have lived the last of his twenty-four years loving and hating everybody at the same time.

And eventually, I suspect, they would've addressed those gathered at Queen of Heaven's Tuesday night prayer meeting in hushed and solemn tones, and shared not only finger sandwiches and cups of hot mint tea but the wisdom of their experience.

"It's just the way the world is," June would have declared in summary. "Charley may be burning in hell for what he did, but it's not his fault. It's all the world's doing."

"It's not easy being young these days, even for the sons of farm people," Malcolm would have said. "There are so many temptations, so many crosses to bear."

The end that awaits the truly sorrowful is redemptive, I think, but I would not have told Charley's parents that. This probably would have confused them, and I would have been asked to explain myself. "But what of the truly sorrowful who kill themselves?" they might have asked. "Can there be redemption in such a death?"

I would have struggled to find an answer. "Yes and no," I might have said. But how does one adequately explain a life built on yes and no—on everything and nothing? Perhaps in time Malcolm and June Harwood would have learned to believe as I do: that redemption is a need of the spirit, and it belongs to the believers.

I was more than a little frightened driving south again on Highway 2, headed to the Harwood's farm to pick up Charley and carry him away. I knew that it was a mistake to have left him alone the night before in the enormous grave he had dug for himself, sitting stoned in front of that dying fire and trying to make sense of his ridiculous, wasted time on this earth. There was no making sense of it. Harwood was like too many other young men who talked of opening their arms to embrace and gobble the world, but who knew their arms were not long or strong enough and their mouths not big or powerful enough. In truth, he had little appetite for grand achievements. Charley Harwood didn't care about the world or even himself. He was full of sin and regret and was too lazy and dull-hearted to change. He wasn't even a good gravedigger. Like so many other young men, Charley believed that nothing he could ever hope to do had not been done before him. And nothing he could ever hope to undo could make things any better.

I stopped and parked at the swing gate at the front meadow and started to walk back down that long muddy road in the direction of the Harwood family cemetery. The rain had slowed and now was little more than a misty drizzle. Blackbirds moved and chattered in the fields. For the first time in days, streaks of light crossed the sky, and there was the bruised promise of sunshine in the clouds. Approaching the downed tree in the road, I saw it had not been struck and felled by the weather after all—the red-painted blade of Harwood's ax was planted in the trunk. Only Charley would've left the gate open to signal where he was and then chopped down this tree to make reaching him difficult. Only Charley's mind worked that way. Just on the other side of the tree, my flashlight lay in a shallow puddle.

By the time I reached the end of the road and started down the path through the briars, the misty drizzle had stopped altogether and the sun was reflected in the standing pools of water in the field. I saw sun on the rusty tin roof of the impoverished hay barn, and the willows seemed to reach toward the heavens, their glistening yellow-green branches stirred by the wind. It was suddenly beautiful—everything was—and I thought this was no good day to die. But I was full of thoughts, most of which included a picture of my friend as a dead man. I pictured him hanging from a tree, shot in the face, wrists cut to the bone. I pictured him cold and blue, his heart a quiet fist of meat. And yet I was propelled forward—on to the little yard of dead Harwoods, on to the poor fool's grave. My legs took me there.

His Jeep stood in the new sun, the mud at its wheels no less deep than the night before. I was certain he hadn't tried to move it. The tall grass of the graveyard, unmarked by footprints, swayed in the breeze and smelled wintry and clean. Nothing remained of the flare at the top of the dirt hill, and the tin pail and shovel were still at its base. The tent was stained black with carbon, but no firelight showed through the green canvas. "Shit, Charley," I said in a strong clear voice. "You come out of that hole right now—right this very second, you hear?"

When at last I stood at the mouth of the shelter and looked in, I could not see the floor of the pit through the darkness. I bent to a knee and leaned over the edge of the hole, and I made out the charred bones of wood in the far corner and the food supply standing against the earthen wall and the cooler and clothes trunk and fishing gear. Then I saw a large heap in the corner directly below me.

"Charley," I said. "Charley Paul Harwood. You dumb asshole. You sonofabitch." I dropped a handful of dirt on the heap, but it didn't move. My eyes adjusted and I could see an overcoat with a fur-lined hood, hiking boots, a shotgun and the scratchy old horse blanket Charley liked to take on camping trips. From what I could see, there was also a body beneath the coat, boots, blanket and gun. "Dumbfucker," I said into the dark hole. "Dumb stupid fucker. Why'd you have to go and do it?"

As I had learned some months before, it is possible to hear the sound of air being forced from your lungs before feeling it. The sound that fills your ears is terrible, but the sudden feeling that there is no air to breathe is worse. When Harwood ran from his hiding place at the back of the yard and buried his same twisted face into my back, I heard my lungs explode before I knew how to interpret the pain. In fact, I slammed onto the floor of his grave and was struggling to breathe again before I knew how badly my chest and back and shoulder hurt. The noise was screaming and white. I landed on my right side with him on top of me, and both of us tumbled against the wall and the firewood in the corner. He was laughing as maniacally as he had the morning he tackled me at Bellevue, and this time I joined him. "You asshole," I struggled to say. "You dumb sonofabitch. You dumb sonofabitching asshole."

"You thought I was dead," he said.

All of a sudden the smell of urine filled my nostrils, and Charley said, "Look where you fell. Right in my piss hole. You got piss all over you. You're full of piss." Laughing and spitting blood, he walked unsteadily to the other side of the grave, lit his kerosene lantern and revealed the body beneath the coat and boots and horse blanket. It was a young deer. With both hands, Harwood grabbed the animal's hind legs and swung it over to the middle of the floor. A syrupy rope of blood ran from the animal's mouth, and its eyes were open black bulbs glaring at nothing. Shit had streaked the white hair of its hind legs. I pressed my fingers into the large meaty wound on its neck and felt the buckshot. There was blood all over its hide, and it felt greasy on my fingertips. The body was still warm.

"It's just a baby," I said. "Why'd you have to kill it?"

"I was hungry," he said. "I wanted some meat. I wanted some barbecue for the road. You always liked barbecue."

"You killed a little baby deer," I said.

"Just a deer, John."

"Just a deer?" I said. "Just a deer?"

He was laughing now. "That's all. Just a deer."

I could feel the blood beating in my head. "But it's wrong. It ain't legal, Charley."

"Fucka buncha legal," he said. "Fucka buncha wrong."

He climbed out of the grave and left me alone with the deer, and after a few minutes I heard the distant sound of an ax chopping wood. Each blow of the ax, though dull and faraway, made me flinch. Suddenly I was as breathless as I had been minutes earlier when he knocked me into the grave; the blood beat louder and louder in my head. I felt faint. "Come back here!" I shouted once the blows stopped. "Charley, come back here!"

He returned dragging a thick green branch that must have been twelve or thirteen feet long, and I watched from my seat on the floor as he set the branch across the top of the hole and tested its strength by hanging from its middle. With a piece of rope he tied the carcass to the branch by its hind legs and let it hang all the way to the floor. Gummy strings of blood began to pool on the ground. Although there was now enough sun to see by, Charley disassembled the canvas tent and packed it in the short bed of the Jeep. Then he carried everything else out of the hole and packed it carefully in the Jeep—the food, the sporting equipment, the books and spare clothes. I remained seated, watching him, and said nothing.

"Thanks for giving me a hand," he said after he finished.

"You're welcome," I said.

He gutted the deer in the great new wash of light. The bag of entrails spilled onto the floor of the grave and made a wet liquid gurgling sound. The odor was everywhere, more sickening and pervasive than the urine. When he stripped the hide, I saw how small the deer was and how little meat there was. "It was just a baby, Charley."

"It wasn't no baby. It was a deer, John. I wouldn't shoot no baby. I like babies. I always liked 'em."

I climbed out of the hole, leaned against the trunk of a willow and watched him work as he whistled a song I didn't recognize. He made a huge wood fire in the graveyard—at the place where his parents were to be buried—and threw what remained of the deer on the old horse blanket next to the hill of dirt. Once the fire had died down to a bed of burning wood chunks and coals, he cut off a slender strip of meat from the animal's loin, impaled it with a stick and began to roast it over the busy white flames. He roasted the meat until it was crackling and charred black. "I like my deer well-done," he said. "How do you like yours, John?" His lower lip was cut and swollen, and there was dried blood on his chin and neck. He bit off some of the meat and chewed, studying the larger piece on the end of the stick. His lips glistened with the blood and juice. He said, "Little deer tastes like rubber," and spit it out and wiped his tongue and mouth on the sleeve of his shirt.

"Tastes like an old used tire," he said. "Come try it."

"No," I said.

"It's chewy and dry, but the flavor's there." He held the stick out to me, the meat burning its thin ribbon of smoke.

"No," I said again. "I don't want it." He took another bite of the black strip of meat. "I wish you hadn't killed it. Not a baby. And then to cook the poor damn thing."

"It was nothing personal, John. Not that it matters, but I swear it was nothing personal."

He ate until I moved out from under the willow tree. Then together we struggled to drive one of the tent poles through the bony breast and out the rear and set up a spit over the coals. I helped Harwood gather more kindling, and we stoked the fire generously. Yellow fat and skin melted and dripped from the deer and hissed on the coals, and soon I couldn't see the animal for the enveloping wall of flames. Charley ran and filled his tin pail with water from a puddle and threw it on the open stove. The black wood smoked and black ash rose and clung to the charred body, now shriveled down to the size of a large dog. Crusty and black, it crackled and steamed in the sun.

"Little bastard was eating on those berry bushes over by the pond," Charley said, staring absently at the ruined meat. "I shot for the big one first, the mama, but she ran off and left him. He looked right at me, John. I mean, he looked me right square in the eyes as if to say 'I dare you, I dare you.' When I shot him, he must have flown ten feet high before coming down. He landed like a bag of rocks."

"It wasn't a he," I said. "It was a she."

"Well, whatever it was," he said and laughed, "it thought it was better than me. It thought it was superior."

We stood a long time by that smoldering fire, and perhaps Charley was thinking as I was of all the days that were gone and behind us now. This was not the best of them, but it was the last. I knew before he said anything that he had changed his mind about leaving. It seemed to me that I knew what he was incapable of doing better than I knew what I was incapable of doing, but I didn't tell him that. "Fucka buncha dying," he said.

"Yes," I said. "Fucka buncha dying."

"It's too damn serious, John. I mean, it's all there is."

"It's the end of things."

"It's also a sin," he said. "I'm tired of sins and sinning and being so damn serious. You tired of being serious, John?"

I was silent for a moment, but then I shrugged and pointed at the deer. "Let's bury her, Charley. Why don't we?"

"Good idea. She deserves a burial. Let's bury her."

He grabbed one end of the tent pole and I grabbed the other and together we walked with the deer to the grave and dropped it in, the body disintegrating in a storm of dust and black crust. Charley looked over the edge of the grave and said, "It was just a deer." And I said, "That's right, Charley. Just a deer." Then, as if to get in the last word, he said, "Good-bye, old girl."

We took turns filling in the hole. We worked until the sun went down and nothing was left of the dirt hill but a wide dusty circle on the grave of Joe Wendell Harwood. The wind was cold and strong and kept us from sweating. Charley stomped the earth over the grave with his feet and said, "You know when I say I love you, John—you know I mean it, don't you, John? I love you like I love life." He kept his eyes down on his feet.

"I know," I said after a moment.

He was standing only a few yards from me. "I'm sorry I can't leave yet," he said, his voice breaking. "I've left once already, and you know what happened. I can't hurt June and Malcolm, John. You remember what happened to Malcolm last time I left, John? I'm tired of being scared and ashamed. You know what I'm talking about?"

I didn't say anything.

"And I've got other considerations—I've got Mabel and my art. You know what an artist I am, don't you, John? I'm a line artist. I got graves and graves and graves—all these graves to dig. Somebody dies every day, John. People die every minute. You know what I'm saying?"

He began to weep violently, and I did not know if it was because he lacked the courage to leave home or was sad to see me go. I was the only friend he had. I shook his hand and left. I left without saying good-bye or wiping the blood from his face or telling him that I, too, loved him like life. The immense winter darkness crowded against me as I started across the graveyard, but I knew where I was going. Blinded, I knew my way.

I was walking to the front gate and my mother's Pontiac, following the set of tracks in the road, when I heard him calling behind me. "Confiteor," he called. "Confiteor, confiteor, confiteor!"

I took my time driving north to Old Field. I told myself that this was the last time I would ever drive this stretch of highway, that it was important to see and memorize everything. I drove down Union Street and saw the storefronts dressed for Christmas—all the trees and Santas and nativity scenes standing in the show windows. It was after seven o'clock, and the sidewalks were empty. Everything but the pool hall, Toussaint's Grill and Maxwell's Newsstand was closed. I drove in front of the place that once had been Girlie's Men's-and-Boy's and looked to see if anyone was staring out of the upstairs window. I braked the car and pumped the horn, but the building was dark and the curtains didn't stir. I drove on and parked between two cars near the back gate of the cemetery at Saint Jude, and for a long time I just sat there, smoking cigarettes and listening to news reports on the radio.

As I sat slumped against the headrest, gazing off at the blinking red nose of the reindeer on Bubba Toussaint's roof and feeling the chill, Emma Groves crossed the boulevard behind me and walked quickly along the familiar path, her eyes on the ground and her hands in the pockets of her long, dark coat. I suppose she would've stopped and come to the car if she had seen me, but as it happened she walked on through the stones under the tall bare trees and found the ground that awaited her. I tried to hear what she was saying, but it was no good. The wind blew. The town moved toward bedtime. I heard nothing.

When she finally came back across the worn path, I moved farther down in my seat. Through the crack in the window I heard the clicking of her heels on the concrete walk. Before entering her building, she stopped and looked in my direction. For a moment, I was certain that she knew I was there, watching her and feeling the shamefully loud beating of the heart I had invented for myself, and I moved to open the door and step out onto the pavement. But something stopped me—what was it that stopped me and kept me from telling her to hurry along, to run and get her things, it was time to go?

I waved. "Emma," I said. But she opened the door and was gone.

20

ow I return to Old Field only in memory and dreams.

In one dream, I return to the great house on Ducharme Road and we are all together, seated at the elaborately dressed red-oak table in the dining room—my beautiful mother; my father with his hard athletic chin and hands like stone; my brother, Sam; my grandfather Jason in an ancient three-piece seersucker suit and scarred saddle shoes, smelling of liquor and stale cigar smoke; my grandmother Marie, wearing expensive clothing she had tailor-made at a New Orleans boutique; and Emma. Oh, yes, Emma is there.

It is a new life we are living, and we're happy. My mother is happiest. She is the soul of our family, the one who wakes us up in the morning and puts us to bed at night.

"Right and simple," I announce to all over the clamor of silverware on china. "I just want to make things right and simple."

My mother smiles and says, "Do you really, John?" She loves hearing this. It makes her giggle like a child.

"Yes, I do, Ma. Right and simple."

Sam is Sam Girlie again, a brooding, fiercely competitive boy disturbing his plate of food with his fork and restless to bolt from the room. He has an elbow on the table, his face in the palm of his hand. "Get your elbow off the table," Marie says, but he doesn't move, so pleased in his quiet rebellion. He grumbles instead. Marie likes giving orders, even when they are not obeyed. "You heard me, Samuel Daniel Girlie. Off with the elbows," she says. She is old but tough when she has to be. She knows her place among us.

My father, who has said little, asks me, "Son, how do you suggest making things right and simple?" He is so young, so handsome. I think he is the most handsome man alive. "How do you begin? Where do you begin? It seems such an unlikely ambition."

"I don't know how," I say.

"Then how do you expect to do it?"

"I don't know," I say. "But this time I'll do it."

"I don't know that you can," Jason says, raising a glass of port to his lips. "You can't have again what's already lost."

"You can't reach for what isn't there," Marie says.

"Oh, let the boy have his dream," my father says.

"What's past is past," Jason says.

My mother comes to my defense. She runs her fingers through my hair. She adores me. "He wants to make things right and simple," she says. "Does that sound like such a difficult thing to do?"

"What can be so difficult about making things right and simple?" Emma says. "Johnny can. Let him show you."

Dreaming of Old Field is probably an unhealthy preoccupation, but after these years of living away, I still allow myself an occasional indulgence. I know I will never go back, but I have known other things that have proven themselves wrong. I knew, for example, that Emma Groves was mine, and in one moment of startling clarity I saw the future of our lives together. It was the night I first met her in the yard at Saint Jude—the one night of the year it snowed—and we were going to live as people who love each other are supposed to live. But of course we didn't. We never married. We never produced a child to fill the void left in her by the death of her first. We never found the place we so often and fervently promised each other. And when finally I left Old Field, I went alone.

I was eating breakfast in the cafeteria of a hotel in West Jacobs, some one hundred miles to the north, when I learned how she died. Because of the manner in which she took her life, the news coverage reached all points of the state and probably drifted by way of the wire services into papers all over the country. I do not mean to imply that her sudden notoriety was something I seized upon—that on the January morning when I was made aware of her death I exhibited any loss of conscience and went out and bought a stack of racy tabloids with news accounts to be distributed among friends. On the contrary, I wanted to hide. I wanted to be dead myself. I wanted to leap into the days that were gone, and to recreate them. And I wanted to be someone other than the person I had been only a few weeks earlier: John Girlie, the friend and lover of the same orphaned mother who thrust a carving knife into her lower belly while lying naked on the grave of her son.

Although the sound was turned way low and the report barely audible, I learned of her suicide while watching the small color television screen above the cafeteria grill. The screen held a succession of familiar images—the wintry cemetery at Saint Jude, the police cars and the people, some of whom I recognized, and the grave with the red, uncut stone where they found her body. The photograph of Emma, situated behind the solemn-appearing anchorwoman, was not one I had ever seen before. I stared past the fry chef flipping breakfast steaks to the television and saw the picture of a mere child, her bright red hair unevenly parted down the middle and supported by mousy little ears, her eyes wide and sad despite the smile on her lips. She was wearing a white graduation gown and holding a mortar board—her high school graduation portrait, I decided, more than sixteen years old, taken when she was still Emma Dupuis. She looked less like the woman I knew than a girl—the girl who ran through cow fields on her way to catch the school bus, an imaginary swarm of giant bottle flies chasing at her heels.

"Could you turn that up," I asked the man at the grill. "Please."

"Broke," he said. "Been broke. Always will be broke."

I hurried outside for a paper. The same picture of Emma at seventeen was played below the fold on the front page of the Baton Rouge *Morning Standard*. I didn't read beyond the headline and first few paragraphs, which said enough.

I think now of another oft-dreamed dream of Old Field, one that comes to me like the others—when I choose to create it, when I allow it a place in me. Emma and I are naked, sitting on the sandy edge of the Samms River. It is warm and dark; late night, early

NIGHTS

morning. The river moves. We are older and have known each other a long time—for years, in fact. We have returned to this place to remember how we began. She holds a bottle of cheap fruit wine that she now pours into a glass. The wine spills on her flat brown belly, spreads like a cloud and runs parallel to the thick raised scar on her lower stomach. The wine runs down into her bed of hair, down into the slick place below. She says, "Oh, John, it's cold," and leans back when I move to clean the mess. I put my tongue on her flesh, on the spot where she spilled. The wine is sweet and gritty. I close my eyes and see a wild incoherent wash of red. I lick off the wine. I lick the scar, lick the wet spongy hair, lick the place below. This is one of the acts of love that has become us; it is old and familiar, new and strange. "John," she says, her back arched, her knees lifting off the ground. "Baby. John. Oh, John."

I need to hear her speak to me. Talk to me, I want to say. Tell me something. I love the taste, the smell of her.

At last she says, "What is it like?"

"Like you."

"Like me," she says. She whispers.

"Like you."

Eventually, I think, there will be no place for these dreams, and my memory of Old Field will fade, and I will make my peace. I will stop listening to the loud, unending sound of what is gone, and no longer will I need to address that time so boldly in my heart.

Perhaps some things I will never forget—the smell of the fields, the blue fragility of night, the bare elegance of the tupelo trees in winter—and I will see them as something old and faraway, something hardly lived. And then, perhaps, I will laugh at the thought that anything, anything at all, could ever have mattered so much.

But on that January morning I continued north on Highway 3, climbing, climbing, there was far too much behind me to think I could ever simply drive away from where I'd been.